I0664008

BLOOD
MONEY
POWER

Inspired by a True Story

An epic political saga of wealth
and greed leading to murder.

by Michele Marie Tate

Blood, Money, Power

Tate, Michele Marie
Revised October 2010, ISBN 978-0-9831148-0-2
First Edition—August 2010, ISBN 978-0-9826428-0-1
Library of Congress Control Number: 2010906843

Book and cover design by Holly Eve Adams

Printed in the United States of America

www.michelemarietate.com

Dedication

In loving memory of Charles and Irwin.

Acknowledgements

This story was completed with the guidance and expertise of many special people. I am truly grateful for the faithful support of my dear husband and sweet daughter.

I'd like to express my appreciation to those who counseled me. Holly Adams, my designer, did a great job of walking me through the publishing process. Her creative input, expert advice and personal help, encouraged me to be a better writer. She was always there when I needed her. A special thank you to *The Mighty Pen* of Portland, Oregon for their excellent job of copy-editing and comments. Also, R. Craig Hindley, LLC, Attorney at Law for his expert legal advice.

Blood, Money, Power would never have been written if it weren't for my good friend who asked me to give a voice to her dramatic story. I truly appreciate and hold dear to my heart my close family and friends who never gave up on me, or my dream of becoming an author.

My acknowledgement wouldn't be complete without thanking my creator and his angels for the higher guidance I've received throughout my life.

Table of Contents

Part One
Otto Preston, Elizabeth Preston 1920–1940

Part Two
Cynthia Preston, Barbara Preston 1940–1970

Part Three
Sandy McDaniel, Clark McDaniel, Amber McDaniel 1970–1997

Preface

"When I despair, I remember that all through history, the ways of truth and love have always won. There have been tyrants, and murderers, and for a time they can seem invincible, but in the end they always fall. Think of it—always." –Mahatma Ghandi

Blood, Money, Power was inspired by a true story that was meant to be told. This fictional political saga reveals hidden secrets, lies and the unscrupulous deeds of the Preston family over a span of nearly eighty years and three generations. Otto Preston, a power hungry attorney, will do anything it takes to build a legacy and erase the pain of his own personal past.

Follow his journey that begins in one of America's most beautiful coastal cities, Santa Barbara, California. While palm trees sway, you'll relive the colorful folklore of Hearst castle, 1920's widely wicked ways and the dazzling lives of Hollywood's legendary movie stars.

In the following pages you'll discover the families dark secrets, callous deeds and personal trappings. You'll experience foreign intrigue in Thailand, which leads to adventure and danger. Mystery appears when you learn about a love that is worth dying for.

You're invited to join Amber as she fights for justice in a land known for its natural beauty–Portland, Oregon. She struggles to find the answers from the past that led to her personal nightmare. Will she win her battle for the truth?

Come explore this action-packed world, filled with drug and diamond smugglers, international mafia and powerful vipers that murder their victims and leave a trail of blood, money and power.

Disclaimer: While this story does include actual places and events, the majority of characters appearing in this work are fictitious. Any resemblance to real persons, living or dead, is purely coincidental.

Part One

Otto Preston
Elizabeth Preston
1920-1940

Chapter One
The Preston Legacy

1920
Santa Barbara, California
Otto Preston

In the snap of a finger, I gingerly mounted the sideboard of my 1920 Model T Ford with its shiny black hood, spindle tires and bug-eye headlights. After making a last-minute check of my appearance in the rearview mirror, I smiled with satisfaction at the dapper image I saw.

Then I frowned. Even though I was wearing a custom-made suit, spit-polished shoes and was driving a spanking new automobile, I couldn't erase the haunting, disappointed words of my father: "Otto, you can do better than that."

Thinking of my old man—the bastard—back in Chicago, I wondered, will I ever be good enough to earn a note of praise from that demanding old man? For the moment, I tried to put my father's judging words behind me.

I pressed down hard on the gas pedal of my new Tin Lizzie to see how fast it could go. As I sped down Highway 101, my body filled with the same exhilaration I used to feel watching my mother undress through her bedroom keyhole. I took a deep breath of the Pacific Ocean's fresh air and the sight of California's untouched coastal beauty renewed my hope for the future.

What a gas, I thought as I felt my thick brown hair toss playfully across my forehead like a teasing feather. When the four-cylinder engine reached its top speed of 45 mph, my heart raced with the thrill of a champion who'd won his first round.

Although not a soul was in sight, I knew my father surely would have cursed, "You damn fool."

I thought about my German parents, who were working like slaves back in Chicago at our family's kosher delicatessen. By now they would have received my letter informing them that I had decided to remain out West.

In my correspondence, I expressed my profound gratitude for their financial sacrifice. It had allowed me to attend Hatfield College of Law in San Francisco, which in turn had led to the position I'd just obtained at the reputable firm of Mitchell and Blaine in Santa Barbara. Of course, I could never reveal to them the exact circumstances through which I had come into contact with the firm. They would be devastated if they ever found out about my personal relationship with Gordon or about how I had obtained my new set of wheels.

As I continued to traverse the endless miles, my mind returned to a painful childhood memory I can't seem to shake to this day. I had just turned thirteen and recently completed my Hebrew school classes.

I was looking forward to my upcoming bar mitzvah ceremony with great anticipation.

The morning of the event, my burly father had announced, "Today you become a man, Otto. It is time you learn exactly what that means."

We had silently walked the two blocks together to our family's butcher shop while questions raced through my mind. What did he mean? Would this end in another of his angry outbursts of which my mother and I lived in fear? As we entered the front door, I trembled, dreading the sting of the marks he often left on my backside with his spankings.

My body had stiffened and I swallowed hard, watching him puff on his Cuban cigar as he put on his bloodstained meat-cutting apron. Beads of sweat formed on my brow as he walked over to the sink, washed his pudgy hands and ordered, "Otto, go stand and face the side wall."

I stood there shaking in fear's choking grasp. The lingering scent of slaughtered beef made me dizzy and I clamped my eyes shut. In the darkness, my body flinched when I felt him yank down my trousers.

What did I do wrong? I wondered.

With the jar of an electric shock, my father's full body weight crushed against me. I gasped for air, letting out a loud shriek while my hands slammed against the wall. With a sudden push of his hips, my father forced his rock-hard penis between my bare buttocks. Pinned like a trapped animal, I struggled with every ounce of my strength, but still I couldn't move.

Suddenly, I felt my father's hand grasp my penis. He began pumping it with repeated strokes.

I nearly choked on his nasty cigar breath when he said, "Now that you're a man, Otto, the lesson is you have to control your meat."

As my body automatically responded to the physical act, tears of humiliation rolled down my cheeks. Relief came for both of us, and with a loud moan, the old man's rapid panting stopped.

I heard the belligerent tyrant zip up his pants. He handed me his handkerchief as I tried to collect myself, still facing the wall.

In a commanding voice, he said, "Son, this is part of what it means to become a man. Always remember, your meat is a tool for private pleasure. My advice is to keep it in your pants. Take care of yourself until you find a woman from good stock."

Though neither he nor I ever spoke about it again, the scar of the experience has remained throughout my life.

In high school, I wondered if the erotic thoughts I entertained while watching the playful interactions of my male teammates at football practice had anything to do with my father's assault on me. I couldn't stop thinking about how I wanted the pleasure of penetration again.

I was especially confused by my homosexual desire because I felt equally excited when I looked at any girl who had beauty reminiscent of my mother's. Anxiety and guilt tormented me. This kind of homosexual behavior was socially unacceptable. I chose to suppress my feelings, but could not deny them.

As an only child growing up in a home where we strictly observed the Sabbath, holy days and kosher dietary laws, I felt great pressure from my family. My parents had made their expectations clear. It was an unwritten law that I would complete a formal education, marry into my own religion and raise my children in the faith.

I knew my recent unorthodox behavior at college went against everything my parents believed in. How could I ever face either one of them again?

I didn't think that even my loving mother, who had smothered me with attention, would understand. But to be fair, I never understood her, either. It angered me that she had tried to cover up the marks my father left on her without ever saying a word to anyone about it. She was kind and beautiful—too beautiful, I often thought, to put up with my father's mistreatment of her.

She had flowing, long, dark brown hair that was highlighted by a prominent widow's peak. Nothing brought me more comfort than her warm and gentle loving hugs. Even her sparkling green eyes never gave away the pain she silently carried.

The sound of a passing car made me refocus on the highway ahead, but when the road was clear again, I retraced my thoughts. Now I had to face my greatest fear. Could what I did in the past destroy my future?

I had studied hard in high school and had earned a partial scholarship. In my freshman year, I decided to study law.

Coming from an immigrant family, I never felt I had learned what Americans considered social skills. That fact combined with my obsession with neatness and my small stature made me somewhat of an outsider. To my embarrassment, my dormitory classmates nicknamed me Pretty Boy. Before long, the name had spread among my classmates. I was stuck with it.

Since I had to watch every penny and couldn't afford to party like my fellow students, I had few friends. To distract myself from my solitude, I buried myself in study and tried to block out my classmates' constant bragging about their good times at the local nightclubs.

One afternoon, to my surprise, my Legal Writing and Research professor, Dr. Sorenson, invited me to his home for dinner. Professor Gordon Sorenson was a tall, thin, middle-aged man who always tipped his black, half-rimmed reading glasses down his nose as he addressed his students. From our first meeting, Gordon's penetrating blue eyes raised a passion in me that brought me to my knees.

Sitting in his classroom, I enjoyed listening to his proper British accent. He would stroke his trim goatee as he pointed to the equations on the blackboard with a wooden yardstick. Every day, he greeted his students wearing a neatly pressed tweed suit, a starched, white shirt and a bow tie.

On my first visit to his home, I discovered the respected scholar lived in a two-story colonial brick manor in an upscale neighborhood several blocks from the college. His butler served us dinner, which was when I inquired if there was a Mrs. Sorenson. I was delighted to hear there was not.

After our meal, the friendly instructor invited me to stay for a game of chess. My mother had taught me to play as a child, and I'd always retained a fondness for the game. Gordon was a great storyteller. He impressed me with his travel stories while we moved the ivory-carved pieces across the marble chessboard. In his large library, filled with exquisitely carved antique furniture and colorful Persian rugs, I smoked my first Cuban cigar.

"Like me, Otto, you don't seem to fit into the party crowd," he observed.

"True," I told him. "I appreciate your invitation, Professor. I really admire you."

"Call me Gordon," he insisted. "Otto, I'd like to mentor you. I'm impressed with your conscientious study habits and high level of academic achievement."

I felt Gordon press his knee against mine beneath the table.

Slowly our relationship evolved, and we became intimate partners.

In the following months, his private lessons coached me in a positive way what my father's lesson had not. Sometimes my visits became weekend stays. Gordon schooled me to understand how to satisfy a man's needs. Even though he was as mild as a lamb on the outside, in the bedroom he roared like a lion. Gordon knew that for me to attain complete sexual satisfaction the act had to be rough.

We remained lovers for nearly two years. No one ever questioned where my fancy gifts and extra money came from. Though I was never ashamed of our relationship, the social pressure of our secret weighed heavy on my mind.

It was mutually understood that when my schooling was complete, we would part. Gordon often encouraged my hopes for the future. "Be proud of your heritage, Otto," he would say. "You have the tools to achieve your dreams of financial and social success."

Upon parting, each of us acknowledged to one another that we had attained exactly what we needed from each other. At graduation, this kind and generous man presented me with my Tin Lizzie and with the letter of high recommendation that had opened the door to the distinguished Santa Barbara law office of Mitchell and Blaine.

Like the highway that stretched before me, I had to continue on to whatever the future might bring. When I saw an unpaved road that headed inland, I decided it was time to take a new direction. I had to slow my motorcar on the bumpy road. I looked around while driving, taking in the rural country setting filled with rolling hills painted in rich greens and golds. Endless fields of alfalfa bloomed, ready for harvest, next to open ranch land dotted with Black Angus cows. I'd never seen anything like it.

The scenery brought to mind something Gordon had said. "Owning land measures a man's worth." What I saw before me would yield a potential fortune.

The breathtaking view distracted me, and moments later, the agonizing sound of crushing metal filled the air. I slammed on my brakes, bringing my automobile to a halt. A cloud of dust remained in the air as I hurried outside to survey the damage. I couldn't believe I'd hit something. A large rock had bent my front right fender so badly that it was pressing into my tire.

"Damn! Why here? Why now?" I cursed and threw my hands in the air.

I banged my fist onto the hood of my car and kicked the dirt.

My mind went wild with questions. Where the hell am I? How far am I from the nearest town? Will I starve to death before someone comes along?

I took off my topcoat and for the next hour I tried, without success, to fix the fender. The only thing that I accomplished was getting all sweaty and covered with dirt. I felt like an idiot, dressed in a suit on a dirt road without a clue what to do next. I slumped down onto the sideboard to assess my situation.

My clothes were ruined. I felt like a weakling. I didn't know exactly where I was. If my father were there, he'd have been saying, "You're worthless."

And, just then, I would have agreed with him. Soon the afternoon sun would disappear behind the hills. It was time for me to start walking. I hated to leave my prized possession behind, but I knew I didn't have a choice.

Not long after I had started out, I saw the silhouette of a man on horseback in the distance. Boy, was I relieved when he kept heading my way. The muscular cowboy remained on his horse, but tipped his ten-gallon hat and grinned. "Looks like you might be in need of some help."

"These roads are a mess." I frowned and pulled out my handkerchief to wipe the dirt off my face.

"Is that your fine piece of machinery back there?"

"Yes. I hit a rock. It bent my fender into my tire and it won't budge."

"I'll see what I can do. You can climb up and ride back with me."

"I'd be mighty grateful. Please excuse my unpresentable appearance." I swallowed hard as I took the rancher's outstretched hand and he pulled me up onto his horse.

"Hold onto the back of the saddle," his gruff voice ordered. "My name is Hank Thurman."

"Otto Preston. I'm a lawyer in town," I explained. As we rode back to my car, the warmth of Hank's body penetrated his plaid flannel shirt and passed on to me. For a moment I yearned to press my body closer to his, but I held back. I was afraid I might offend the helpful stranger.

When we approached the impaired vehicle, Hank yanked on the reins, signaling his horse to stop. He helped me slip down from his brown mustang.

"Out here, a horse and buggy still do the job," he commented, removing his hat and gloves in preparation to work. Hank's wide shoulders and muscular arms matched the rugged look of his stubbly beard and calloused hands. He took a moment to check the damage. "I can fix this in a jiffy." Hank opened his saddlebag, took out a hammer and proceeded to pry the metal back to where it had been originally.

"You're a good man, Hank," I praised him. "I meant to ask, where are we, anyway?'

"Cayuma Valley. It's part of Santa Barbara's North County. My homestead isn't too far from here. Follow me, and I'll fetch you some refreshment."

"My mouth's as dry as tumbleweed," I nodded and hopped back into my Model T.

As I followed Hank, something deep inside me stirred at his good looks, muscular body and friendly manner. I was tempted to make a move on him. Too soon, I thought and pushed the idea out of my head.

We arrived at Hank's single-story ranch house with a wide, covered porch. "Come inside, Mr. Preston, and we can talk over a glass of fresh-squeezed lemonade."

We washed up and climbed several wooden stairs. When Hank opened the door, the sweet aroma of homemade apple pie welcomed us. It reminded me of my mother's great home cooking. Inside, gray, weathered hardwood floors and an enormous stone fireplace marked the modestly furnished, open-beamed room. Sunlight filtered through a large picture window at its far end, which highlighted a huge, pine, drop-leaf table with ladder-back chairs.

A woman with long, black hair tied back in a ribbon and wearing an apron appeared from the kitchen. She carried two glasses of lemonade and set them before us. Hank introduced her as Molly Thurman, his wife.

Too bad, I thought. The cowboy is off limits.

"We don't get many visitors out here," she stepped away.

I couldn't help but notice that her rough hands contrasted with the softness of her voice. "I appreciate your generous hospitality, madam."

For a moment, I gazed out the window at Hank's field of alfalfa that stretched for miles. I took a long swallow of my drink. The kindness of his welcome brought a memory of my mother's warm greeting when I returned home from school.

A pleasant picture of my mother and I playing chess after school came to mind. I recalled how her hands were small and delicate as she moved the pieces across the board. I had learned the strategy of the game from her.

The late afternoon sun beat down from the window and sweat covered my brow. I removed my topcoat and instantly felt better. I asked Hank, "How far does your homestead reach?"

"I've got over a thousand acres of crop land and pasture," he grinned. "It's a great life, but we battle Mother Nature to hold on to every bit of it."

"What do you mean?" I questioned.

The rural farmer inched closer and recounted, "A city slicker like you might not understand this hard way of life. Our land is our livelihood. Out here, we struggle to survive."

For the next half hour, I listened to the hard working farmer describe the woes of his occupation and those who lived in the North County.

"Getting supplies, overcoming water shortages and procuring a good education for our young ones are tough achievements we struggle to reach."

"Hank, I'm a lawyer. What I understand most is the law. Let me see if there is anything I can do to help. Maybe I can do something about those rough roads, for example."

Just then a young boy wearing a white t-shirt and dungarees peeked out from the kitchen door. I noticed that he was missing an arm. His freckled face and sad brown eyes reflected the harshness of rural life.

"No medical doctors close by, either," Hank sighed.

"I promise to see what I can do to help."

On my way home to my apartment in Santa Barbara, I let my mind wander. I pondered Hank's and the other farmers' troubles. I fantasized about Hank's muscular body rubbing against mine. I wondered if I could acquire a piece of this golden land for myself.

When the dazzling ocean view shimmered before me, I caught sight of a handful of iron-horse oil rigs pumping out at sea. Instantly Gordon's voice filled my mind. "Gold, stocks, oil and politics are all means to power." Could this be my way to strike into my own pay dirt?

My first thoughts of a political career began to take form. What if I could represent both the North and South counties? It might be an avenue to acquire assets of my own. I believed a political career could offer me unlimited possibilities, holding the key to the sort of wealth I desired.

Back in my private office at Mitchell and Blaine, I drafted a long-term plan to create an everlasting Preston legacy. I vowed to erase my father's painful words: *"Otto, you'll never amount to anything."*

Chapter Two
Opportunity Knocks

1922-1924
Santa Barbara, San Simeon and Santa Monica, California
Otto Preston

My hard work and sacrifice at the firm proved worthwhile when Gene Mitchell arrived at my office, dropped a leather case on my desk and told me about my next project. "Otto, you're being assigned to a high-profile client. His name is William Randolph Hearst, a well-known publishing tycoon with a reputation for being clever, shrewd and extreme."

I'd heard about him. Hearst was a multi-millionaire with controversial political views, a big-hearted pocketbook and a long history of indulgences in life's finer pleasures. His name was a familiar sight in daily newspapers and magazines across America.

Gene outlined the assignment for me. "I've set up an appointment with him on Friday morning at his ranch in San Simeon. He requested someone smart, honest and able to travel for the special assignment. You're the best fit for the job."

"I hear Mr. Hearst is a man who resists playing by the rules. Is it true?"

"You can handle him, Otto. Just do it with kid gloves." Gene winked and walked out the door.

I opened the briefcase and shuffled through the large file on my prospective client. It described a man who went after the things he wanted and did whatever it took to get them. A personal background summary was included with the papers.

His history stated that he was the only son and heir to George and Phoebe Hearst, whose vast fortune was acquired through silver mining. As a young boy, he had traveled extensively with his mother around Europe, learning to speak German and French while there. He had acquired collections of stamps, coins and porcelain while abroad.

It was obvious that he'd continued his excess of accumulation, judging by the large number of import receipts tucked inside the files Gene had left. Mr. Hearst definitely had an appetite for fine things, and an abundance of money to satisfy his every whim.

Reviewing his information further, I learned that as a young man, he had attended Harvard College, but did not graduate due to a school prank. I smiled upon reading a note in pencil explaining that he'd sent several of his professors chamber pots with their names engraved on them.

What a unique sense of humor, I thought. Here's a man unafraid to state his mind. He definitely lives a flamboyant lifestyle most people only dream about.

A list detailing his vast holdings and assets was included in the portfolio. The entrepreneur owned an inventory of twenty-two newspapers and magazines from coast to coast. Some of the names I recognized: the *New York Daily Mirror*, *Cosmopolitan* and *Harper's Bazaar*.

Mr. Hearst's political achievements were noted in some attached news clippings. Upon reading them, I saw that he had promoted his personal political views though the various editorial machines of his newspapers and magazine. He had to be a multifaceted man who thrived on sensationalism in all areas of his life.

The record stated that he had married Millicent Veronica Willson in 1903. They had five sons, including their twin boys. Officially, they all resided in New York City. But in a folded note marked *Confidential*, it was revealed that Mr. Hearst spent most of his time at his California residence where he resided with his mistress, the actress Marion Davies.

The information was not a surprise. I'd heard rumors from some of my colleagues about wild parties at his secluded residence. I only hoped his personal life, so different from mine, wouldn't interfere with our business relationship.

A map and directions were included in the file. Mr. Hearst's sprawling abode was located in the town of San Simeon, about halfway between San Francisco and Los Angeles. This could be a lucky break for me, I thought. If Mr. Hearst likes my style, I could learn so much from him—a man who has already achieved the success I crave. A tinge of doubt swept through me as I wondered if I could win him over.

Friday was a clear, beautiful, sunny day as I headed north on Highway 101 to meet Hearst. The breathtaking coastal drive took about two and one-half hours. It gave me time to think. Lately, many invitations to social gatherings had come my way. I was beginning to feel the pressure of remaining a single man. I realized there would be social and political advantages to having a wife. Yet nagging thoughts of the professor remained.

I knew homosexuality was not acceptable in my social circle—really, in few, if any, social circles at the time. I worried that my secret might sabotage me.

Soon I was approaching the winding road that led up to the 240,000 acres of ranchland Mr. Hearst called home. Giraffes, zebras and bison roamed the rolling hillsides with wooden stables that looked like a small zoo. As my father might have noted, the man had good stock.

Two giant concrete Spanish cathedrals stood like guards at the entrance of the expansive hilltop fortress. A colorful garden and a flowing fountain surrounded the mission style entrance with a life-sized nude statue as the centerpiece.

A uniformed servant approached me when I stopped my car, "Sir, what is your name and business here?"

"My name is Otto Preston. I have an appointment with Mr. Hearst."

After this was confirmed, he instructed, "Your motor car will be parked for you. Please follow me."

We ascended a long, concrete stairway where massive European double doors were opened. The butler ushered me into a lavishly decorated sitting room filled with centuries-old furniture and Renaissance tapestries. Sitting there, I wondered, what could this man, who seemed to have everything, need from me?

After a while, the butler returned, and we walked down a long hallway that was outlined with arched windows. They were elegantly dressed with floor-to-ceiling green velvet drapes. Imported, inlaid ceiling tiles, several suits of amour, and priceless artifacts were a delightful visual feast along the way.

As the door of the master study opened, the bright light coming from inside momentarily blinded me. The arched ceiling overhead was lined with skylights and a row of massive hanging crystal chandeliers. I managed to focus on the sixty-foot-long table that stretched down the length of the room. It was completely covered with scattered newspapers.

A tall figure stood at the table's end. For a moment, a fleeting thought of Gordon crossed my mind. But he was soon forgotten when Mr. Hearst's steel-gray eyes seemed to stare right though me as he extended his hand. I repressed a flinch as I took in his oversized stature. I was surprised to discover his handshake couldn't slay a dragon.

He motioned me to sit down and seated himself in a high-back chair that looked like a throne. My eyes were distracted by the looming shadow of a Gothic lion's head behind him. I soon realized the reflection was created from the carved stone mantel of a nearby fireplace.

"Mr. Preston, your outstanding reputation at Mitchell and Blaine precedes you. I look forward to your representation in my business and personal affairs," the businessman began. His pipsqueak voice certainly did not match his superior prominence.

Mr. Hearst paused until the butler closed the door behind him. "There is a personal and very private endeavor that I'd like you to oversee in order to protect my interests and keep me informed," he explained.

As I sat and listened to his proposition, I squirmed in my chair when he mentioned that it was regarding his mistress, Marion Davies.

"I'm in the process of negotiating a business contract with Mr. Thomas Ince, a well-known Hollywood producer. It involves adding a new location up north to my present company, Cosmopolitan Productions in Los Angeles."

As the details became clear, I was disappointed that my services seemed a minor assignment in relation to his giant empire. Without asking, I immediately deduced that his intention was to promote the career of his mistress. A part of me didn't want anything to do with Hollywood or any actress. Still, I realized it was an opportunity to prove myself to a man of high stature.

I intently listened as he told me more about the assignment.

"We need to seal the deal, Mr. Preston. I've planned a weekend meeting in LA, where your presence is required. You will be informed of the date and time of our departure." He paused and added in a serious tone, "It is very important that anything regarding this matter be kept in strict confidence."

I was wondering if he was questioning my loyalty, when a phone rang that was located on a small desk at the rear of the room. Mr. Hearst excused himself to answer it.

I tried to relax, but worried about my future performance. It bothered me that during our conversation, Mr. Hearst seldom had looked me directly in the eye. I was unsure if I'd won him over. Had he judged me by my ethnic look? I wondered. Gene surely had commented on my expertise in drawing up contracts. From what I'd heard about the Hollywood scene, it wasn't up my alley. The toughest question was, could I fit in and be comfortable with that crowd? I felt compelled to reassure him that I was up for the job.

It was a relief to see my client smiling upon his return. "Miss Marion," he said.

"Mr. Hearst, I understand the strict confidentiality of this matter, and I'm prepared to do whatever is necessary to complete your request." I did my best to mask my inner fear that the unscrupulous reputation of the motion picture industry might test my personal discipline. Gordon had taught me the importance of good social interaction, but I still doubted my abilities. This new situation would definitely be my greatest challenge.

In our following conversation, Mr. Hearst outlined his expectations and goals. Based on my research of the relatively new industry of motion-picture films, I advised my client, "Your venture has the potential of lucrative profits, but it also comes with high risks."

"I feel the rewards more than outweigh the risks," Mr. Hearst stated.

There was a note of classy charm in the way he chose his words and in the wry smile that almost revealed itself. "Mr. Preston, my reputation is of the utmost importance. I will count on you to keep my private life out of the newspapers. Anything negative, of course," he grinned. "Oh, by the way, please call me W.R."

With this announcement, we shook hands, and I finally began to relax. "Please call me Otto," I told him.

"How about I show you around the ranch? I try to make my visitors feel right at home," W.R. offered.

I followed him along several corridors before we ascended a spiral stairway. The fifty-seven-year-old magnate recounted the fascinating history of each exquisitely furnished guest room. I was impressed by the Gothic furniture and French mantels. There were breathtaking views of the Pacific Ocean from each tower we climbed in the castle.

W.R. detailed from which of his worldly travels each elegantly displayed antique had originated. There were works of art from every continent. Such luxuries exceeded my wildest dreams. As the tour continued, I vowed to one day treat myself to that kind of extravagance.

Shortly we arrived at a magnificent Roman-style indoor pool. From a nearby dressing room, a stunning blond beauty waved to us. She blew a kiss toward W.R., and I recognized the curvy, talented actress, Marion Davies. Her intoxicating silhouette made my heart swoon. I quickly understood why my client desired to challenge Mary Pickford as the nation's number-one leading lady and wanting such a beauty on his arm.

A warm glow radiated from W.R.'s face as he shyly said, "Nothing keeps you young like the vision of a daisy in spring."

I was surprised when Miss Davies' steamy image, in her wet bathing suit, brought heat to my veins. I'd learned about sexual fulfillment from Gordon. My experience with women was limited. In that aspect, I was the novice and W.R. the expert.

W.R. turned toward me and asked, "Is there a Mrs. Preston, Otto?"

I gave him my standard answer: "So far no one fills my rigid requirements."

Not missing a beat, he snapped his fingers. "We'll have to do something about that."

As a private attorney for a man like Mr. Hearst, I conceded to myself that the time would be right to take a wife. She would be a valuable social asset when entering the political arena, as I was now qualified to do, with Hearst's backing.

After slipping on a silk robe, Marion strolled over and W.R. officially introduced us. I was delighted with this dame's spirited personality and captivated by her whisky style and irresistible charm.

Even though there must have been at least thirty years between them, I could feel their magnetic attraction. It had to be the origin of W.R.'s seemingly ageless vitality and motivating drive.

After some socializing, W.R. told one of his servants to retrieve my automobile and we said our good byes. On my way home, I realized that the tantalizing taste of a rich man's lifestyle had brought an enhanced vision to my dreams of the future.

Researching and planning for my client's project would be a valid test of my academic talents and social adaptability. Was I ready to rise to the occasion?

Several weeks passed before I received a telegram that gave me the details of our upcoming weekend meeting in Los Angeles. On Friday morning, I left my office in Santa Barbara and headed toward W.R.'s estate. I was escorted to the private airstrip where W.R. and Marion were waiting to board the six-seat propeller plane. The noisy plane landed after one hour at Clover field, located only a few miles from Marion's beach residence. A chauffeured Rolls Royce picked us up to take us to our destination.

Stately concrete columns lined the entrance of the Georgian-style mansion, which was nearly equal to W.R.'s home base. "Welcome to the Ocean House," Marion smiled as we drove in.

She proceeded to babble about her stunning abode. "The u-shaped structure has three stories, one hundred and ten rooms, thirty-four bedrooms, fifty-five baths and three guest houses. But all the fun happens in the two swimming pools and on the tennis court."

She gave me a private tour of the house. I noticed several full-length oil paintings of her wearing costumes from her motion picture roles. As I walked through, I thought, this looks more like a museum than a home.

A pretty, young maid escorted me to one of the dramatically designed two-story guest bungalows, where she set down my small leather carry bag. It was amazing to discover the four-thousand-square-foot guesthouse had six bedrooms, four bathrooms and a full-length balcony.

On a coffee table by the glowing floor-to-ceiling fireplace, I found a tray of assorted cheeses and bread accompanied by a bottle of vintage wine. The fully equipped kitchen, spectacular ocean view and general luxury of the place overwhelmed me.

Later the maid knocked at my door. "Sir, is there anything I can get for you?"

"No, thank you," I replied, wondering how things could be any more perfect. Downstairs, I stretched out on the pillow couch and enjoyed the tranquil beachfront view. It was the perfect vacation spot. For the next few hours, I unpacked, cleaned up and relaxed.

Some time later, the butler summoned me to the main house. In the courtyard gardens, we stumbled upon a knockout, handsome young man in a white linen suit. His clear blue bedroom eyes made my heart skip a beat.

"Tom Ince." His white teeth gleamed as he stretched out his hand. Before I had a chance to say anything, he continued, "You must be Otto Preston. W.R. told me you'd be here."

"It's a pleasure to meet you." I felt a sting of envy in acknowledging the producer's sophisticated charm and enchanting voice.

Together we followed the butler to a poolside table where Miss

Davies and W.R. were waiting. I took a step back when I saw Mr. Ince warmly embrace Miss Davies and plant a kiss on her cheek. The stranger possessed a sense of classiness unlike anyone I'd ever known. The casual affection made me uncomfortable. A throb of jealousy passed through me.

W.R. invited us to sit down. We did, and he began, "Gentlemen, we're here to ensure there is no limit to Miss Davies' future."

In conversation, I revealed the details I'd compiled for the proposed partnership.

W.R. looked over at Tom. "There are unlimited resources available for this venture."

Tom smiled, but did not respond immediately. After a pause, he said, "My primary concern is that we haven't determined an exact location for the new studio."

"Our plan is to expand the film industry farther north. I've assigned Otto to the task. He will keep us informed of his progress," W.R. explained.

"The location is important. I want it written into our contract that I have final approval where it will be built," Tom requested.

While W.R. pondered the thought, I added, "Mr. Ince, this is an extremely fair agreement that offers great benefits to everyone."

"Put it in the final contract, Otto, if that's what it takes to seal the deal," W.R. announced and instructed, "Draw up the contract exactly as we've discussed. We'll meet here Sunday morning for the final signing."

With business completed, the conversation took on a lighter tone. Mr. Hearst requested lunch. Several bottles of vintage champagne were popped open. W.R. ordered a special glass of gin for Miss Davies.

We enjoyed appetizers of fresh shrimp cocktail, baskets of plump fruit and imported cheese. Some time later, a food cart arrived with our meals, each covered by a domed silver warming plate. Once everyone was served, the staff opened all the covers at once.

Everyone erupted with laughter. I was stunned to see a large dead fish on my plate, its slimy skin shimmering in the sunlight. All eyes were on me.

I took a deep breath, raised my head high and announced, "Fish is my favorite dish." The roar of laughter continued as a waiter removed the platter, which I had correctly guessed was another of W.R.'s practical jokes.

"We do this to all our first time guests, Otto. You know, to break the ice. Popsi always likes to mix pleasure with business," Marion giggled.

"I certainly got caught on that one," I smiled as my racing heart began to slow down.

"You're a sport," Tom snickered.

It felt good to know I had passed my first social test.

We all drank to the occasion of Tom and W.R.'s partnership. The liquor brought out a childlike playfulness in Marion. "Popsi, we've got to have some fun. Let's have a costume party tomorrow night," she pleaded, snuggling up to her beau.

W.R.'s smitten face couldn't say no.

She jumped up from her chair with excitement, "Got to go and telephone my friends."

Tom directed his baby blues toward me, "How about a swim?"

I fidgeted with the papers in front of me before answering, "Forgot to bring my suit."

"I'll have one sent over to your room," W.R. quickly offered.

The idea was appealing. It wasn't just the temperature that was rising; the fire in my groin flared as I imagined that Tom might be suggesting more than just a swim. I headed back to my guesthouse to wait for a bathing suit to be delivered to me.

Soon I heard a knock at the door. A servant handed me a large package. Inside was a giant beach towel, a terry cloth robe, rubber sandals and a swimsuit, all my size. When I arrived back at the patio, Tom was already in the pool.

I felt awkward and unsure of the encounter, so for a few minutes I sat poolside on a chair.

"Afraid to get your feet wet?" Tom yelled.

Not wanting to look foolish, I quickly dropped my robe and dove into the water. Tom swam over and teased me with a splash. Soon, an all-out water fight began. Once we were both out of breath with laughter, we started to swim the length of the pool together.

"Otto, what's your story?" Tom asked, staying in near proximity to me as he swam.

Uncertain exactly what he meant, I disclosed, "W.R. recently hired me to negotiate the deal between you and he."

"So you're not familiar with the Hollywood crowd?"

"Not much."

"Well, my friend, tomorrow night you're in for a taste of many candy-land characters," he chuckled.

I had been feeling a charge of sexual energy grow between us and was tempted to make an advance, but reconsidered, reminding myself that I could not risk damaging my professional relationship with W.R.

Nonetheless, an enticing picture of Tom and I together in the shower filled my mind. I quickly erased it, reminding myself that a liaison of that sort was no longer appropriate for a man in my position. With regret, I informed Tom, "My unwritten law is that I never mix business with pleasure."

"Ah, my friend, I commend you. One day you should learn to mix pleasure with business."

We both laughed. I was grateful that he had backed off graciously, but it was torture to watch him towel himself dry.

On my way back to my room, I bumped into Marion. "Otto, I can't wait until tomorrow night's costume party!" She casually slapped me on my shoulder. "All my closest friends will be there. You'll just love them."

"Marion, no doubt you have lovely friends, but I'm not a party guy. Anyway, I don't have a costume." I tried hard to make an excuse not to go.

"Not to worry, we always supply our guests with costumes. Besides, you might meet someone interesting." She winked one of her sultry eyes, clearly scheming something up.

It was difficult to discourage such a charming dame, even though I knew her crowd didn't fit my bill.

"But I need my beauty sleep," I tried again.

"No. No. No. Otto, you will not weasel your way out of this. You've got to be at the party to meet my friends." Then she squealed suddenly. "Okay, I've got an idea," her eyes fluttered. "How about at the party, you keep count of how many of my costumed friends you can identify?"

"W-well ..." I stuttered, still not wanting to commit to her game.

"Come on, Otto. For each person you guess correctly, I'll give you a one-hundred dollar bill."

I couldn't refuse that offer, so I finally agreed. It was rather amusing, after all. One thing I'd figured out, spending time with Marion and W.R., was that when you're with the big players, you go along with their rules.

For the rest of the afternoon, I enjoyed the comforts of my own private palace. I realized then it would be easy to get used to others taking care of my every need. I watched a miraculous ocean sunset from my window and went to bed.

The next morning, a knock at my door announced the delivery of my costume for the evening. Inside the package was a red velvet tunic with a jeweled cross on its chest, black satin knickers and a silver cowl to put over my head. I marveled at the fine detailing of the medieval knight's outfit. Tucked inside I found a silver-studded leather belt, a shiny sword and tall leather boots. When I saw a fake brown beard and eye mask in a pocket, I laughed out loud.

As a kid, my mother had made every Halloween outfit. None of hers compared to the one before me. I knew it had to be from one of the studios' wardrobe supplies. To my surprise, it fit perfectly. I stared at the dashing image of myself in the full-length mirror.

Later that day, I received a note slipped under my front door. It was from Marion: "Good luck, Otto. Hope you can recognize Willy and me at the party."

As evening approached, I peeked out my upstairs window and saw a line of chauffeured limousines outside, signaling that the time had come to get dressed and go to the main house. I sneaked unnoticed into the high-domed ballroom with its many crystal chandeliers and headed for the bar. For a moment, all seemed surreal as a circus of masked characters surrounded me. From behind, I heard my name being called.

The legendary Zorro spread his black cape open, flashing his toothy smile, "Care to join me for a drink?" Of course, it was Tom Ince. He looked delicious in his all-black silk outfit, complete with a flamboyant Spanish hat and tights. We found a table, put down our scotch glasses, and had a smoke.

I told Tom about Marion's challenge. We made a separate bet as to who could guess the most real names of the costumed actors and actresses at the party.

Tom pointed out Marie Antoinette, whose plump assets overflowed from a revealing bodice gown. "I'd recognize that hot dish anywhere," he smirked and brushed his hair back from his brow.

With a closer look, I did not doubt he'd found our hostess, Miss Davies. A giant of a man stood close by, wearing the gold, jeweled crown of a king. The full-length cape trimmed in fur fit W.R.'s status.

The game continued as I recognized the famous pair, Douglas Fairbanks and Mary Pickford, dressed as Romeo and Juliet. She was wearing a low-cut, purple gown, a gold choker and a brocade hat. He was quite the picture with his white panne shirt, stockinged legs and feather hat.

"There is something to be said about a man in tights," Tom mimicked a slow bump-and-grind move.

I struggled to control my urge to reach under the table and grab Tom to release the explosive heat that welled within me upon seeing his gesture. The sound of the orchestra playing, the smell of booze mixed with smoke, and the strange cast of characters all made for a bizarre fantasy. My heart raced with fear that my discipline might fail, and the consequences might jeopardize my future. Through the haze of my madness, my father's voice drummed in my ear. *As a man, you have to control your meat.*

Just then the crowd's focus shifted to an elevated stage where the well-known jazz singer, Al Jolson, appeared. He had donned his famous comedic-jig persona. He held the microphone with his stark white gloves as he welcomed the crowd. Soon his mesmerizing voice echoed through the ballroom, and sighs of joy erupted as he broke out singing his hit song, *"You Ain't Heard Nothin' Yet."*

The air buzzed with music and laughter. I pointed to W.C. Fields as he staggered by in a straw hat, overalls and a rosy nose. Tom picked out Rudolph Valentino, who was dressed as Napoleon. When Valentino looked over at us, he gave a wink.

As the hours passed, the body heat in the room climbed. I noticed several couples disappear down the hall only to return with their costumes disheveled. With every drink, I felt my sense of will power diminishing. As the level of naughtiness peaked, I knew it was time to leave before I was too weak to avoid embarrassing myself. "I'm going to call it a night while I can still make it to my room," I told Tom.

"I'll stick around, Otto. I want to see what this party has to offer."

Even though a part of me yearned to stay, I bid my friend goodnight.

The next morning was brutal. I awoke with a pounding headache. I took a long shower and emerged to find, to my delight, that a servant had brought a light breakfast with steaming hot coffee and a bottle of aspirin. A note was attached to my tray requesting that I come to the pool at noon. For the next several hours, I cleared my mind and focused on preparing the partnership contract.

Upon arriving, I found Tom crouched low in his chair, looking like a damp dishrag. I softly whispered, "Good morning."

"Otto, it is the morning after the night before..." Tom slumped down further in his chair.

I wanted to ask my friend if he got lucky, but kept silent.

Marion shuffled to the table, hiding behind large, dark sunglasses.

W.R. was bright eyed and seemed happy as a lark. He motioned me to sit down and instructed, "Otto, you and I will be leaving at 3:00 o'clock to return to the ranch. Marion will stay to finish work on her new film, *When Knighthood was in Flower*."

The table stayed quiet while hot coffee was poured all around.

Out of the blue, W.R. announced, "I've decided to conduct a contest for the best plan to end this lawless Prohibition."

Marion's head bobbed up. "Popsi, what are you talking about?"

"Booze. Free-flowing Hooch," he grinned. "I'll offer a prize of $25,000 for the best plan. It should sell lots of newspapers."

"Go for it, Pops." Marion rested her head inside her palms. "Let me know who wins the prize."

Everyone at the table knew W.R. never touched the bottle. They also knew he offered the highest quality liquor to those who embraced the intoxicating spirits. He seemed to enjoy watching the entertainment it offered.

It dawned on me that this was just another child-like game for Marion and W.R. to play. I'd learned that it was one of the strange parts of their relationship. Who was I to question the king and queen who lived in the magic castle by the sea?

Once all the contract papers were signed, Tom excused himself and said his goodbyes.

Marion suggested, "Let's cool off and take a dip in the pool, Otto."

It was an irresistible invitation.

The two of us left to change and met back at the pool. The California sun blazed overhead and the nearby palm trees swayed. With the famous bathing beauty close by, I couldn't have asked for more. We swam across the 110-foot heated pool with the grace of a pair of swans.

"So how many film stars did you recognize last night?" Marion questioned as she swam close by.

"Six," I answered. "You outshined all of them, Marion."

"Really? You're just being kind."

"You were the highlight of the show," I reiterated.

"I like you, Otto. Popsi knows how to pick 'em." She laughed as her streamlined body crossed the pool.

At the shallow end of the pool, I sank my body down into the water and made up my mind that I would do whatever it took to enjoy this kind of comfort. Mr. William Randolph Hearst was my role model from there on out.

On the flight home, W.R. asked me to oversee all legal matters connected to Marion's career. "She likes you. Keep me informed of all movie offers, any negative publicity, or current affairs where she's involved. You know that my goal is to make her the number-one film actress in America."

"Yes, Mr. Hearst," I acknowledged. *But are you man enough to do it?* My father's voice chimed inside my head.

Chapter Three
The Bride

1925
Santa Barbara, California
Otto Preston

Months passed, and my professional and personal relationship with Mr. Hearst deepened. He introduced me to many movie starlets, powerful business associates and high-ranking political officials during my visits to his ranch. Those connections helped me plan and achieve my political ambitions.

In May, I received my first invitation to a dinner party at the mansion. It was in honor of Tom.

The dinner invitation came at a bad time. Between the pressure mounting to find an appropriate location for the new film studio and local opposition to having one in Santa Barbara that had aired at the last town meeting, I found myself in the midst of a conflict of interest. When I called W.R. and informed him of this, he responded, "Otto, film making is big business. Just get the job done."

I wasn't in the mood to attend the party that night, knowing I had no good news to give them. The only reason I decided to go was because it was for Tom. It rained all the way there, and I arrived feeling cold and grumpy.

The darkness faded when the platinum-blond bombshell, Gloria Swanson, cruised by in the hallway wearing a slinky, white satin gown. I remembered seeing her at Marion's costume party dressed as Cleopatra.

I joined a small crowd of guests wearing cocktail attire who were mingling near the dining table. It was set with formal white linens, silver candelabras and fine china. Place cards marked each chair.

I recognized some of the celebrities attending—Charlie Chaplin, Seena Owen, Theodore Kosloff and Elinor Glyn—but no one else was familiar except the host, hostess and Tom. Walking through the crowd, I felt like an everyday dish in a china cabinet.

I noted that W.R., Marion and Tom were sitting in the center of the long table as I took my seat at the far end. As names were exchanged, I unhappily noticed that only females surrounded me. The new acquaintances were friendly, but they talked mostly to each other. Feeling uncomfortable, I wanted to skip out before dinner, but knew that would be rude to the hosts.

It wasn't the first time W.R. and Marion had arranged this type of setting. As a single man, I knew others felt compelled to set me up. The atmosphere made me feel like I was a spectator at a theatrical play.

Soon, W.R. stood up to give a toast to the guest of honor. Clinking his champagne glass, he began, "Tonight we recognize a genuine hero, a man dedicated to promoting the film industry to its highest level. We celebrate his success and toast Tom Ince for his accomplishments."

Everyone clinked their fine crystal goblets in unison as they admired the fashionable man of the hour. Flaming dishes, elegantly dressed silver trays of gourmet food and bottles of vintage wine streamed into the room. From my dinner partners, I learned more about Tom's impressive accomplishments in the creation of motion-picture films. I intently listened to each glitzy dame who gave high praise to Tom for his creativity and hard work in that imaginative world.

Before long, I felt a tap on my shoulder and realized it was the man of the evening himself. "Congratulations, my friend. You look tops tonight," I told him while we shook hands. His touch made my heart beat faster.

"Where have you been since our interesting night at the Ocean House?" Tom asked, giving me his million-dollar smile.

"I've been searching for that perfect new film studio location."

"Good luck, Otto," Tom encouraged. "I believe in you."

His words meant a lot to me.

After speaking to me, he went on to engage in conversation with several gorgeous women. I noticed his ease—like a bee flying from one flower to another. Tom must be drawn to both sides of the gender coin, like me, I thought.

Later, W.R. stopped by for a brief hello. "Pick out one of these beauties," he whispered in my ear.

At that point, I felt obligated to put some effort into his offer. I directed a question to Sally Haver, the voluptuous brunette across from me. "What is your association to our guest of honor, Sally?"

After taking a long drag from her cigarette, she answered, "Oh, I'm an old acquaintance of Marion's." Sally blinked her long lashes at me, bent forward slightly, and exposed her perky breasts. "We go way back."

I couldn't stop myself from staring at her hard nipples, highly visible though her clinging flapper dress. As she chattered on about how Marion was her best friend while continuing with her blatantly flirtatious behavior, I recognized that she didn't come from good stock.

Though I tried to be polite, she continued to rattle on about herself and it annoyed me. Deciding she was a complete waste of time, I turned toward the more conservatively dressed dame who sat on my right, asking her the same question I had asked Sally.

Her serious brown eyes scanned me up and down as she answered, "I'm Louella Parsons, a Hollywood columnist, an employee of Mr. Hearst and a friend of Tom Ince. And you?"

"I'm a lawyer for W.R. I met Tom through that association."

We continued to discuss the day's headlines, which included a recent fire at the Ambassador Hotel, the new maximum speed limit (thirty-five miles an hour) and the latest fad: beach rompers. It was clear Miss Parsons was all business when she handed me her card, but did not ask for mine.

As the evening wore on, you would never know that Prohibition existed outside La Cuestra Encantada—the Enchanted Hill, as the ranch was called. With every drink Sally consumed, her high-pitched giggle, vulgar tone and obnoxious advances became more irritating. Finally, I decided to leave.

Before departing, I stopped and thanked W.R. and Marion for the invitation and gave Tom a pat on the back for all his achievements. On my drive home, I thought again about how W.R. had purposely set up my seating arrangement, hoping I would find someone who fit my expectations. It definitely was time for me to seriously look for an appropriate spouse. Politically, it was a requirement.

In the following months with W.R.'s influence, I attained my first political goal and got elected as a Santa Barbara City Councilman. My streak of good luck continued when several real estate lots became vacant and therefore available as options for the new location of the studio.

One day while on the telephone with W.R. discussing the available real estate, he informed me that Marion wanted to host a political gathering in my honor. He revealed, "We're going to invite many high-ranking state officials."

I was excited after Marion sent me a guest list and said, "The party list just keeps growing."

The names on it were very impressive. They included many legendary movie stars—Greta Garbo, Lew Ayres, Clara Bow and Harold Lloyd—and powerful business associates—Louis B. Mayer, Florenz Ziegfeld and, of course, Miss Julia Morgan. I was delighted to see the names of our local mayor, George Hyland and our city commissioner, Dick Thompson.

The party would take place in the master ballroom. It would be a black tie affair.

Marion excitedly spouted, "I've hired the Tommy Dorsey jazz band to play throughout the evening."

I decided to order my first custom tuxedo, a new top hat and a pair of patent leather shoes for the occasion.

Upon my arrival, Marion fussed over me and complimented, "If I wasn't already spoken for, I'd be looking your way."

Her words gave me confidence for the evening.

Mr. Hearst walked over and told me, "I personally invited the supreme court judge, Mr. Stanley Terrell and his daughter Elizabeth to sit at our table."

The special guests stood up when we arrived at the head table.

"Your honor and Elizabeth, I'm proud to introduce my legal counsel, friend and newly elected city representative, Mr. Otto Preston."

"Thank you, W.R., for those kind words," I said. When I took Elizabeth's delicate hand, I instantly recognized that it held the tenderness of my own mother's. Elizabeth's innocent hazel eyes were hypnotizing. My heart skipped a beat as I took in her hourglass figure, highlighted by her crimson silk dress. Her ivory skin looked smooth as a pearl. I managed to get out the words, "It is my pleasure to meet your honor and your enchanting daughter."

The honorable judge shook my hand. "Congratulations, Mr. Preston, on your appointment. I think highly of anyone whom W.R. calls a friend."

As we all sat down, I thanked him. "I appreciate that," I nodded, turning my eyes back to Elizabeth. It was difficult to take them off of her.

Soon Marion joined us, and W.R. stood up and cleared his throat to draw the other guests' attention. "Tonight, we're here to honor Otto Preston, city representative, outstanding lawyer and personal confidant—a hard-working man whom I believe will be a righteous leader for our great city of Santa Barbara." Applause followed as my host motioned for me to stand up. "Congratulations, Otto, and good luck on your new job." W. R. gave me a hearty handshake as I got up, and he took his seat.

"Thank you, Mr. Hearst." I paused for the crowd to quiet. "I sincerely appreciate this vote of confidence. Our growing city has many needs, and it is my goal to offer the highest quality of life to every citizen. I promise to work hard, root out government waste, build better roads and put more jingle in all your pockets." There were chuckles throughout the room. "Most of all, it is an honor to serve you. Now please, I invite you to enjoy the fine hospitality offered here this evening." When I sat down, my whole body was electrified with the admiration that filled the air.

"What made you decide to go into politics, Otto?" Mr. Terrell asked.

"It is my desire to serve a broader public spectrum," I answered, my eyes again straying to take in Elizabeth's tantalizing green eyes, finger-waved auburn hair and dainty, heart-shaped lips.

Marion joined in the conversation. "Otto, you and Judge Terrell are both alumni of the same college. He lives in San Francisco and went to Hatfield, like you."

"A fine place to get an education," I affirmed. Thoughts of Gordon crossed my mind. I quickly pushed them aside to focus on Elizabeth. "San Francisco is a great city. Will you be visiting long?" I addressed my question to her.

"One week." Elizabeth warmly smiled. "This is the very first time I've traveled with my father. I couldn't resist the invitation to visit Mr. Hearst's ranch," she confided in a voice as sweet as the piano playing.

After dinner, I offered to light Marion's and Elizabeth's cigarettes. I'd overheard them speak about a beach picnic planned for the following day. While I chatted with his honor, Judge Terrell, about his home city, my father's nagging voice brought fear to my heart. *Are you good enough for her?* Elizabeth's sophistication sparkled like the fine Waterford crystal on the table. I had to find a way to impress this breathless vision of elegance whose every move teased me with temptation.

As views on foreign politics were discussed, I added my thoughts. "As an American, I feel it is my personal and political responsibility to fight the spread of communism, fascism and national socialism across the world."

With this comment, Elizabeth turned my way. "I commend you, Otto. That is the responsibility of our democracy. Every citizen should appreciate the right of freedom here in America."

Judge Terrell agreed.

Everyone at the table applauded my comments.

Just then Tommy Dorsey and his band stepped up the beat with some ragtime rhythm. Marion's body swayed to the music, and she tilted her head toward W.R. "Popsi, let's take a whirl out on the dance floor."

I felt a slight kick to my shoe under the table. Acknowledging Marion's hint, I turned toward Elizabeth and asked her to dance. She was a delight to watch as her long, curvy legs kicked to the high-energy beat. When a waltz followed, she swished her platform heels across the floor in harmony with my step.

After the dance, we exchanged views on Sinclair Lewis's newly released book, *Main Street* and our fears of Hitler's rising power in Europe. It didn't take me long to realize that Elizabeth's Jewish heritage, educational background and political standing were the assets I'd been looking for in a wife. She met all my requirements, and there was no doubt she came from good stock.

I acted the perfect gentleman that night. Like an eraser on a chalkboard, Elizabeth removed all thoughts of Gordon. By the end of the evening, her charms made me feel as though she were my master and I her servant.

In the following months, we arranged to see each other while her father stayed with W.R. We took long walks in the lavish gardens, she accompanied me to several political dinners, and I traveled by train to San Francisco, where we attended the theater. Though I had never contacted Gordon since college, the thought of never seeing him again weighed heavy on my mind; but I refused to entertain thoughts of him while I was courting Elizabeth.

Six months later, I purchased a three-karat diamond solitaire engagement ring from Adan Shariff, one of my overseas clients. When I approached Judge Terrell and asked for his daughter's hand in marriage, he questioned me about my intentions. I told him, "I hope to become as successful as your honor," which sealed his blessing. Our engagement was announced in the local paper, the *Mariposa Daily.*

It was a wonderful surprise when Marion and W.R. offered their mansion for our wedding and reception. Elizabeth decided that our ceremony should take place the next June, outside, in the main garden terrace. Marion helped her handle all the details appropriate to our large wedding with 250 guests.

Lately my business and political career was filled with town meetings and problems due to a devastating drought in North County. Such pressing issues forced us to schedule a short, one-week honeymoon in San Francisco.

Elizabeth's captivating beauty, spice-scented perfume and voluptuous body wildly aroused me, but the nagging thought of my personal sexual needs worried me. When I reached a certain point in the actual act, an animalistic hunger took over that was brutally unstoppable. Will Elizabeth reject me for it? I wondered. My father's voice tormented me; *will you ever be the man that succeeds?*

On our wedding day, I worked to push these thoughts from my mind as I drove toward the castle. The lavish scene had the glamour of an elaborate movie set. White lilies and pairs of caged doves were the romantic theme. Violins played while servers poured champagne with the ease of the surrounding fountains. Some of my associates, including Gene Mitchell and Harry Blaine, had agreed to stand up for me. For a moment, I wished my mother could have been there, but I'd received a letter that my father had suffered a stroke and was now confined to a wheelchair. Somehow, the timing had seemed just right and I decided to tell my parents that I'd eloped so nothing could spoil Elizabeth's and my special day.

On that perfect, sunny day in June, the early-morning fog had already burned off by the time the ceremony was set to commence. W.R. was my best man and Marion the maid of honor. I was waiting in the wings with W.R. for things to get started, when my generous friend slipped an envelope inside my tuxedo jacket.

It was a big step in my life, and I felt confident enough to discard my father's nagging voice. *Prove to me you're not a loser.* I felt that with Elizabeth by my side, I already had. I truly loved her and hoped, in time, she would come to understand me. As I walked down the rose-petaled aisle, I felt like a king. Elizabeth looked stunning with the sex appeal of actress Clara Bow as she stood by my side in front of the chuppah.

I smiled at her, knowing that night, she would be the servant and I her master.

My loins filled with warmth as Elizabeth teased me with her tender touch during the train ride to San Francisco. In our honeymoon suite at the Fremont Hotel, I cleaned up before Elizabeth emerged from her separate parlor adorned in a white, fur-trimmed negligee made of silk and lace. My mouth watered as I devoured her seductive image. When she dropped her robe to the floor, she revealed a body as irresistible as a goddess.

The satin sheets couldn't cool the fiery passion between us. The momentum built as I slipped into my role as master. In the darkness, I heard Elizabeth's sighs of pleasure soon turn to moans of pain.

Elizabeth fought in bed with the spirit of a wild horse. I finally had to clamp her hands down to take her as I needed to. Beads of sweat moved down my forehead as I tried to ignore her screams of "*Stop!*" I hoped one day she would understand my sexual needs and accept them.

As I lay back, exhausted, Elizabeth turned toward me. Her face was flushed and she was sobbing. "You hurt me," she accused.

When I reached out to console her, she shouted, "You selfish bastard! You will never do that to me, ever again."

"I'm sorry, Elizabeth. I got carried away," I tried to explain, knowing that it would take time to break her in.

"All my life, I've been looking forward to this day." She trembled, stumbling up to put on her robe. "You've made it into a nightmare."

"Please forgive me, Elizabeth. I'll make it up to you somehow. I love you and promise to do whatever is needed to make you happy."

"Right now, Otto, I'm not sure what I want. Just please leave me alone." She raised her hand and pointed toward the door.

I obeyed her request and left the bedroom. Elizabeth had a choice to make, and I had to patiently wait to hear her verdict. So I had a smoke and poured myself a glass of leftover champagne.

Chapter Four
Family Legacy

1926
Santa Barbara, California
Elizabeth Preston

My whole body shuddered from the pain and humiliation of the physical trauma I'd endured. I stumbled back to the bedroom and locked the French doors. Tears streamed down my face as I crawled back onto the bed. When I envisioned my wedding night, it was a picture of Otto and I face to face. Instead, I was mounted like a dog without a touch of tenderness.

He had transformed into a crazed animal, using force to have his way with me. Right then I hated him. I needed to pull myself together and took a deep breath. My tears were easy to wipe away, but the memory of his harsh treatment still penetrated my mind. I needed time to sort through my feelings and contemplate my next move.

A part of me never wanted him to touch me again. Yet earlier that day I made a vow in front of God, to take my husband in sickness and in health, in good fortune and in adversity. The ring he gave me symbolized my commitment to that love for that day and forever more.

How could I walk away now?

Before tonight I thought Otto was the man of my dreams. He always acted the perfect gentleman. I was so proud that he was a politician like my father and shared my Jewish heritage. There wasn't a doubt in my mind that our life together would be everything my heart desired. He was the man I'd loved and wanted to spend the rest of my life with. Now, that love felt tarnished like a neglected piece of fine silver.

All my life I strived to maintain the pride and honor my father instilled in me, ever since my mother died when I was twelve-years-old. If I walked away from my marriage, this news would devastate him.

I needed to be strong and figure out an answer that I could live with. Many questions crossed my mind. Would Otto and I ever be able to overcome our differences in the bedroom? If we couldn't, would I be faced with a lifetime of un-fulfillment? I realized that these questions would only be answered with time.

Slowly, I regained my composure and planned my next move. I made up my mind that I would walk back through those doors filled with determination and dignity.

I sat up, opened the French doors and stood a distance away from Otto and said, "I made a vow of honor today that I will keep." I cleared my throat and continued, "As your wife, I have a duty. But there are boundaries to this union that you must promise to keep, too, Otto… I need to know right now if you're willing to respect them."

Otto never took his eyes off me and stood perfectly still.

"I will try to respect your rules because I love you, Elizabeth," he promised and took a few steps toward me.

"Sleep on the couch tonight, Otto. I want you to think about what I need." I stepped back, returned to the bedroom and locked the door behind me.

This had created a distance between us, and I was unsure of what the future would bring.

The next morning a bellboy delivered breakfast to our suite. Otto requested that I join him. As we ate together he informed me, "I have commissioned a local contractor to build a seven-bedroom Victorian home in the heart of Santa Barbara. Elizabeth you will have an unlimited budget to decorate it."

I was speechless and wondered if he thought this would compensate for his cruel behavior. In the following months we portrayed a happy couple to the outside world, but our struggles in the bedroom continued. We both tried, but failed to satisfy each other's needs. The conflict built a barrier in our relationship, yet we mutually decided it was best to keep our vows of marriage.

Chapter Five
The Preston Children

1926
Santa Barbara, California
Otto Preston

Six months passed. One evening after returning home from the courthouse, Elizabeth gave me some shocking news. "Otto, I'm pregnant."

The tone of her voice reflected the harshness of a scolding rather than the sort of joy that might be expected from such a revelation. Though I was thrilled, I saw sadness on Elizabeth's face.

"I'm not happy about it," she confessed. "The whole idea of how this baby was made, makes me sick. I wish it would all go away."

"Don't worry, Elizabeth," I tried to soothe her. "I promise to hire a nanny to help you."

She turned away, and I heard her whisper beneath her breath, "You don't understand me."

As the end of her pregnancy grew near, Elizabeth's health declined. Her doctor ordered her to remain in bed. She spent most of her time reading or sleeping. I distanced myself from her, not wanting to hear her constant complaints and whining.

While our coastal city of Santa Barbara grew, so did my political responsibilities. The different needs for the North and South counties increased. A major drought created a water shortage in the agricultural area in the north. This forced me to spend more time away from home to appease the struggling ranchers and farmers.

Not long after, due to an untimely resignation, I was appointed to complete a term on the Santa Barbara Board of Supervisors. The new job brought more stress, but also presented new political opportunities for me to wash the hands of local businessmen and in turn lock in my position for the future.

That spring, when Elizabeth went into labor, I was out of town. I got there as soon as I could, but she had already delivered our newborn baby girl.

When I entered Elizabeth's hospital room, her first words to me were, "Damn it, Otto, you're never around when I need you."

I tried to hold her hand, but she pulled it away.

"How are you doing?" I asked.

"You have a daughter."

"I'm grateful. I've seen her through the nursery window. She is as beautiful as you."

"Don't try to buy me off with compliments. You should have been here."

"I'm sorry, Elizabeth, but my career is important to us, and sometimes it has to come first."

"You're a father now and that means added responsibility. I hope one day you have a closer relationship with your daughter than you do with me."

Elizabeth's complaints trailed off in my mind after a while.

Later that evening, I held Cynthia for the first time. I was amazed that the physical act I had performed with Elizabeth had created such a perfect, tiny, pink bundle. Cynthia's face had delicate features like her mother, but my own genes were realized in the prominent widow's peak on my daughter's hairline.

At home, our newly hired nanny, Maria, took full charge of Cynthia. Elizabeth remained distant from the baby, devoting her time to regaining her old physical stature.

I was so proud of Cynthia that I ordered several boxes of pink Cuban cigars to hand out to friends and colleagues to celebrate her birth. I instinctively tucked one inside of my desk drawer for Gordon, as I couldn't seem to forget him, just in case I ever decided to contact him. Several times I'd thought about picking up the phone to catch up with him, but I never had followed through. I worried if our secret was revealed it would ruin my up and coming career.

I relished the fact that the Preston legacy would continue. The accomplishment of having a child was as important to me as the diplomas on my office wall. Now I had a little princess as part of my own royal domain. I would not deny her anything. Since Elizabeth had little interest in her, I would claim her as my prize.

In the following months, I devoted as much attention as possible to my new daughter. Cynthia was always smiling. Sometimes when I looked at her, it made me think of my own mother. I vowed that my new daughter would live a life of status and wealth.

In time, Elizabeth's health improved and we tried once more to mend our relationship, but had little success at taking care of one another's needs.

Two years later, Elizabeth became pregnant again. I was annoyed. I'd told her more than once that I had no interest in having more children. But after our daughter Barbara was born, Elizabeth's motherly instincts suddenly appeared when the infant became ill. Struck with chronic chest infections, Barbara spent several weeks in the hospital. Her weak physical condition infuriated me because I had always equated physical strength to success.

When we were finally able to bring Barbara home, I watched Elizabeth handle her as delicately as a porcelain doll. She babied the child as though she were an invalid. When my wife insisted that our sick child sleep with us in our bedroom, I announced, "I'm going to sleep in the guest room."

Six months later, one evening, after I got home from a rancher's meeting up north, Elizabeth told me that Barbara was back in the hospital. "I'm on my way there. It would be nice if you came along, for a change."

"I'm too tired and have a lot on my mind," I answered and sat down on the couch.

"Otto, you worry more about this city than you do about your own family," she angrily flared.

"You can baby her, if you want," I mumbled to myself. "City business will always come before an ailing child."

Elizabeth slammed the door on her way out. I shook my head with disgust. I never said anything about her extensive social gatherings, lavish purchases and continued bedroom follies, but the sick baby was not something I had asked for. It was just one of many things we didn't see eye to eye on. Our separate daily lives, limited communication and different ways of thinking had created a giant wedge in our relationship. Still, I had to maintain some peace to keep our family image.

Over time, our disagreements led to permanently separate bedrooms. It was easier. My hours had become erratic with late town meetings, city duties and Mr. Hearst's increased demands. I got so tired of Elizabeth's complaints that I hired a live-in housekeeper besides the nanny to help her with the growing girls.

As the years passed, Elizabeth's freedom from the children gave her time to establish a high-society social life filled with tea and garden parties. I was pleased that the group of women supported the community. It reflected well on me.

Three years passed and the two of us spent less and less time together. It seemed my wife was happiest when she was tending our garden and decorating the house with flowers for every season.

One evening when I arrived home late, she confronted me a few steps from the front door, but did not come any closer. "Otto, we can't go on like this. You're never home. Even when you are, you spend more time with Cynthia than Barbara or me. I need more from you as their father and as my husband," she sighed.

"Elizabeth, isn't it enough that I hired a housekeeper and nanny to help you? What else do you want from me? I have a growing city that's facing a water crisis. If I don't find a solution soon, the citizens will demand my resignation."

"Why don't you just go live at the county courthouse?" Elizabeth yelled as she stormed upstairs.

I followed her and softly knocked on her bedroom door. "We need to talk, Elizabeth," I demanded.

"The door is open."

I breathed in the fresh smell of roses as Elizabeth looked up at me from the edge of her quilted bed. "I don't know you, Otto. You supply me with every comfort, but I feel a vacant hole in my life," her head slumped down.

"It is not my intention to hurt you. I will try to spend more time as a family, but all these comforts come at a cost."

"I'm probably more upset than usual because I've received some disturbing news. A letter arrived from my uncle Leo overseas. He says war is looming there. He was also concerned about an increased threat to his family due to the advancement of the communist front. On the radio, they say there are bloody massacres of Jews taking place." Elizabeth began to sob. "We've got to do something. My father knows a banker in San Francisco who might be able to help."

I sat down next to her and let her head rest upon my shoulder. "Yes, I've heard that, too. I understand your concern, but my priorities are with local issues, not world events." When I saw tears streaming down her face, I offered, "Tomorrow I'll make some inquiries and see what can be done."

As I turned to walk away, Elizabeth whispered, "Thank you."

Later that night, she appeared at my door wearing a sheer negligee and nothing else. I was enticed by her poise and her long sexy legs. I dared not refuse her offer.

Our mutual heritage was in danger. For that night, we stopped being enemies and became mutual supporters. We both were servants to a higher cause of the religious heritage we shared. For this one night we surrendered to each other's needs, which lit a fire of passion between us that took all night to extinguish.

The next day Elizabeth gave me Mr. Goldman's number. He was the banker in San Francisco that her father knew—the president of West Coast Trust, Inc. Later in the day, I called him.

"Financial aid can be wired overseas, Otto, but I will need your signature and some personal information and documentation to secure the transaction," he informed me.

When I opened my desk to obtain the legal information needed, my eyes fell upon the wrapped, pink Cuban cigar I had set aside for Gordon years ago. The trip to San Francisco I would need to make to visit Mr. Goldman would be a fine opportunity to give the cigar to Gordon. So much had changed since my college graduation. I wondered how he would react if I contacted him now.

I picked up the phone and waited for the operator to come on the line.

She asked, "In what city is your party located?"

"San Francisco."

"What is the name of the person you wish to speak with?"

"Professor Gordon Sorenson."

Chapter Six
The Visit

1928
Santa Barbara and San Francisco, California
Otto Preston

My heart skipped a beat upon hearing the professor's voice. "Gordon, it's Otto Preston. I'll be in town this weekend and I was wondering if we could get together." I anxiously tapped my foot, waiting for his reply.

"I'd love to see you. We have a lot of catching up to do."

"I'll be staying at the Fremont and I have some business to take care of. I'll call you and maybe we can meet for a drink in the lounge?"

"I look forward to seeing my favorite pupil."

I took a deep breath and hung up the phone. It had been nearly ten years since my graduation and I often wondered if Gordon ever thought about me. Even though are lives were separate, I'd never forgotten my teacher's lessons of social skills and sexual satisfaction. If nothing else happened, at least I could sincerely thank him for all that he'd done for me.

My train arrived in San Francisco on a foggy Friday morning. From the station, I took a carriage directly to the Fremont Hotel where Mr. Goldman had made my reservation. While waiting in the lobby, a hotel clerk disclosed to me that several presidents and a king had stayed in the six-thousand-square-foot penthouse suite on the eighth floor where I would be staying. Even though I'd never met Mr. Goldman, I was impressed with his fine taste and generosity, equal to Mr. Hearst, my favorite client.

I had the requested stocks and bonds I'd purchased as collateral for the overseas transaction. By wiring the money, I would secure Elizabeth's uncle's entire family a safe passage to the United States. I also enclosed a large donation to support the Allied cause.

Later that day, a courier picked me up and I arrived at the bank's five-story brick building, located downtown. I was greeted by a doorman, who showed me the metal cage elevator that would take me to Mr. Goldman's private office on the top floor. Goldman's secretary announced my arrival. As I walked into his wood-paneled private office, I was pleasantly surprised to find the aged bank president with a full gray beard and bushy mustache like the kind my old Hebrew school rabbis wore. Mr. Goldman's compassionate brown eyes, warm handshake and greeting of "Shalom" created an instant rapport between us.

I listened closely to what he had to say.

"Adolph Hitler is a threat to all Jews, and we have to stop him," he asserted. "Your contribution toward the fight against anti-Semitism is greatly appreciated. Please give Elizabeth my warmest regards and assure her that her family will be taken care of." The affluent businessman, about my father's age, told me, "I will bring the final receipt of this transaction to the hotel later this afternoon."

We shook hands, and I sincerely thanked him for his generous hospitality, business expertise and compassion.

Outside while I sat in my carriage, I thought about my father. Recently, my mother had written to say that he was completely bedridden. It was a relief for me to know that he couldn't hurt anyone anymore. I had no sympathy in my heart for the estranged man that had bullied me all through my childhood. I had pity only for my poor mother, who had to take care of him. I was certain that she had known, once I left home, that I would never return. I made sure to let her know that I would care for her financially when my father passed away.

On my way back to the hotel, I asked my driver to go by Hatfield College of Law. It seemed strange to see the young students more casually dressed as they bustled about the campus. The school hadn't changed a bit. The scene brought back fond memories of Gordon and I wondered if he'd found a new student to mentor.

Back at my hotel, I looked around my elegant suite. It had four marble fireplaces, three bedrooms, Persian rugs and a grand piano in the living room. Exotic hardwood floors led out to a balcony with a sweeping view of San Francisco Bay. I had a smoke, cleaned up and unpacked the box of fine Cuban cigars I'd bought for Gordon in addition to the one I'd set aside upon Cynthia's birth.

After a quick nap, I received a message from the bellboy. It was a request from Mr. Goldman that we meet at 6:00 PM in the dining room restaurant on the main floor. I would telegram Elizabeth when the bank transaction was complete. She knew I would not be returning until Sunday morning. I had other personal business on my mind.

Mr. Goldman arrived promptly and the paperwork was quickly completed. We had dinner together and he left around 8:00 PM.

In the lounge, I ordered a scotch. Soon, memories of my relationship with Gordon were turning through my mind like pages of a scrapbook. Though I'd been busy these past years since our last meeting, I never had stopped thinking about him. Gordon understood and enjoyed my need for sexual rough housing, deep penetration and urgent desires and supplied them willingly. Elizabeth would stop me cold, if I got at all rough with her.

Gordon arrived timely and neatly dressed as usual, wearing a beige, three-piece cashmere suit with a matching hat. His hair was grayer, but I felt immediate comfort in his presence and had a renewed desire for more. I ordered him a drink. As the chatter of small talk commenced, the time that had elapsed since we had last seen each other vanished as though it had been only yesterday.

I'd forgotten how much I enjoyed listening to his British accent, breathing in his Old Spice cologne and getting lost in his clear baby blues. In the darkness, our knees touched, and with the speed of an electric shock I once again felt the savage attraction between us.

"I have something for you to open later." Gordon smiled as he handed me a small briefcase.

While we casually consumed our drinks, I felt my savage urge flame. I boasted about my business and political success to compensate for my flustered feelings. "I owe much of it to you," I admitted.

"Otto, I'm so proud of you. My years as a teacher now have greater meaning." My old companion tilted his head down toward the table and sighed, "I've missed you."

I warmly put my hand on his shoulder and squeezed down. "Let's go upstairs, Gordon, where we can enjoy the view."

I could feel the sensual heat between us as our elevator climbed toward my room. Once behind closed doors, the raging passion we shared seemed to explode. We teased and stoked each other with the intensity of new lovers. "You bring out the beast in me," I said.

Our clothes fell to the floor, and we headed toward the bathroom for a ritual wash and a steamy shower. With our hands filled with foaming lather, we stroked each other's bodies. I felt every muscle in my lower body tighten. With the skill of masters, we guided our fingers toward the other's hungry pleasure points. My body quivered with pleasure at the pull of Gordon's mouth devouring my cock. When he crushed his full body against me, thrusting into me, my hands slammed against the wall.

We packed a lifetime of passion into one night of lovemaking. I had to admit there was something to be said about a man knowing what a man needs. Even though such human experience has taken place throughout history, we both knew it was not accepted in mainstream social behavior.

I did not understand or deny my desire for certain members of my same sex. I only knew that my feelings were as real as the flesh on my bones. There are those who would say this behavior was a crime against God, but I believed people were just displacing their personal judgments onto Him. My feelings were always natural. The exchange between Gordon and I was always simply an act between two consenting adults.

Even so, by morning we both knew that had been the final chapter of our illicit affair. Neither of us could afford the public embarrassment of its disclosure, were it ever to come out.

Before saying goodbye, I opened Gordon's gift. Inside was a beautiful, hand-carved ivory chess set. After a quick embrace, I handed him the box of Cuban cigars. Tucked inside, he would later find the pink one. At the bottom of the box, I had slipped inside a photograph of my daughter Cynthia, sitting on my knee.

Chapter Seven
Political Clout

1928
Santa Barbara, California
Otto Preston

Upon returning home, I soon realized the problems Elizabeth and I had were small compared to the challenges I faced between the North and South counties. Outside the courthouse, my once long-time supporter Hank Thurman confronted me, "What are you going to do about the water shortage? We need answers now, before this drought takes all our crops." His voice shuddered in desperation.

"My friend, that issue weighs heavy on my mind. Please be patient, and I promise to address this and other issues at Friday's Town Hall meeting," I explained.

"I've heard talk about a demand for your resignation, Otto. I'm warning you now. Both the city folk and ranchers are unhappy. They mean business."

"Thanks for the warning, Hank. You'll get those answers at the meeting," I promised.

After Hank left, I closed my office door to contemplate my next move. I had to take immediate action to keep both sides happy. It called for the strategy needed to win a challenging chess game.

So far I'd been lucky. In the north, political favors I had performed for others had brought personal pay dirt in return—property ownership and financial donations to my campaign. I'd already acquired several hundred acres of agricultural land to build the Preston empire. In the city, Mr. Hearst had printed a favorable article in the *Mariposa Daily* that nearly guaranteed my reelection.

But none of that could help me now. If I didn't come through at the next town meeting, I might lose my job. I made a quick assessment of my options. The plan to secure federal funds to build the dams necessary to prevent future water shortages was already drafted, but being unfamiliar with that part of the government, I was unsure about my success to obtain them. I had to keep Mr. Hearst and myself in good standing with the citizens, yet it was difficult with opposition was on the rise against an additional film studio in Santa Barbara.

I needed to figure out a way to appease everyone. An asset I often used was the political clout that came with my job. Sometimes I had to walk a tightrope to get what I wanted done, but I felt like it brought out the best in me. With a sudden idea, I picked up the phone and called the director of the local department of transportation, Mr. Thompson. "Ted, your brother-in-law's construction company has a bid on the Spenser development project that goes before the board next week, right? I'd like to award him the contract, but find myself undecided."

"He is a good man, Otto, and his company is highly rated in the county. Is there anything I can do to make your decision easier?" Mr. Thompson offered.

"Maybe. I have a zoning issue with a piece of real estate. Is that something you can help me with?"

"I believe so. Let's talk over lunch, Otto. We can discuss the details then," Ted suggested.

The transaction would be an exchange of favors. On many occasions, my legal expertise had helped key individuals through personal crises. Some were judges, others local city officials. I had even aided the police chief during an ugly divorce. In return, I expected to be able to call in favors. After all, the expense of my political campaign ran high.

I sat at my desk and reviewed the large amount of funds made available for Mr. Hearst's special project and decided to make another call. "W.R., I believe the zoning issue on the studio property can be solved. As you are aware, the citizens of Santa Barbara oppose this venture. If you offer a substantial cultural donation, it could bring you into public favor."

"Brilliant idea, Otto. Do whatever it takes to get the project moving." My busy schedule had forced me to limit my legal clients, but I always made time for Mr. Hearst.

Friday evening, I heard loud chatter spilling out from the nearby assembly chambers where the town meeting was held. Before leaving my office, I washed up, had a cigarette and did a last minute check of my appearance in the restroom mirror. When I arrived at the assembly room down the hall, businessmen, farmers and city citizens had already filled the large gathering.

I had to bang down my gavel hard several times to call the meeting to order. "Thank you all for attending. Tonight, several issues will be addressed, including the water shortages, proposed property developments and long-range city goals. I'd like to begin by making some announcements that will benefit both the North and South counties."

"We need answers now!" an angry citizen called out. "Rumors of water rationing have surfaced. Will the government be imposing such regulations?"

Heated voices echoed throughout the chamber at the prospect.

I slammed my gavel down again and demanded, "Order! Quiet down and give me time to address your concerns. First, I have prepared a proposal to secure government funds for the construction of several dams as the solution to our ongoing water problems. No rationing is anticipated. Second, I've appointed a Project Review Committee to submit an evaluation of all pending land development for public review. Third, an outline of short-and long-range goals for the growth and development of the city will be made available for viewing at our new library, which will be funded by our local entrepreneur, Mr. William Randolph Hearst."

With this announcement, applause followed. I took a deep breath and opened the floor for questions. Before the night was over, all fears and issues were addressed as I promised my fellow citizens a brighter future.

While I headed back toward my office, a tall, heavy-set man with a handlebar mustache approached me, smoking a big cigar. "Mr. Preston, we haven't met. My name is Antonio Marcello." He held out his hand. "I own *Marcello's*, the new Italian restaurant in town. Maybe we can do some business together," he offered me his business card.

Antonio's gangster-grip handshake, inset beady eyes and thick Chicago accent reminded me of the men who frequented the town's local pool halls. Still, I tucked the card inside my jacket and promised, "I'll stop by sometime."

The next day, I telephoned Ted to meet me at *Marcello's* for lunch. "It's located on Main Street in the center of town."

Diamondback leather chairs with blood-red tablecloths and the aroma of sizzling garlic welcomed us as we entered the upscale diner. Immediately, a bottle of wine appeared "Compliments of Antonio," the waiter smiled as he served us.

I was not surprised when the robust Italian sat down at the table right after Ted left. He offered me a smoke and lit my cigarette. "We have something in common. You're from the east side of Chicago, right?"

I nodded.

"Something tells me you're a man of opportunity. I think there is something you might be interested in."

I put my cigarette out. "Well, Mr. Marcello, that depends."

"Call me Tony." He stood up and waved his arm and said, "Follow me." Tony headed toward the kitchen.

Always drawn in by the curiosity of forbidden fruit, I accepted his invitation. We walked past the kitchen toward the back of the restaurant where he opened a tall wooden door. Before us was a dimly lit stairway leading up.

Tony gestured for me to follow him. My palms filled with sweat as I heard the heavy man's footsteps creak while we climbed to our unknown location.

At the top of the stairwell, he spoke what I presume was Italian to a big guy standing guard at the entrance way. The giant man pushed open a set of velvet drapes, and the air behind him burst forth with piano music, smoke and laughter.

Through the hazy, muted light inside, I could see the outline of jovial patrons enjoying illegal liquor. I had known hidden places like it existed, but had never stepped foot into one of them myself. It didn't take me long to figure out what Tony had on his mind. He knew if a police raid were scheduled, I would know about it. What could be worth this kind of news scoop? I wondered. Tony and I sat down at an empty table in the back of the room.

Just then, I felt a tap on my shoulder and turned around. Standing before me was a platinum blond bombshell as sultry as Hearst's mistress. She was wrapped in leopard and black lace with mounds of exposed flesh that cast a spell on me to come and have a taste. The dame was the vision of my wildest sexual fantasy.

"This is…Stella." Tony's words trailed off as my I consumed every inch of her buxom silhouette.

"Can I have a seat, big boy?" she teased, running her tongue across her hot, ruby red lips.

Stella's body intoxicated me. I felt sweat bead on my forehead as the sex kitten rubbed her long, slim, gartered, stockinged leg against mine. She sat her bottom in my lap, like a bitch in heat, while lifting a cigar out of Tony's pocket. Stella wrapped her hand around the rolled tobacco leaves, opened her mouth wide and deep throated it. I swallowed hard as I watched her sumptuous tongue flick across the cigar's tip like a snake's. "Just a sample of my talents," the sexual tigress chimed.

I reeled back, not wanting to look too anxious.

"Are we talking about a trade agreement here?" I asked Tony with my eyes still on Stella, my heart racing.

"Peace of mind for my business, and a high-class piece of ass for you." I caught Tony's grin out of the corner of my eye.

"My name is Stella Barnes," the enticing bait purred. "I can take care of things from here." Like a sex goddess, she motioned Tony to leave.

For the next few moments, Stella's hips performed a striptease bump and grind. When she pressed her firm breasts forward, my entire face was nearly drowned in her flesh. I took a deep breath and inhaled her piquant perfume. The scent completely melted away any resistance. I was rock hard and my animal urges craved more of the lovely vision.

I could tell Stella was a dame that understood what a man needed. We headed toward a private back room as she pressed her tight ass against my rock hard cock. From the last doorway down the hall, I roared like the king of beasts in an explosion of ecstasy.

Chapter Eight
The High Cost of Games

1928
Santa Barbara and San Simeon, California
Otto Preston

Some political favors came at a high cost, and keeping *Marcello's* under wraps was one of them. I made sure the police chief received a regular supply of imported cigars, provided unlimited legal advice for the county sheriffs and made sure the cops on Tony's beat were supplied free meals.

Power became my drug of choice. I craved it. The city became my kingdom. I could rule it with the power of a king. With clever moves, favors called in and knowledge on how to bend the law, I could easily fulfill my personal needs and cover up any unethical deeds.

Then late one evening, my private phone rang. It was Mr. Hearst calling to summon me immediately to his estate. "There has been an accident," he said, offering no further details.

I grabbed my overcoat and hat, left a note for Elizabeth and headed out the door. Upon my arrival, I was quickly ushered into W.R.'s private office. I was shocked to see my client's face pale and forlorn. In the distance, I heard a woman crying and wondered if it was Marion.

Mr. Hearst let out a deep sigh before disclosing the unfortunate events that had transpired. "Otto, our casual outing at sea came to a tragic end. Tom Ince is dead. The details of his death must remain confidential. Those involved cannot afford the publicity of a scandal."

Oh my god, Tom's dead. How can it be? I wondered. My mind fought the notion of his death with disbelief. Lots of questions crossed my mind, but I knew better than to ask them. From the distressed look on W.R.'s face, I realized there was more to the story than he wanted to reveal ... or than I was willing to confront.

"I need your help, Otto, not only as my lawyer, but as my friend." He buried his face inside his hands.

With the control of a taskmaster, I crushed any personal sentiment for Tom, recognizing the desperation in my mentor's voice. Wails of grief continued to echo from down the hall while I struggled to find an answer to the dilemma. There was no doubt that any action I took would be consequential, but it was my duty as his legal advisor to offer assistance.

"I'll take care of it," I told him, although I didn't have any definite plan.

One hour later, two Mexican laborers loaded Tom's body, wrapped up in a sheet, into my trunk. I headed down the long driveway, noticing my white knuckles on the steering wheel as I shivered in fear.

A mist hung low over the highway on the eerie ride back to Santa Barbara. After a while, I discovered a small, alligator skin case stuffed with hundred dollar bills that rested on the front seat of my Bentley. I was haunted by Tom's million-dollar smile. The shadows of the night conspired to cast a reflection that suggested blood on my own hands. The creepy image, chilly air and my heavy mood gave me a maddening urge to drive faster. Even though I had taken no part in the events leading to Tom's death, I knew I was involved way over my head. As the miles slithered by, I desperately tried to think up a plan.

Once in town, I went straight to the county morgue and located Jerry Cahill, the coroner, who was an old client of mine. His apartment was behind the old building. In the past, I'd helped him out of several legal jams. Jerry reminded me of a buddy I'd had in college—they were both notorious for getting into trouble, and they had the same short stature, carrot-red hair, pale skin and broken noses. Jerry was a smart enough kid, but he had no luck with women. A year earlier, he'd been caught with a prostitute and I'd bailed him out.

I was relieved to see a light on. When my client opened the large swinging metal doors, I instantly told him, "I need a big favor, Jerry. I'm in dire need of your services. There's been an accident involving a high-profile client of mine."

In the middle of the night, not a soul was around to see us carry Tom's body inside.

I unzipped the alligator wallet and placed a stack of hundred dollar bills on the nearby desk. "This has to be handled with kid gloves. Can I count on you to take care of it?"

Jerry picked up the blood money from the table and answered, "You bet. Looks like a heart attack to me. A doctor friend of mine can confirm it," he assured me.

I breathed a sigh of relief as we shook hands. Jerry prepared to slide

Tom's corpse into a refrigerated unit. "Wait a minute, Jerry," I ordered.

Standing beside my dead friend, I pulled back the sheet. I felt the blood drain from my face when I saw Tom's chalk-colored skin, his once-shining baby blues gone out forever. I noticed a small hole by his left shirt pocket that may have been the real cause of his demise. Replacing the white sheet, I reminded myself that the potential rewards for this deed would definitely outweigh any risks.

In the morning newspapers, Tom's death was listed as heart attack at sea. Few details were given, and no foul play noted. Yet as news spread of the incident, suspicions were raised.

I made it my job to make sure no guilty fingers were pointed. At Tom's funeral in LA, anyone who was anyone in Hollywood attended. In time, the mystery surrounding his death only slightly echoed at the mention of his name. The castle's secrets remained safe on the hill.

Back at work one afternoon, my secretary alerted me that a group of angry ranchers had stormed the courthouse. I stood at my office doorway and addressed them, "Gentlemen, please come in."

"Otto, we need those dams you promised now! Our crops are drying up." Hank Thurman threw his hands in the air. "Exactly where and when will the dams you promised be built?" he demanded.

"I've completed two government grant proposals. Next week, I will travel to Washington, DC to obtain the funds and the final approval."

"That's not good enough." Hank shook his head. "If you don't start rationing water now, come fall, there won't be any crops to harvest."

"Rationing is a last resort, Hank. You have to be patient. We need the guarantee of government funding to begin these projects. It is the only permanent solution to the problem. Once we have approval, the work can be started immediately."

"Two weeks, Otto. That is all we can give you. If there is no word, we want your resignation as supervisor," Hank declared.

It bothered me that Hank Thurman, one of my strongest supporters, was now my biggest threat. "Hank, you'll get those dams. I guarantee that I'll return from Washington with it in writing."

After they left, I sat at my desk. As a precaution, I needed to approach the Santa Barbara Utilities Board with the prospect of water rationing, just in case the dams didn't get approved.

Later that day at a meeting, I presented my case to the Committee Board, but they expressed some opposition.

"The town's citizens do not share your sympathy for the rural community, Mr. Preston," the chairman retorted. "It's your job to secure the government funds for this project. Do you have a backup plan?"

"I have a proposal ready and a trip to Washington planned for next week. There is no reason to believe that the funds will not be approved." I stood my ground.

"We respect your confidence, but the citizens have expressed disappointment with how this crisis has been handled. We need results, Mr. Preston, and if you don't obtain them, your position as supervisor is in jeopardy."

"I understand," I told them and slammed the door behind me.

Inside my private office, I thought about how difficult it was to please both the urban and rural citizens. The city demanded improved streets, more public transportation and better cultural activities, while the agricultural region needed a guaranteed water supply, more schools and health facilities. It seemed like an impossible job to comply with all these demands. It was like trying to arbitrate a civil war.

If I didn't come through, my political future was over. I sank down into my chair and felt defeated. How can this be happening? I wondered.

I'd worked hard and made the city a place anyone would be proud to live in. Despite all my work and help, my local lawyer friends, city officials and county supporters could do nothing to help me with the endeavor to secure funding from the federal government. For the past few years, I'd worked my ass off trying to keep everybody happy. This was not how I wanted the Preston legacy to end.

My affiliation with W.R. had taught me the importance of staying in favorable public opinion, of going after what you want and of doing whatever it took to get it. For the first time I was deeply worried. Would I fail?

Still in my office, I somberly gathered together the documents for my trip. I wondered, what if the amount of money I'm asking for doesn't cover the full cost of building the dams? Since I was not familiar with that higher part of the government, my confidence waned. I heard taunting laughter inside my head.

Without warning, everything around me began to shake and rumble. The floor seemed to slip right out from under me, and I desperately grabbed hold of the sides of my desk. Books flew off shelves, papers scattered to the floor and the deafening sound of breaking glass filled the air. Chills ran down my spine when I heard screams of terror echoing down the courthouse hallway.

It seemed like an eternity before the severe rattling stopped. I realized a severe earthquake had just occurred. I yelled out to my secretary, Mary,

"Are you okay?"

Mary stood trembling at the doorway, her face as white as a ghost's. As a young woman of twenty, pretty and petite, she would be worthless in the catastrophe. "I'm scared, but not hurt," her voice trembled.

"This is an emergency. I've got to assess the city's damage."

"The phones aren't working and the electricity is off. What should I do?"

"First we need to check and see if anyone here needs medical attention. Just stay put, Mary, until I can get things under control." I ran out of the door.

I knew my first priority was the safety of my citizens. The fire brigade, police force and local government aid agencies had emergency programs that had to be implemented fast.

I did a quick assessment of the courthouse and found that it had only suffered minor damage. It was a relief to learn that there were no serious injuries. I went back to my office and told Mary, "Walk down to my home and make sure Elizabeth and the girls are safe. I can handle things here."

After Mary left, I decided to go out to the second story balcony of the courthouse. Before me were many damaged buildings and collapsed roofs. Piles of rubble lay like carnage on the ground. Sirens howled and smoke filled the air, while dazed citizens poured into the streets. Everything had changed in one moment.

Maybe, I thought, if I played my cards right, this disaster can make me into a hero instead of a villain.

Several hours later when the phone lines were restored, the mayor gave me a call. "Otto, your emergency plans are working. Help is on the way to all who need it. Several fires and collapsed buildings have been reported. Farmers and ranchers from the north have arrived to help. It is amazing how our city can come together when in need."

We met later to further evaluate the situation. I was informed that several burst water pipes had been turned off. It seemed Mother Nature had her own rationing plan.

When Mary returned, she said, "Elizabeth and the girls were shook up, but they were unhurt. Your house sustained minor damage."

Later I received a message from the editor of the *Mariposa Daily* newspaper: "Sheffield reservoir cracked and sent a wall of water into the ocean. The police chief declared martial law. Hospitals are receiving the injured and a number of deaths have been reported."

By the end of the day, it was confirmed that a 6.3 magnitude earthquake had struck Santa Barbara and had caused an estimated $8 million in damage to my city. Thirteen people had lost their lives.

The mood was grim as city leaders came together. They looked to me for answers on how to deal with this new crisis.

In the counsel chambers, the mayor requested that I address the town leaders: "Our fine city has suffered a natural disaster. We have millions of dollars in damage to property, buildings and homes. We will survive. The task at hand is to make Santa Barbara come back, bigger, better and stronger than before." The forlorn group patiently listened. "We need federal assistance, and I will leave for Washington, DC immediately to seek help. Refer to the mayor in my absence."

The next morning, I got a call from Mr. Hearst offering to accompany me on my cross-country trip. Inside my aging friend's luxurious private train car, we penciled out several different proposals for federal grants to reconstruct the city and to build two new dams.

On that trip, I learned the true importance of knowing the right people in high places. Through a critical meeting arranged by W.R., I met with Mr. Neal Johnson, the director of the Bureau of Reclamation. As the arm of the federal government renowned for the dams, power plants and canals it had commissioned for construction since 1902, the Bureau of Reclamation had the power to approve multi-million-dollar projects. W.R. knew Johnson's agenda. In the past, W.R. had offered his influential status to raise public support for government initiatives Johnson wanted passed.

I was impressed with the ease with which our goals were accomplished as we secured the first ever, directly funded $80 million federal grant. The deal was sealed with a handshake and only one stipulation: somewhere in Santa Barbara county, I had to designate fourteen acres of land to be set aside for a nuclear waste disposal site.

On our train ride home, W.R. and I opened a bottle of vintage champagne to toast our success. It was unspoken between us, but I knew W.R.'s debt to me had now been settled. Afterwards, we sat together like two kings enjoying a friendly game of chess.

Chapter Nine
Long-Term Plans

1929
Santa Barbara, California
Otto Preston

The planning of the enormous dam construction projects and the reconstruction of the city brought daily problems that mounted like steam in a boiler. Issues like sandy soil, earthquake requirements and safety concerns drew my immediate attention. The North and South counties both indicated that they wanted control of the dams' water rights. I had been elected Chairman of the Board of Supervisors and this now increased my duties and power.

The morning assembly was scheduled for 10:00 AM at the courthouse. Outside the boardroom, I heard the familiar roar of angry voices. I took my place in front of the packed crowd of businessman and ranchers. "I call this meeting to order."

The roar continued.

"Fellow citizens," I called to them. "I demand respectful behavior in this courtroom. Open discussion of town issues will not begin until everyone is quiet and seated." I looked around to see if my commanding voice and vocal sternness had made their point and it had.

"Our agenda includes discussion of financial assistance for rebuilding our city, locations for the federal dams project, the disposition of water rights and the proposed nuclear waste site. I must limit each speaker to three minutes of floor time. Each citizen will be recognized by name; please state your occupation and place of residence. No interruptions or outbursts of any kind will be tolerated."

There was a buzz of conversation between people in the audience, and I slammed down my gavel. "This meeting will be canceled if I do not get your cooperation in these matters. I will not stand for this kind of disrespect in my courtroom."

Hank Thurman requested the floor. He gave his name and continued, "I'm a farmer representing the rural community of the North County, Mr. Chairman. With respect, I feel we are entitled to the water rights of the federal dams. Our livelihoods depend on the water supply, and we more effectively understand the requirements for the area."

When Hank sat down, angry voices of city dwellers filled the chamber. Again I called the meeting back to order.

Tony Marcello stood up and requested the floor. He gave his name and said, "I'm a business owner in the city, Mr. Chairman, and I disagree. The water rights should belong to the city. We reflect a higher number of citizens, all of whom contribute to the prosperity of the town. Our concerns are for the future population of our growing city. We need a guaranteed water supply."

Hank jumped up from his seat. "You city slickers only think of yourselves!"

Several individuals from the rural community and from the urban community began to call each other vicious names, arguing bitterly as to who deserved the water more.

I shook my head with disbelief. In a loud voice, I demanded, "This childish behavior cannot be tolerated here. I need order in this meeting." I pounded my fist down on the wooden desk several times.

Finally, the crowd quieted. I stared out at the diverse congregation. "Gentlemen, arguments are getting us nowhere. The control of the water rights to these dams should not divide us, but instead unite us. The dams will ensure prosperity for both the North and South counties. Can you at least all agree that our only feasible long-term water source is the Santa Ynez River?"

For the first time, concurrence came from both parties.

"I propose a compromise. A water reclamation committee will be created to represent both parties. One dam's location will be diverted to the North and the other to the South. The sooner these projects are completed, all water rationing and fines for overuse will be terminated."

A round of applause filled the air.

When a vote was taken to move the motion through, it passed by a large margin. I was pleased about transforming the local war into a truce. Moreover, I had achieved my ultimate goal: the city council would keep control of all water rights and I would have final say over all decisions in regard to this matter.

Afterward, I disclosed a possible location for the nuclear

waste-dumping site just outside of the city limits, still far from agricultural terrain.

When I pointed to the location on a nearby map, the new superintendent of schools raised an objection. "As our city expands, can you ensure us that this land will remain publicly safe?"

"The sealed containers are guaranteed by the federal government not to hold any public threat. There will be full disclosure if any risk is evident," I answered.

The long meeting closed with the appointment of two committees. One was designated to oversee the water rights issue and the other to distribute the grant the government had given us for rebuilding after the earthquake.

With the meeting adjourned, I told my secretary I would be unavailable for the rest of the day. I left the courthouse and ventured to the apartment building where I was keeping Miss Stella in finery.

Heat permeated my groin as I thought about the delicious treat Stella would soon offer me. I headed toward the private elevator to our secluded apartment, this way I had her all to myself. When I opened the door, my seductive mistress greeted me wearing her low-cut corset, black garters, nylons and nothing else. Stella put out her cigarette and motioned me inside. I squeezed her plump exposed breasts and slid my tongue deep down into her cleavage. She planted her moist red lips on mine, and I yanked her body close.

Her hand slid down my trousers and she gave my cock a quick, teasing squeeze. "Otto, slow down, there is plenty of time for that. Let's have a drink first."

My eyes followed her firm buttocks while she poured me a scotch and performed a slow striptease, removing the rest of her garments. My mouth watered in anticipation of our time in bed when I'd ride my prize like a bull in heat.

Stella knew what I needed. She willingly got the job done and never denied my S & M requests.

Afterwards, she worked the tension from my back while she sat on my naked ass. With her, all business was forgotten. Our partnership was a perfect trade agreement: physical satisfaction for me and financial comfort for her in return.

Chapter Ten
Fear, Lies and Cover-Ups

October 1929
Santa Barbara, California
Otto Preston

With an election looming, I needed to secure my political position. I wouldn't let rumors spread by disgruntled citizens jeopardize my reputation at such an important time. I knew several rising political figures were after my job.

Tom Barker, a local hardware store owner, had already decided to run against me. I was furious when I heard him say, "It's time for a change." With the help of my friends in the media, we fabricated a rumor about Mr. Barker's possible association with the mafia. By the time his name was cleared, my reelection was already a done deal.

I felt like a champion, leaning back in my chair in the office that day. I was at the top of my game, again in control. For once, my father's voice wasn't there to reproach me.

Abruptly disrupting my moment of satisfaction, my secretary, Mary, rushed into my office with a panicked look on her face. "New York City is in chaos because the stock market has crashed. My phone is ringing off the hook from your associates with desperate cries for help. What do you want me to do?" she frantically asked.

Her words felt like a one-two punch. After a moment of thought, I answered, "Take messages and tell them I'll get back to them as soon as I can, Mary." She hurried out the door.

I turned on a nearby table radio and eagerly listened to the broadcaster. "An unexpected New York stork exchange collapse is making its effects felt across the country. Black Tuesday will forever remain a dark day in America's history. No one knows the full extent of this catastrophe. The economic fallout will impact the entire nation."

I felt a sudden lump in my throat and I couldn't move. This couldn't be happening at a worse time, I thought, a sick feeling filled my stomach. The cost of the dam projects had dried up the original federal grant money, and I recently had given the bank a personal guarantee that any additional debt would be paid.

After turning down the volume of the radio, I immediately called Mitchell and Blaine.

Harry advised me, "The banks are closed, Otto. Your personal assets are frozen, and most of our clients will be forced to liquidate their stocks due to margin calls."

After I hung up the phone, I slumped down into my chair, feeling as useless as a deflated balloon.

Mary again appeared at the door, her face sunken and distraught. "What should I tell them?"

"Hold all my calls," I ordered. "I need some time to plan a directive."

My mind was consumed with the priority of my own financial survival. I could make a total assessment of the crisis later, but just then I had to gather as much information as possible. I turned up the radio to hear more.

"Overextended investors have flooded the stock exchange with sell orders, resulting in the market crash. Many folks have had their life savings wiped out overnight. This is a dark day in American history as many families face financial ruin," the announcer groaned.

As my head reeled with this devastating news, my father's old familiar voice echoed in my head. *Loser—nothing can save you now.* I aimlessly walked around the room trying to accept the life-changing event that could ruin everything I'd worked for. My investments were as worthless as yesterday's newspaper.

To fail after having climbed so high would destroy me. I had to save the Preston legacy. I vowed to do whatever it took to stop this from disgracing Elizabeth, my children, or me.

I sat down at my desk, buried my face in my hands, and for the first time in years, prayed for an answer. My elbow jerked forward, my eyes opened, and I looked down.

Within my view was a large manila envelope. It had been part of the mail Mary had brought to me earlier. The return address was marked *Official Business, Washington, DC.* I quickly ripped it open and saw a $10,000 check from the federal government marked for payment for the fourteen acres that were designated for the required nuclear waste site location.

I realized the check was made out in my name. Gordon's words popped into my mind: *A man without money is as useless as a pen without ink.*

A desperate idea came to mind. What if I switched parcel numbers and listed a property I owned instead of the actual parcel number that had been designated for the toxic waste site? I could then use the payment for myself. Such illegal action would offer me financial security and protect my family from ruin. At a later time, I could fix the parcel numbers and pay the city back.

Even though the potential discovery of such an action was a threat that could ruin my reputation, I felt the reward would more than outweigh the risk. With my knowledge of the law, I would figure out a way to cover my tracks. Unfortunately, I knew it was only a temporary fix. Taking the money would save me, but it wouldn't be enough money to keep my status and help my friends. In time, I would have to come up with another form of revenue.

It was then I recalled a conversation that I had some time back with Adan Shariff, one of my overseas clients, who traded in diamonds.

"Otto, I have a lucrative offer that could secure your financial future," he had said when he approached me.

Before the stock market crash, I had had no interest in the offer, knowing the risks of engaging in the illegal activities he had in mind would be too high. But with my financial status in jeopardy, I knew his was an offer I couldn't refuse.

My first priority as supervisor was to keep my city running. Now that I knew how I would look after myself, I made a promise that the national financial crisis wouldn't destroy everything I'd worked for.

Chapter Eleven
Little Princess

1930-1939
Santa Barbara, California
Otto Preston

I did what it took to guarantee my financial and political survival. In the coming months, there were few quiet moments. By granting many personal loans to my friends and colleagues, I secured future favors they would owe me.

As the political arena became ever more cutthroat, I savored the evenings when I could return home and spend time with Cynthia, who at that time was already ten. At the end of my busy day, it was Cynthia's bright smile and hazel eyes that perked me up like a healthy dose of medicine. I would never forget the first time she said, "I love you, Daddy." It nearly brought me to my knees.

Barbara's illnesses remained constant, and Elizabeth spent all her spare time with her, so it was only natural that my oldest daughter longed for my attention. I enjoyed watching Cynthia dress up in fancy clothes. She loved to put on her mother's high-heeled shoes and fine hats.

We would pretend that she was my princess and I her king. Her bedroom was our castle where nobody could enter without permission. I helped her line up the music boxes that I'd bought as presents for her so that she could dance in front of me. Afterwards, she'd always run toward me with open arms, offering a big hug and kiss.

By the time she was age eight, I had already taught Cynthia how to play chess. It was another favorite pastime for us. I was glad I could share the tradition my mother had passed on to me with my daughter.

Five years flashed by. Elizabeth attended to the girls' social graces. I figured she knew what was best for them. Birthdays came and went. Our calendar was filled with piano recitals, political fundraisers and city celebrations. I never connected with Barbara. Cynthia kept me wrapped around her little finger.

Being a private person with hidden secrets, I could never let those around me get too close—not even Cynthia. I guarded my personal behavior and actions with the strength of a four-star general. What happened in my private life was strictly my business. I was always careful to cover my tracks and never allowed any type of disgrace to be tied to our family name. Protecting the Preston name was paramount to me.

When Elizabeth announced that it was time for the girls to go to a private boarding school on the East Coast for their higher education and etiquette lessons, I was saddened. I knew I would miss Cynthia dearly. While she was gone, I often took the picture of her I kept in my billfold out to show her off, bragging many times to those around me that she was my little princess.

During those three years, Cynthia wrote to me regularly. She mailed her letters directly to my office at the courthouse. I'd saved all of them in the locked desk drawer I used to store personal items. Cynthia expressed an interest in becoming a nurse. So as a special surprise, I sent her a complete medical reference library.

Finally, the time neared for the girls to return home. Elizabeth announced that I would be presenting my blossoming teenage daughters at the upcoming debutante ball. I was delighted that they would have completed the social requirement of a proper education. It was hard for me to imagine that they were already old enough to begin making decisions of their own. My hope was the ritual introduction into society at the debutante ball would insure that they both married worthy of the Preston name.

Just days before the girls' train was scheduled to arrive, I came home early to discover Elizabeth was not there. Heading upstairs, I saw her bedroom door ajar and checked inside. I noticed an open journal laying face down on her bedside table. Standing near the kerosene lamp, I opened to a marked page and began to read:

Sitting at my vanity table, I look in the mirror and I do not recognize my reflection. My physical state is as well preserved as that of a thoroughbred horse, but the spirit inside me has faded from my eyes like a wilting rose. Surely, I am a product of my own choices.

Those who see me from the outside do not know the pain I endure. At a glance, anyone would envy my status, luxurious lifestyle and position as Otto Preston's wife. What they do not know is that it is all a lie.

My home is immaculate, my hats and clothes custom-tailored and monogrammed. They are neatly cleaned and pressed by others. I have no want for strings of pearls, diamonds or furs. Beautiful flowers from my garden decorate our home throughout every season.

Yet the haunting voices that surround me at elegant parties, formal teas and political fundraisers are echoes of mockery. I play my role as the perfect wife and mother, shielding myself as a victim of heartbreak. Here in my private parlor is the only safe haven where I can express the ache of my lonely heart for the one thing money can't buy: True Love.

I swallowed hard, feeling the cutting truth of Elizabeth's written words. Yet I was drawn to read on.

I want to scream out, "I'm vibrant and alive. Why can't you see me as a woman with emotional and physical needs?" Yet, I dare not. I find comfort in financial security that sustains, like the warmth that emanates from my bedroom fireplace. Still, somehow, the chill of lost personal fulfillment seeps inside.

It is obvious that Otto has a mistress and no longer desires me for that part of his life. Even though no physical scars are visible, my self-confidence has taken a painful and savage beating. My husband's actions tell me he feels that there is nothing to lose.

Yet for me there is everything. For now I am silent and remain faithful for social standing and keep this emotional pain as my constant companion. My lesson learned is that a life of status and money comes with sacrifice.

Replacing the journal, I quickly returned downstairs.

Not long afterward, Elizabeth arrived with her arms filled with packages.

"You're home early, Otto. Maria came with me to pick up the girls' formal dresses for the debutante ball," she smiled.

"I look forward to Cynthia and Barbara's homecoming." I helped her with the packages.

Thoughts raced though my mind about what I'd read in Elizabeth's journal. It never occurred to me how she might feel or that she'd be disappointed with her role as my wife. Elizabeth never expressed her longings or suspicion to my face. Now with the girls returning, I knew some changes must be made. I would have to be more cautious about my private life and spend more time at home.

Part Two

Cynthia Preston
Barbara Preston
1940-1970

Chapter Twelve
Sisters: One

1940-1945
Santa Barbara, California
Cynthia Preston

I'd always been glad to be the oldest daughter in the Preston family. My favorite childhood memory was when my father and I pretend-played that we were a princess and a king. I have often recalled how I loved to dance for him and how I looked forward to his big hug and kiss at the end of each song.

Papa's busy schedule often kept him away, but when we were together, he made me feel like no one else existed in the world. All my life, he called me Princess. I still remember how exciting it was when he'd return home with his hands filled with music boxes for my sister, Barbara, and me.

During our childhood, Barbara spent a lot of time in the hospital or confined to bed because of her constant medical problems. She had asthma and chronic chest ailments that often kept us apart. If mother wasn't watching over Barbara, she was attending charitable luncheons or political support groups or working in her garden. In those early years, we spent most of our time with our nanny, Maria.

I never felt close to my mother. At times I thought she might be jealous of my relationship with Papa. When mother informed us we'd be attending boarding school in New England, I cried for days. Later at the train station, I promised Papa I would write, and he whispered, "Send them directly to the county courthouse."

While at boarding school in New England, my sister and I finally got to spend lots of time together, and her physical health improved. One night she revealed, "I never really felt like I had a father."

This made me sad. It was hard for me to be mad at Papa. He always filled my world with the warmth of the sun. On visits home, he let me attend city ceremonies and let me watch him speak to the citizens of our city. Since I was the eldest, he permitted me more than Barbara. He became my hero, and I'm so proud to be his daughter. I am certain all who know him respect him.

Lately I'd been thinking about becoming a nurse. My sister had shared wonderful stories with me of her special caregivers. I thought it would make Papa proud of me, too.

While we waited to take our train home, I was nervous thinking about the upcoming debutante ball. I wanted everything to be perfect and believed it would be one of the happiest days of my life.

In our boxcar, on our ride back home, Barbara excused herself to go to the bathroom. I watched her put down the journal she was writing in. Curiosity tends to get the best of me, and so I picked it up and began to read an entry.

Throughout my childhood, my father rarely turned his head in my direction. Not even these passing years can erase the painful rejection I feel inside of me. I really did try to please him. I got good grades, obeyed all the rules and did my best at everything. Still he didn't notice me, and no matter how I tried, it was never enough.

I really think my mother cared, but I always sensed a deep sadness that kept her distant. Maybe now that it is time for the debutante ball, things will change. Father is going to escort Cynthia and me that night. I'm so excited to finally stand by his side.

Her feelings cut my heart with truth. I set her diary down before she returned, and the rest of the ride home, we giggled and laughed about our soon-to-be coming-of-age party.

It was a wonderful homecoming. Papa, Mother and Maria waited with open arms for us at the train station.

"My, you both look like such polished young women," Mother commented.

"Princess, I couldn't wait to see you," Papa embraced me with a warm hug and kiss. He completely ignored Barbara.

Mother embraced Barbara and gave my father a disapproving stare.

The scene made me wonder how two sisters from the same parents could grow up to feel so different.

Chapter Thirteen
Sisters: Two

1940-1945
Santa Barbara, California
Barbara Preston

I always hated being the younger sister. My childhood memories are filled with sadness. Even though Maria and Mother looked after me while I was sick, Father had little patience for my constant illness and coughing bouts.

When mother first told us we would be going to boarding school in New England, I was so happy. Spending time with Cynthia and my other classmates helped me get beyond my physical weakness. I envied Cynthia, who knew what she wanted to be and who had won over our father's heart. I didn't understand his rejection, and I couldn't help being angry about it.

I was anxious and excited about our homecoming. Would I be able to win my father's affection? What if I got sick again? With the debutante ball coming up, I couldn't wait, to finally get to stand by father's side.

On the morning of the celebration, Mother called us upstairs for her final inspection of the clothes we were wearing. Our formal dresses were made of fine white satin with shoulder cap sleeves and a square neck. Each of us was to wear a matching sash with our name embroidered on it.

Maria helped us put on our dresses and we stood still as soldiers when Mother entered the room. One at a time, we got up on the stool for her to measure our hemlines with the yardstick.

"Your hair comb is crooked," she told Cynthia, proceeding to tug down on the diamond-and-pearl hair clip.

I watched my sister squint in pain while my mother snickered.

"Now put on your long white gloves like polite young ladies," Mother instructed us with the tone of our boarding-school teachers.

To my horror, I saw a bright red smear of lip paint across my glove. Mother grabbed the soiled accessory and yelled for Maria to quickly fetch another pair.

My body tightened as Mother's judging eyes scanned our bodies up and down. Before leaving the room, she stopped and straightened the shiny gold locket hanging around my neck.

"Girls, make your father proud," she ordered before leaving the room.

I was so nervous that night, I almost got sick to my stomach before we left. Cynthia gave me a hug and told me, "Everything is going to be fine."

I felt like my heart would jump right out of my chest when our names were called for presentation. Taking a deep breath, I thought, so far, so good, as Father took our arms to escort us onto the stage.

Like two glamorous movie starlets, we strode alongside our leading man. Soft music played as we took our place in line with the other girls. It was electrifying to be on stage with so many pretty young girls.

Afterward, groups of young and older tuxedoed gentlemen gathered around us, praising our youth and beauty.

Father commenced the evening with a champagne toast, standing to represent all the fathers present. "Today is a day of celebration. Each of us here has at least one beautiful young daughter to be proud of. Let us all take this moment to toast them with pride and to acknowledge their womanhood."

A loud round of applause followed as the servers poured the chilled, bubbling drink as generously as fountains.

Those of drinking age consumed their alcoholic beverages in the style appropriate to a party. It had been that way since Prohibition ended. After a short program and the meal, a group of musicians began to play. My father turned to Cynthia and asked her to dance. I wished it had been me instead.

To my surprise, one of my father's business friends at the table, Mr. Perkins, offered to be my partner. Without hesitation, I said yes. But once we were on the dance floor, he drew me close and I was overwhelmed by the strong smell of liquor on his breath. As the night progressed, I often noticed his vulgar gaze and seedy smile, further accented by his handlebar mustache. It made me increasingly uncomfortable. Cynthia and my father seemed oblivious to it.

My father soon received an urgent message of a crisis downtown. He apologized, telling us he had to leave, as it was an emergency. I was dismayed when Mr. Perkins offered to take us home and Father agreed.

When Cynthia left the table to meet with some friends, my heart sank. I knew I was lost and alone. The father-daughter high-society introduction was not turning out as I had hoped.

Cynthia eventually returned to the table to inform me that several of her girlfriends wanted to ride home together. Within that group was Mr. Perkins' daughter.

"Barbara, I'll personally take you home," he offered, his thin lips curling.

I wasn't sure what to say, but I finally agreed. My heart raced with fear as I lifted my formal dress to step into Mr. Perkins fancy, spanking new Rolls-Royce.

Once inside, the old coot motioned me to come closer. I shook my head, remaining silent as he started the car and we headed on our way.

Before I realized what he was doing, Mr. Perkins had pulled over to the side of a deserted road and turned off the engine. I tried to open the door to get in the backseat only to find it already locked. A wave of panic crashed over me.

"You stay away from me!" I yelled, my trembling voice trailing off in the darkness.

"Barbara, don't be afraid. Come closer," he demanded with a crazed look in his blood-shot eyes.

"No!" I frantically screamed, desperately looking for a way to escape. My whole body started to shiver, but I was so terrified that I couldn't move.

With the jar of an electric shock, Mr. Perkins forced me down flat against the front seat. I fought like a wild horse to get him off, madly kicking with my high-heeled shoes. He was much stronger than me, though, and my distress calls for help echoed inside the automobile to no avail.

Thrashing about, I used every ounce of my strength to fight him off. It was only from pure exhaustion that I finally surrendered to his agonizing attack. He had his way with me quickly, but a searing pain remained between my legs. When he finally lifted his odious weight off of me and I heard him pulling up his trousers (my eyes were still tightly closed to block out the horror), I burst out crying.

"You bastard!" I spat.

The foul smell of his breath permeated the air and I nearly threw up. When I finally managed to look up, I couldn't believe that Mr. Perkins was just sitting there, combing his hair.

Turning toward me, he yelled, "Damn it, girl! Pull yourself together." He finished the last of his attack with "If you ever say a word to anyone about this, I will destroy you and your family's reputation."

His harsh words stung as badly as the pain of my father's rejection and the ache between my legs.

I couldn't stop my tears, knowing I had to hide the secret. I wondered, Who would believe my story, anyway? Will Father blame me for this? Those thoughts cut through me as deeply as the evening's repulsive events. When we finally arrived at my front door, I ran inside, went straight to my room and locked the door.

I was relieved that Cynthia wasn't home and that my mother was fast asleep. In my safe haven, the terrorizing night brought endless tears. What I had hoped to be one of the best memories of my life had turned into an ugly nightmare. Pushing my face deep down into my pillow, I made a vow to never say anything to anyone about it.

It wasn't until several months later that I realized something was wrong. I couldn't keep my food down, and my abdomen had started to swell.

It didn't take long for Cynthia to notice. One day, she pulled me into her bedroom and closed the door. "Barbara, is something wrong?" she asked, waiting patiently for my answer. "Please confide in me," she prompted when I gave her no response. "You haven't acted like yourself since the debutante ball and I've noticed that you have gained some weight."

I remained silent, not knowing what to say.

"Something is bothering you. I just know it. Please tell me. No matter what it is, I promise not to tell anyone."

I bowed my head as I blurted out the torrid details of that horrible night.

When I looked up, my sister's face was pale. "Damn it!" she cursed and wrapped her arms around me. "I'm so sorry. Why didn't you tell anyone?"

"I was so afraid no one would believe me. What would Mother and Papa think of me?"

"That creep Mr. Perkins belongs in jail." Cynthia shook her head. While she held my hands, Cynthia confirmed my worst fear. "Barbara, I think you're pregnant."

We agreed that the truth could never be revealed to anyone. Anxiously, she promised, "Don't worry. Somehow I'll take care of it."

Even though I knew she could be trusted to keep my secret, I was still nervous and wondered what would happen if Father somehow found out. The next day, Cynthia carried several medical books up into my room. Closing the door, she announced, "I think there is a way to fix this."

Her words scared me to death, but Cynthia assured me it was the only thing to do. "In a few days, Mother and Papa have a charitable ball that they will be attending. It is Maria's day off. I'll get everything ready and you won't have to worry about anything after that."

Even though I trusted Cynthia with my life, I was still concerned about her plan. She never told me exactly what it was, and as the days passed, my apprehension rose.

Wearing loose clothing helped me cover up my new figure, and when the day arrived to be rid of it, I was relieved that no one had noticed the change in me. Cynthia hadn't said much those last few days, and I realized that no matter what, I just had to trust her. Right then, I wanted to get it over with and put it all behind me.

Once my parents had left, Cynthia instructed me to wait one-half hour and then meet her in the basement. My body shuddered as I made my way down the basement stairs. A kerosene lamp glowed in the dim room and I made out the outline of a makeshift bed. Several stacks of neatly piled cloths were nearby and there were blankets scattered over the floor. I froze in my tracks, seeing a small bucket and twisted iron coat hanger resting on a wooden crate.

Even though it was never said between us, both Cynthia and I knew a bastard child would never be tolerated in our house. The loss of social grace would kill our mother, and the public embarrassment could ruin our father's career.

Cynthia told me, "You'll have to remove your clothes from the waist down."

I complied with her orders without question. My body shivered as I slipped onto the pillowed frame she'd made. Cynthia tenderly placed a blanket across me and then looked away. The tension between us weighed as heavy at the deed she was about to commit.

"Barbara, this will hurt some. You'll have to spread your legs open as far as you can," she flatly stated.

I could have dug a hole for myself right there. Sisters are supposed to share many things in their lives, but this wasn't one of them. With each passing moment, I wanted to yell "Stop!" but I kept my lips sealed. Silently I prayed, just let me die.

Then Cynthia handed me a small clothespin and commanded, "Barbara, when you need to, bite down hard on this."

My mouth clamped over the wooden piece, and seconds later I felt her insert the cold hanger within me. In the darkness, I heard Cynthia choke as she filled the pail beside her. Suddenly, I felt dizzy and closed my eyes.

The next thing I remembered was cold water pouring over my face.

Cynthia was sobbing. "I thought I lost you."

I felt weak and couldn't move. There was a sickening smell in the air. As I tried to lift my head, I saw piles of rags filled with blood on the cement floor.

"What happened?" I questioned.

"You started hemorrhaging." Beads of sweat covered Cynthia's brow, and she was pale as a ghost. I began to sob when I heard, "I'm done."

In the uncomfortable moment, my emotions bubbled over in a murmur of relief combined with tears.

Cynthia instructed, "I'll help you get upstairs to bed. You need your rest. I'll finish here."

I struggled to mount each stair, but leaning on Cynthia helped me make it to the top. My own bed offered me comfort, but the searing pain inside me prevented deep sleep.

My body trembled when I heard the sound of metal piercing the earth in the distance. My eyes clamped shut trying to erase the picture of my sister disposing of the evidence of our deed. When she returned, she told me, "No one must ever find out, but I marked the grave with an iron hanger." I knew our secret was buried, but the cruel act would surely haunt us for the rest of our lives.

Chapter Fourteen
Sacrifice for Love

1940-1945
Santa Barbara, California
Cynthia Preston

A life was sacrificed that night to save Papa's unblemished career, to keep Mother's social grace and to save Barbara from shame. What I had done went against everything I had believed in and dampened my hopes of becoming a nurse. How could I work in a field dedicated to saving lives when my hands were marked by murder? When Barbara had started hemorrhaging, I panicked, feeling alone and helpless. What if she had died? How could I have faced Papa?

Our secret was buried, but the bloody deed would never be washed away. It was a sacrifice for love. Even so, my heart felt cold, dead, like the steel shovel I had slammed into the dirt.

Standing before the makeshift grave, it had seemed important that I mark its place. I quickly had bent the hanger in the shape of a P in memory of the Preston life I'd stolen, and placed it on top of the blanketed remains. The hole was deep and far away from the back of the house where it surely would never be found. Walking away, no tears fell, for I had done my duty to secure the Preston name.

Several weeks later, a tinge of fear rose within me when Barbara complained of lower back pain. Returning from the doctor, Mother announced, "Barbara has a severe kidney infection and needs her rest. The doctor gave her daily medication and told her to drink more water. He said that she should recover soon."

"That girl can never stay healthy for long," I scoffed and headed upstairs to Barbara's room. Upon entering, I noticed that she looked tired and pale.

"Did you say anything?" I demanded.

"Of course not." She grimaced, "Cynthia, the pain is excruciating."

I said nothing, but before I left, our eyes met, and in the silence we both knew what was to blame.

Several months passed and Barbara's infection lingered. This built tension between us. I spent little time with her, feeling it was now her burden and no longer mine.

In my room with the door closed, I would escape into the fantasy world of my Harlequin romance novels. My favorite part was when the prince charming rescued his damsel in distress just in the nick of time. Many times I closed my eyes, trying to imagine the man of my dreams. Oftentimes, his face resembled Papa's. These stories were filled with tales of sacrifice that others made for love, which often came with a personal price. I believed what I did for Papa was a sign of true love.

Over time, Barbara finally got better.

Papa was traveling more and I saw him less. His political career kept him busy with several dam-building projects and business trips. Then one sunny afternoon in May, Papa declared, "Princess, I've invited Jim McDaniel and his son, Jack, for dinner on Saturday evening. Have you met Jack before?"

"Yes, we've met briefly," I answered, feeling a suspicion that he had a purpose for setting up the meeting.

Jack, a handsome beer-and-football-type guy, had been introduced to me at the debutante ball. I had watched all my girlfriends compete for his attention. His notorious reputation as a womanizer was common knowledge. His bedroom baby-blues cast a spell on all who looked into them.

Saturday night arrived and the mood was festive with Mother playing the piano. Purple and white violets and our fine china set decorated the table. I was seated next to Jack.

"Cynthia, you look lovely this evening," he complimented. "I've heard you were schooled on the East Coast. What a fine experience that must have been."

"The New England fall is incredibly beautiful, but an all-girl school can be quite boring," I politely smiled.

"It is the perfect place for a young girl to get an education," Mother added.

When our meal was finished, Papa stood up and suggested, "Why don't you two go into the parlor and chat while Jim and I have an after-dinner cigar?" Papa's stern expression didn't give me a choice.

I swallowed hard as Jack offered his arm, and we headed toward our cozy sitting room. Even though the fireplace glowed with warmth before us, a shiver ran down my spine as his hips rested next to mine.

"Did you hear what happened to Albert Einstein while he was visiting Santa Barbara?" Jack pulled a hanky from his pant pocket and proceeded to blow his nose.

"No, I haven't," I replied, wondering if he was sickly like my sister Barbara.

"Well, Dr. Einstein, though a world-famous scientist, didn't know better than to eat a ripe olive right off the tree," Jack chuckled outloud.

I crossed my arms and looked away, not finding much sense of humor in his tale.

"Father is giving me flying lessons, and I'd love to take you for a ride sometime."

I could tell he was trying to impress me. "No, thank you. Actually, I'm afraid of heights."

Some awkward silence followed.

"Your father told me you liked to dance. I'd be honored if you would accompany me to our annual Spring Barn Bash next weekend," Jack persisted.

"I'd like that," I answered, thinking I'd better play into Papa's plan. We set the date, but Jack didn't stir the passion in me that I'd read about in my novels.

After Jack and his father had left, Papa sat me down. "Princess, Jack comes from good stock and would make a fine husband."

His words cut into my heart with the sharpness of a butcher's knife. I bowed my head, "Papa, I've heard he's been around with some girls with questionable reputations."

Papa checked behind us as we sat on the davenport to be sure Mother wasn't around before saying, "Boys will be boys, Cynthia. It doesn't make him bad material, Princess. Jack is smart, an only child and Jewish. He also is the son of the most successful dairy farmer in the North County. He can give you a good life." Papa put his arm around my shoulder. "Princess, your marrying a fine young man like Jack would make me very happy."

For a long moment, I was quiet. I thought, There isn't anything I wouldn't do for Papa. Even though I wouldn't pick Jack, he isn't hard to look at on the outside. And marriage would get me away from Barbara's angry eyes and Mother's judging ways.

Papa's desperate expression reflected the fact this sacrifice would somehow benefit him. "You'll always be my princess, Cynthia." He planted a kiss on my cheek.

I made an effort to get to know Jack from that point on. Our courtship had some exciting moments. He invited me horseback riding, and it was my first time. Jack's patience never waned as I struggled to learn the ropes.

He showed me the rich beauty of Santa Barbara's North County with its lush, fertile green valleys and nature-filled coastal mountains. When we rode our horses side by side, I embraced the free feeling of my hair blowing in the wind. When Jack galloped ahead, I pictured him as Prince Charming on his quest. His wide shoulders, ruggedly handsome face and adventurous spirit did match those of the gallant heroes in my books. We had several picnics near the small lake that his family's ranch-style homestead overlooked.

One afternoon, after drinking wine, his passion went too far and he unbuttoned my blouse. I angrily told him, "Jack, stop. I'm saving myself for my wedding night."

Catching his breath, he abruptly got up and sprinted toward the shore. I was shocked when he stripped naked in front of me and dove into the water. The vision of his gladiator's body aroused me. I was thrilled watching his muscular arms effortlessly take him across the lake. He made me giggle, knowing it was his way of cooling off, but I stayed put until he returned to the shore.

Jack was so different than anyone I'd ever met and I found his crazy behavior intriguing. Not long after, Papa promised to buy us our own farm if we married, and we set the wedding date for the next July. Even though I didn't think that I was in love with Jack, when Papa gave us his blessing, I felt happy.

Mother wanted to be sure that our wedding would be the highlight of the summer social calendar. It didn't bother me that she made most of the decisions about our ceremony. Over three hundred and fifty guests were invited to attend the conservative temple service and gala reception. Soon an endless parade of fine china, embroidered linens and Waterford crystal arrived at our doorstep from Papa's wealthy clients.

On the morning of our wedding, Papa knocked on my bedroom door. He was already dressed in his formal tuxedo. My mouth dropped. His dashing image was equal to the Hollywood heartthrob Humphrey Bogart. He handed me a small, wrapped present. Upon opening it, I gasped, seeing a giant teardrop diamond pendant inside. As he gently placed it around my neck, he whispered, "I love you, Princess, and this is a token of that love."

Tears of joy ran down my cheeks as we hugged. It was a moment forever locked into my memory. When he left, I told him, "Papa, you'll always have my heart."

Staring into the mirror on the vanity, the sparkling gem was the largest I'd ever seen. Papa must have sacrificed a bundle for it. What a beautiful symbol of our love. I was so proud to wear it around my neck, especially that day, my wedding day.

Our wedding took place at the Jewish synagogue downtown. The temple aisles were overflowing with the most prominent citizens in Santa Barbara. Barbara had agreed to be my maid of honor. She looked healthy and vibrant with her new permanent-wave hairdo. She kissed my cheek and said, "I'm happy for you, sis," but I still felt a barrier between us.

Earlier, Mother had checked over every detail of my custom-made dress and veil. The designer-name, French lace and satin, Cinderella gown was form-fitted at the waist and accented with hand-sewn pearls. Barbara made sure my cathedral-length train was straightened before she took her place.

My heart skipped a beat as the wedding march started and Papa took my arm. We were the idyllic image of a king marching with his princess down the rose-petaled aisle. Jack looked mouth-watering as he stood waiting under the chuppah decorated with white lilies. I quickly glanced toward my mother, who held an embroidered lace handkerchief in her hand, but she was not crying. Overhead, a beam of light magically spotlighted our silhouettes from a large, round, stained-glass window depicting the Star of David.

The rabbi looked the part with a full beard, a mustache and a white satin yarmulke. He read the Sheva Brachot, and we drank wine and exchanged our vows and rings with one another. In true tradition, at the conclusion of the ceremony, Jack raised his foot and smashed the glass, followed by shouts of "Mazel tov!"

Once the ritual was over, I felt as though a tight collar had been placed around my neck. Turning toward the crowd, we were proclaimed husband and wife. I tried to smile, but a voice inside my head screamed, *what have you done*?

The whole scene felt distant and surreal as the crowd sprayed rice over us and we climbed aboard our rose-covered, horse-drawn carriage, which transported us to the reception in the courthouse garden. It was a beautiful, clear, sunny day; still, I couldn't shake the dark cloud of sadness inside me.

A photographer's bright flash captured all angles while a melancholy feeling swept over me.

Mother had made every detail perfect. The pink rose centerpieces with lacy ribbons gracing each table held our names in rhinestones. The four-tiered wedding cake had strings of real pearls dangling down its sides and pink rose clusters surrounded the base. Fountains of champagne flowed while a full orchestra played.

Only when the father-daughter dance commenced did I totally come into the moment. Papa's eyes glistened with love and pride as he took my hand and we glided onto the dance floor. I silently wished, If only this dance could last forever ...

For the next few hours, Jack and I were like two Hollywood actors portraying a stunning performance as we graciously accepted congratulations and best wishes.

Jack's father whispered in my ear, "We're so proud to be part of your prestigious family."

The gala event was followed with a delicious steak dinner catered by the Biltmore Hotel. Afterward, my parents approached us, and my father handed Jack a thick envelope that looked like it was stuffed with cash.

"Something to kick-start your life together," he smiled. "Take good care of my princess."

Mother and Barbara offered a warm congratulatory good-bye hug. Jack and I boarded our carriage to the train station where we would depart for our honeymoon in San Francisco. As my family disappeared from sight, the tears began to fall.

Inside our two-room private car, Jack poured himself another glass of champagne; he finished it off in several gulps. "It's been quite a day, my lovely bride." His face filled with a snide grin. "Do your feet ache as much as mine?"

I didn't answer.

"If I hear one more comment about us being the perfect couple, I'm going to throw up."

Jack's comments annoyed me and I grabbed his handkerchief to dry my eyes.

"Come on, Cynthia. We both know this marriage was prearranged. Not necessarily for our benefit, either." Jack refilled his glass. "I figure you went along with it for the same reason I did: greed. I always wanted a farm of my own and you were the ticket. So let's make the best of it." Jack aggressively slipped his hand under my dress and laughed.

"Get your dirty hands off me!" I ordered.

Jack finished his drink and poured another, "Cynthia, you're my wife now and I'm going to take the prize that's part of this package."

Seeing the wild passion in Jack's hungry eyes made me realize there was nothing I could do to stop him from getting what he wanted. His strong arms lifted me up, and he carried me into the adjoining bedroom.

My wedding night turned out to be nothing like the tender romantic moments described in my books. Instead it was a quick, painful, unsatisfying event.

It was a relief when Jack turned over and finally fell asleep. Tears stained my pillow as I tried to block the day's events from my mind. Feeling isolated and alone, I tightly grasped the diamond pendant hanging down from my neck and sighed. True love did come with a high price.

Chapter Fifteen
Too Close for Comfort

1940-1945
Santa Barbara, California
Otto Preston

Cynthia's marriage into the McDaniel family had stabilized my political position in the North County. Barbara was healthier than ever, and Elizabeth was kept busy with her high-society social calendar. That was the good news.

But then there was the bad news. W.R. had recently suffered a health setback, and Stella's financial demands were getting out of hand. I had received news from the mayor that the police commission had initiated an investigation of "higher ups" in my department. They were looking for evidence of corruption and payoffs. There would be shakedowns. The word on the street was that witnesses had come forward and indictments were already being prepared. I'd heard that both federal and state agents had been called in to help investigate.

I hardly had time to worry about the war raging overseas. The newspaper headline had read *"Japs Bomb U.S. Pearl Harbor, Manila."* Franklin Delano Roosevelt had declared World War II. But I had my own war to wage at home.

An FBI agent showed up at my office several days after the investigation began. He introduced himself as Richard Harris. After he displayed his badge, I invited him in. The clean-cut federal agent removed his fedora and sat down. "A number of city officials have received death threats, and it is my job to identify who is responsible," his deep, serious voice paused. "As the chairman of the city board of supervisors, is there any information or persons of interest you think might be involved?"

My palms filled with sweat. I hesitated to answer. I glanced out the window while giving my answer. "Thugs, dope addicts and gamblers that don't respect the law."

The dark-suited agent with his perfect white shirt and tie never looked away. He continued, "As an attorney, Mr. Preston, you understand the importance of building evidence and finding witnesses. I came here looking for answers. Can you tell me anything that might help in this investigation?"

"I have nothing to say."

"For your information, the mayor wants a roundup. He told me that he's ordered a sweep to clean his city of undesirables." The self-assured agent leaned back in his chair. Before leaving, he told me that the chief of police, a police sergeant and a captain had been named, charged and had warrants issued for their arrests.

When the officer got up to leave, his suit jacket opened just enough for me to see the shoulder gun he was packing. He set his business card down on the desk and advised, "Call me if you come up with something."

"I'll do what I can to get the job done," I assured him as my heart raced.

After he left, I wiped the sweat from my brow. I couldn't afford to have my name tied to the scandal and feared my association with the perpetrators might bring more heat. I would have to keep my distance from them. The kickbacks and special deals had to stop.

When I checked around, I learned that a ring of thugs had been collecting money from gamblers, prostitutes and liquor-runners in return for promised protection. Even though I wasn't involved, the criminal activity was too close to people I associated with for comfort.

Like a torrent of floodwater unleashed by a bursting dam, a mass of accusations and suspicions cropped up around me. I protected myself by not admitting to anything and by getting good legal advice. I was able to stop any actions against me with my airtight defenses. Once all those involved resigned without admitting guilt, things started to calm down.

Publicly, I told my constituents, "These developments call for a complete investigation. We must clean house, gentlemen."

Privately, I warned my cohorts. To Tony Marcello, I said, "My advice is to close down upstairs, my friend, or risk jail time."

So far I'd been lucky not to get my hand caught in the cookie jar. Luck only lasts so long. I knew it was time to clean up my act to protect the prestige of the Preston name.

One thing that needed to be addressed was my risky overseas business contract with Adan Shariff. It had helped me during the Depression crisis, but now the risks of the venture outweighed the reward. The illegal shipments arranged offshore were now being more closely monitored because of the war.

The lucrative partnership had already allowed me to personally pay back the bank for the cost of the loans for the dams project. I was able to do this with the diamonds I'd received in payment for my services. I had gotten enough out of the deal that I could end it. I just had to tell Adan.

I also had made sure to hide a stash of loose diamonds as part of the Preston legacy. It would be a security net for future generations. I wasn't getting any younger, and at that time in my life, I knew I needed to have things in order. I'd accumulated enough money, land and diamonds, but I also had to protect the Preston name from future scandal. Elizabeth was set up with long-term security. Nothing was going to stop me from making sure my daughters and future generations would be proud of their Preston heritage.

Chapter Sixteen
The New Generation

1945-1947
Cuyama, California
Cynthia Preston McDaniel

Papa kept his word. He presented us with our own dairy farm in Cuyama upon our return from our honeymoon. It had six hundred acres with a house and a barn. At first Papa visited often, but as time passed, his political duties kept him away.

I slowly learned that there were advantages to being far from the city. We enjoyed many quiet evenings as we sat on our wrap-around porch with only nature providing a sweet serenade. Though it was a challenge to cook, clean and help with milking the cows, Jack and I got the chores done.

Our main problem remained in the bedroom. My frigidity was a blow to Jack's manhood. I just couldn't bring myself to fake passion for him. He'd tell me "Cynthia, you're impossible to please."

Usually, he ended up sleeping on the couch, and before long, Jack was choosing a bottle of scotch over me. In the months that followed, I tried to ignore his heavy drinking problem.

Late one night, he came home reeking from the smell of liquor. Usually he'd stagger to the fireside davenport and fall asleep, but this time was different. Jack's steps were charged with emotion, and his crazed, blood-shot eyes mirrored a toxic humor. Like a proud peacock, he paraded his face before mine, laughter leaking from his lips.

Sickened by his foul breath, I shoved him away, "What's got into you?"

His body straightened, and a brazen grin filled his face. "Tonight I saw something I was not supposed to see in a place your mother would never dare step inside."

I stoically backed away, put my hands on my hips, and shook my head.

"Tonight at *Marcello's*, I saw your high-and-mighty papa embrace another woman. I have no doubt that they are lovers," Jack snickered.

His venomous words struck with the speed of a snakebite. I wondered as drunk as he was, if he could be sure it was my father. Just the pain of the possibility made me crumple down in a nearby chair. "Not Papa!"

Jack's eyes flashed with anger, and his face blushed red as he blurted out, "My God, Cynthia, are you in love with your own father?" His hands rose above his head and he looked me straight in the eye. "Woman, you must be mad!"

I lowered my head. "Jack, that's not what I meant. Yes, I do love my father, but not in that way."

In the uncomfortable silence, I realized what I needed to do. I grabbed

Jack's bottle of scotch, poured myself a shot and drank it in one gulp. It prepared me for my next role.

Recalling a scene from one of my torrid romance novels, I slowly unbuttoned my blouse and exposed my perky breasts. In my mind, I became the sultry heroine who knows what men want. I swayed my hips in striptease-style. I took Jack's hand and slid it down my panties. "Take me. I'm yours," I charmed him.

With Jack's urgent passion, it was easy to persuade him to stay silent about what he'd seen. For me, my personal satisfaction was reached when the face I saw above me turned into Papa's: a perfect fantasy.

Several months later, I discovered that I was pregnant. I was not excited about it. Mother offered to help me with the nursery. Barbara said she would throw me a baby shower, but every time my sister visited, she spent more time talking to Jack than she did to me.

Papa proudly announced, "It will be a great day when I become a grandfather." He kept talking about creating a trust for his new heir.

Every morning over the next few months, I woke up and chucked out my guts. Toward the end of my pregnancy, while looking in the mirror, I silently cursed the child within me for my ugly, distorted figure.

When Sandra was born, I was relieved to finally get my slim form back. I refused to breast feed and let our nanny do the frequent, unpleasant job of caring for her.

I was surprised when Mother stepped up and showed our new daughter so much attention. She smothered Sandra with affection, so unlike her cold and distant relationship with me.

Around the same time, Barbara eloped with a nice fellow named Bernie, who was an accountant.

At first she seemed happy, but after I delivered two more children, our son Clark and our daughter Claire, she confronted me. "You have all the luck. You have three beautiful children now, and no matter how long Bernie and I try for a child, my womb stays empty," she sobbed.

"What do you want from me, Barbara? Do you think I'm responsible for that?" I demanded.

"It just isn't fair," she screamed and stalked off in a jealous fit.

I never understood her. She had a great husband and couldn't imagine how hard my life was. My sister must think happiness was having three children under five, but I knew different. It was noisy, hectic and mentally exhausting, even with a nanny.

Life became even more difficult when our second child, Clark, developed severe colic and hardly ever stopped crying.

Our beautiful daughter Claire was my salvation. She had Papa's innocent green eyes, and they seldom filled with tears. Even though Jack indicated he wanted more children, I had my tubes tied. After Claire, I wanted to be done with motherhood.

It helped that their grandmother seemed to enjoy spending hours with her grandchildren. My mother's heart seemed to soften as their hugs and kisses filled her life. Our relationship remained strained because of the many secrets between us. At times, I wanted to scream and expose all the sacrifices I'd made so she could keep her status and position.

Papa announced that he would be retiring soon. When I'd heard the city would acknowledge his loyal service by presenting him with a hand-painted portrait, I felt that everything I'd done so far to protect him and the family had been worthwhile.

I was glad that lately Jack has been less demanding of me in the bedroom. Sometimes I wondered if he, like Papa, had found someone else to satisfy his needs. Men would be men.

Chapter Seventeen
Settling the Score

1945-1955
Santa Barbara, California
Barbara Preston

More than my unborn child died in our basement that night so long ago. That secret ripped apart my relationship with Cynthia like the cutting edge of the iron hanger. The shovel that pierced the dirt had severed our sisterly bond. My suffering continued with recurring kidney infections and heavy periods. Even though the doctor couldn't pinpoint the problem, I knew its origin.

I felt lost, sad and alone. The truth was that my father never really loved me, and my mother retreated to her own social world. The pain of self-judgment erased any self-esteem I had left. I hurt most, lying in my bedroom at night, feeling like the soiled dress Cynthia and I had burned.

I let the first boy who showed any interest in me find the same pleasure as Mr. Perkins. At least they held me for a while and said nice things that made me feel better.

Not long after Cynthia got married, I went into her room and picked up one of the romance novels she had left behind. Reading those first pages opened a new world of love for me. I got lost in the pictures of dreamy passion and the words showed me the proper etiquette to personal fulfillment. This made me yearn for the man of my dreams, the man who would accept me for what I had to offer.

Searching for more reading excitement, I made a visit to the library. While sitting at one of the tables, a studious fellow reader started up a conversation. "Do you come here often?" he asked.

"Yes, it's a quiet place to read," I answered, noticing there wasn't a ring on his left hand.

He held up a piece of paper in front of me and I was surprised to see he'd sketched a picture of me on it.

"You're quite good," I told him and smiled.

"It's yours. My name is Bernie Baumgartner, and you're very pretty. I hope you don't mind about the picture."

"Thank you for the compliment, Bernie. I just love it."

"Maybe we could have a cup of coffee or a soda together some time?" he timidly asked.

"I'd really like that."

Bernie beamed with joy. He wore black wide-rimmed reading glasses like me, and though he was average-looking, he carried the innocent charm of a young boy. He asked what types of books I liked and later invited me to go bowling. Bernie was the first guy who seemed genuinely interested in me and not just my body. We continued to meet for coffee and I learned that he worked as an accountant with a local firm and had recently moved from Seattle.

One afternoon, he brought me a bouquet of yellow daisies and a romance novel he had heard was good. When I invited him for dinner, Mother and Papa actually approved of his mild manner and earnest intentions. It didn't hurt that he was also Jewish.

Even though Bernie didn't bring up the passion talked about in my books, his kind, gentle and caring nature compensated for it. So when he asked me to marry him, I said yes. Since his family remained in Washington and because Mother showed no interest in planning another big wedding, we decided to elope.

Bernie never pushed to have sex with me and indicated that he thought it should be saved for our wedding night. There were a couple of times when I came close to telling him about my past experience, but I always stopped short.

We were married by a justice of the peace, and Father offered to pay for a bridal suite at the Biltmore as a wedding gift. He knew Bernie was very conservative when it came to money.

On our wedding night, I put on my white lace and silk negligee. As we consummated our union, Bernie realized it wasn't my first time. I think he figured it out because I couldn't fake not having past sexual experience.

"You aren't a virgin." He shrugged his shoulders downwards. "I trusted you, Barbara. Why didn't you tell me?"

I tried to soothe his disappointment with sexual favors, and in time, he said he'd forgiven me. But sometimes I still felt as though he thought he'd bought a piece of used furniture.

We rented an apartment in a nice area close to where Bernie worked. Another couple around our age lived downstairs and had two small children. When Molly, the mother, decided to go to back to work, she asked me if I'd be interested in caring for her two girls. Bernie liked the idea because it brought in some extra income.

Several years passed by as I watched the darling toddlers grow. My sadness at my inability to conceive my own child grew with them. I envied Cynthia, married years ago and already with three children. She seemed to live the perfect life.

Since my husband didn't have family close by, Bernie enjoyed going to Cynthia's for birthdays and holiday celebrations. On several occasions when I wanted to leave early because I felt overwhelmed, Bernie got mad. He couldn't understand my feelings and often took Cynthia's side in an argument. It took all I had not to disclose what she did to me, but I remained silent.

Then one afternoon, Bernie came home and announced that he had been laid off from his job. The economy had slowed down and our finances got really tight. At one point, he wanted to ask to borrow money from my parents, but I forbade it. It would have been too embarrassing for me.

Several months passed and Bernie remained unemployed. I watched as he slipped into a deep depression. After he'd been out looking for work, he would return home with liquor on his breath. We barely got by on the money I made and soon all our savings had vanished.

One evening out of the blue, my sister Cynthia stopped by. She didn't stay long, but offered Bernie a lucrative accounting position with my father's law firm. He was so excited that he gave her a big hug.

I wasn't sure what to think of this development, but he convinced me that it was our only salvation. Once he took the position, I felt better upon seeing him happy again. He even became a more loving and caring partner.

One night approximately six months later, Bernie sat up in bed and faced me. "Barbara, I have a confession to make," he blurted out.

I was startled and confused, but asked him, "What kind of confession?"

"You deserve to know," he began. "I can't live with myself anymore not telling you the truth."

For a moment, I wondered if he had learned my secret and was about to confess for finding it out behind my back. I held my breath and listened.

"After I lost my job, my whole world crashed down. As time passed, I worried that if I didn't find something soon, I'd lose you, too." He sighed. "I'd gone to a bar, had a couple of drinks and even thought of ending my own life. Instead, in my desperation, I called your sister, Cynthia."

"Oh, my God, why did you do that?" I cried.

"I'm not sure why, Barbara, but I did."

My heart raced with fear, because I knew Bernie well enough that his honest soul had something heavy to unload.

"She said she'd meet me and must have recognized the desperation in my voice. Once she arrived, we sat, talked and had a few more drinks together." Something inside me was screaming for him to stop and not say another word, but Bernie continued. "I'm not proud of what I did that night, Barbara. I just need to get it off my chest. We ended up going to a hotel and had a one-night fling."

"You fucking bastard!" I screamed and jumped out of bed. Barely able to catch my breath, I had to vomit and ran toward the bathroom. After wiping my face, I yelled to Bernie, "How could you do this to me?"

The crushing pain I felt made me want to die. Catching a glimpse of my face in the mirrored medicine cabinet, I hardly recognized the crazed woman staring back at me. My volcano of emotions spilled out on Bernie as I called him every dirty name under the sun. Only after my tears subsided did I start to calm down.

"Barbara, you can never let Cynthia know that I told you," he warned. "We promised each other never to tell anyone. It was after that when Cynthia arranged the job at your father's firm for me."

I sat silently at the edge of our bed, yearning to erase the second-worst nightmare of my life. Bernie wrapped his arms around me, and for the first time I saw tears in his eyes.

There was nothing more pitiful than the sob of a man's sorrow. It softened my anger and opened my heart to forgiveness, a feeling I never had found for myself. That's when it occurred to me that what happened wasn't all Bernie's fault.

As I heard him plead, "Forgive me. It will never happen again," I dried his tears and told him we could work it out.

Just then, he reached beneath his pillow and pulled out a long, black, velvet box. At first I refused to take it, but Bernie didn't take no for an answer. I gasped seeing the breathtaking double-rope diamond bracelet inside. He put it gently on my wrist; it was the beginning of the healing of our relationship.

We agreed never to speak about it again. In the months following, our financial position greatly improved.

What Bernie didn't know was that I wasn't going to stand by and let my sister get away with what she did. Over time, I secretly established a relationship with her husband, Jack. I made sure Cynthia and Bernie never knew that we went drinking together when she was out of town.

Later that year, to my surprise and delight, I got pregnant. No one ever knew who the real father is. It only seemed fair that I got back what Cynthia took from me so many years ago.

Chapter Eighteen
What You Leave Behind

1943-1950
Santa Barbara, California
Otto Preston

For over twenty-five years, I'd held my position as chairman of the board of supervisors for the grand city of Santa Barbara. I knew that some viewed me as a power-craving egotist, but everyone kept electing me because they knew I was the best one to get the job done. Because of my shrewd legal tactics, my reputation had emerged unblemished despite my lengthy career. I knew I had generated a political legacy to be proud of.

The city had flourished under my reign. When I retired, I would leave behind long-range plans for the city and the two ongoing dam projects. Both the North County's and South County's coffers were full—I'd made good use of every cent of the taxpayers' dollars. I had established numerous cultural enrichment projects. From a personal endowment to the local hospital a children's wing was dedicated in the Preston name.

I'd even managed to keep the North and South counties in alliance most of the time.

But after twenty-five years, I felt it was time for me to set down my gavel. There were just a few of my political goals that had gone unmet. I had always wanted to meet the president, so when the opportunity to meet FDR presented itself before my term was up, I jumped on it.

I arrived early at the Santa Fe train depot. I was going to be the one to introduce him for the brief speech he would be making on the Union Station platform at 8:30 AM.

After his introduction, FDR addressed the crowd.

"I am on this tour to learn about the state of the American people. I hope for it to be an educational experience rather than a speaking campaign. It is my desire to study conditions in all sections of the country, to get close to the people and to their problems and to attempt to discern the best possible solutions for those problems."

He took questions from those attending and listened to their economic struggles. At the conclusion, there was loud applause from his supporters. Like many there, I appreciated his indomitable courage to serve as the country's president while faced with his fight against poliomyelitis. FDR explained his sweeping program to bring recovery to business and agriculture, relief for the unemployed and help for those in danger of losing their farms and homes. His plans sounded encouraging to everyone, like they might help our country back on its feet.

Afterward, I was able to meet with the president in his private car.

"I congratulate you on your political success here out west," FDR complimented me.

I shook his hand, "Mr. President, you carry the weight of our country's future on your shoulders. It is you who should be commended."

"Our country has hit hard times, Mr. Preston, but I believe Americans have the grit and gut to overcome these hurdles."

"Yes, Mr. President. My city is less economically affected than most," I revealed. "The dam projects keep many employed and the several federal grants we obtained have brought us sustainability."

As we spoke, FDR told me about an acquaintance in LA named William Mulholland, who might help out with the problem-laden dam projects. It was like a dream realized, to be talking on such familiar terms with the president.

Later, the president introduced me to his wife, Eleanor, who had the same poise and grace as Elizabeth. Upon his departure, FDR said, "Otto, your dedicated service is appreciated."

In addition to meeting the president, there was one last task I needed to perform as a government official before I could leave my political career behind for good. The day after meeting the president, I left to see Adan in Thailand. Elizabeth stayed home, preferring to spend her time with our four grandchildren. It was better that she didn't come along.

On the way to deal with my overseas partner, I decided to stop in Chicago to make a visit to my ailing mother. It was a six-hour flight to the windy city. A cold, winter chill seeped through my topcoat when I stepped out of the doors of the Chicago Midway Airport. I was already tired when the plane landed, but rather than head to my hotel for some rest, I grabbed a taxi, eager to visit my mother in the upscale elderly care home I was covering the expense of.

I wondered how my mother, now seventy-eight years old, would look. From the regular letters and calls I received from her, I knew she still had all her faculties. In our last conversation, she'd told me, "Otto, I'm excited to get to see you."

On the way to the home, I asked the cab driver to swing by the old family butcher shop. Mother had sold it after the old man's death, and I was curious to see how it had fared. I noticed graffiti painted on several buildings and trash littering the streets as we drove into my old neighborhood. My once-beautiful memories of the city were tarnished by the realization that so much had changed for the worse.

"This ain't the best part of town, mister," the driver announced.

"It's very different than when I lived here," I somberly told the cabbie.

When we arrived in front of my family's old establishment, I asked the driver to pull over. I was shocked to see the building empty, filth and rust oozing from its walls. It stood there as cold and remote as the childhood I'd left behind.

For a time, I stared at the Preston name peeling off of the front window. The image seemed to reflect the harsh actions my father had taken against my mother and I so many years ago.

It nonetheless disappointed me that time had so erased any evidence of what the Preston family had once been so proud of. I wondered, could this happen to my own legacy?

When the driver headed toward the upper-class rest home, I was comforted to note the appropriately lush atmosphere. I was grateful that I had been able to provide Mother greater comfort through my financial support.

When the cab pulled up, I instantly recognized her waiting in a rocking chair on the wooden porch, even though her once-dark hair was completely gray. She stood up slowly with the help of a cane. As I walked toward her, I noticed her wrinkled hazel eyes glistened.

I lowered my head when she opened her frail arms to greet me. Mother was pencil thin and her once delicate hands trembled, but I would have recognized the tenderness of her hug anywhere. For the first time in my life, I felt regret, knowing the meeting was long overdue.

"Otto, you look so good! Healthy as a horse," she beamed.

"Do they treat you well here, Mother?" I asked while sitting down on the bench next to her.

"Yes, they do. Three fine meals a day. We play cards and are entertained by piano music most evenings. You have been so generous to me. I am truly grateful, Otto," she gently patted my knee. "I do have a favor to ask you, though," she began. "It has been a long time since I've visited your father's grave. Would you take me?"

For a moment, I was silent. I wondered why she would want to go there after all the pain he had caused her and me.

"Your father never gave up hope that you would return," she said. "I didn't, either, but I also knew you could never forgive him as I have."

"He hurt you, Mother. And he hurt me. I don't understand why you ever forgave him."

"I've learned that love and time can heal most wounds, no matter how deep," she held my hand. "In our later years, Otto, your father changed."

After thinking a moment, I realized I owed my mother for loving me in childhood—the one parent who seemed to—and for still caring for me even after so many years. Taking her arm, I let her lean on me so we could make our way back to the taxi.

We journeyed to the old cemetery where my father was buried. She guided me to a tall cement tombstone. I reeled back, seeing a cameo of the old man on it. Age had taken its toll.

Mother placed the roses she'd cut for him into the small hanging vase by his picture. Tears flowed from her eyes and I politely handed her my handkerchief. "He worked hard, Otto," she said. "When someone asked about you, he would tell them you were a big shot lawyer out west. As the years passed and you didn't return, he never mentioned your name. But on his deathbed, he called out for you."

Though I felt no remorse, out of respect to her, I said, "I'm sorry."

Before leaving, I was compelled to place one of my favorite Cuban cigars below my father's picture. It was a symbolic gesture of my feelings that my legacy had to be so different than his.

Later that day, Mother and I played a game of chess back at the rest home.

Though I remembered the good times I had with her as a young boy—all the hugs and care she provided for me—I knew then, seeing her so frail, that my decision to leave had been for the best. Walking away, I held my head high, confident the Preston legacy was still alive.

Early the next morning, I left Chicago and began the journey to Thailand. Since World War II, overseas travel had been unpredictable and dangerous. In my last communication with Adan, I had demanded we meet to discuss our ongoing agreement. I had informed him of my approaching retirement and that we would have to make plans to phase me out of the deal.

I had only become involved in our partnership to save the Preston empire during the Great Depression, when my family's financial status was at risk. In the early years, it had been easy to allow the ships Adan sent to dock outside the harbor. Smaller vessels could transport the illegal goods ashore with little trouble. The arrangement had given me the means to create the Preston family trust, with enough extra cash to pay off the harbor workers. There had been no need for me to ever dirty my own hands with the affair.

But with the war going on, we had to be more cautious to ensure no one discovered the illegal transfers. On Adan's last shipment, a U.S. Border Patrol boat had spotted the foreign vessel. Even though the carrier was cleared after a minor search, the event was a red flag to me that it was time to stop. I could not afford to be linked to such crime, especially with my retirement drawing nearer.

I kept the only real evidence of my transactions with Adan stored in a safe at my estate. No one would be able to trace where the diamonds had come from. They had been hidden in shipments of toothpaste, in cigar boxes and in the inner heels of designer shoes. They had no identifying information to give away their origin.

The closer I got to retirement, the less I could tolerate being involved in anything that might tarnish my political image. Looking back, it was probably a mistake to get involved with that kind of risky business in the first place, but back when I signed on with Adan, I did not feel I had a choice. I was desperate to save my legacy.

Despite my desire to finish the deal, I feared the consequences that would surely come for wanting out. I knew I was playing with the big guys. I knew I wasn't savvy to their rules.

On the noisy plane ride, these fearful thoughts offered me no sleep. I was exhausted when my plane finally arrived at Bangkok International Airport. Outside the window of the airplane, the first thing I saw was an army of soldiers toting machine guns. They were a less-than-gentle reminder of the degree of danger and corruption that existed in that part of the world.

Two large men in black suits approached me at the gate. One of them motioned me over. "Mr. Preston, our instructions are to escort you directly to Mr. Adan Shariff's residence."

I could hear my heart pounding as we walked to the waiting limousine, the two strong men flanking me on either side. Beads of sweat formed on my brow as we drove through the crowded streets packed with local residents. I tried to calm myself by closing my eyes until the vehicle slowed and then stopped.

Armed guards at the entrance—a heavy, wrought iron gate—waved us past. Adan's palace reflected the prominence of the Taj Mahal. A sandstone fortress with several mushroom-shaped domes and narrow towers loomed before us. Tall bamboo trees, giant ferns and rock formations lined the long road to my host's wide circular driveway, which had a large mosaic fountain at its center.

Exiting the car, I realized that the massive double doors equaled the magnificence of those at W.R.'s castle. The same two men who had met me in the airport escorted me in silently. Once inside, I was awed by the tall granite columns connected to the high arched ceiling and by the painted tile floor that was dotted with hand-knotted silk rugs. Looking around, my eyes took in the visual feast of historical relics of full-sized, golden, god-like figurines, giant porcelain vases and jeweled furniture. Several hanging glass oil lamps illuminated the overhead open-domed entry, which led to a massive marble staircase at the far wall.

I swallowed hard, taking in the wealth and opulence of the setting. What was I thinking, trying to back out of a deal with a man who held so much money?

From a nearby archway, the starched figure of my host appeared. Adan's mandarin-colored silk suit, white turban and bright white smile all starkly contrasted with the rich tan of his native skin. "Welcome to my humble home, Otto," he greeted me with an outstretched hand. Adan's clear English and solid handshake eased my fears.

It had been over three years since Adan's last visit to the U.S., but the Asian businessman still had the charisma and dashing looks I had always found equal to my old friend, Tom. Though admittedly Adan's dark, penetrating eyes shone more with the mystery of foreign intrigue than Tom's boyish spirit.

"You will have time to rest before dinner." Adan clapped his hands and a young, barefoot boy appeared. "Zamer will show you to your room."

"I appreciate your hospitality," I said.

I stood watching Adan disappear and was relieved when my two escorts followed him. Free of the menacing guides, I walked behind the youngster who was balancing my heavy suitcase on top of his head. I followed him up the marble stairway. When Zamer opened the door to the guest room in which I would be staying, I found my breath momentarily taken away by the strong scent of incense that filled the air. I welcomed the sight of the bedroom suite. It was decorated with a red and gold tapestry, fringed pillows and a floor-to-ceiling fireplace that was lined with gilded tiles.

After Zamer left my luggage and closed the door, I sat down on the king-sized canopy bed and lit a cigarette. The antique furniture was tall and pillow-soft. I removed my shoes and stretched my aching muscles, yet when I laid back and closed my eyes I couldn't fall asleep.

I tried to focus on the ticking coming from my pocket watch resting on the side table, but I couldn't block out the disturbing thoughts that filled my mind. What if Adan wouldn't agree to end our association? Was I safe? What would happen if I didn't make it back home? Right then, I felt more like a prisoner than a guest.

My body finally surrendered to sleep out of sheer emotional exhaustion and I felt like I had slept only moments when I flashed awake at the sound of a loud knock at the door. I slipped on my shoes as I heard a man's voice on the other side demand, "Mr. Shariff requests your presence."

"Just a minute," I told him.

But before I even had a chance to wash my face, one of my escorts crashed through the door, brandishing a small pistol. "Cooperate and you won't get hurt," he ordered as he pushed the gun into my side.

The tough guy grabbed my shirt and pushed me back out the door. My legs nearly buckled from the sharp pain of the gun jabbing into my side. The creep held onto my shirt as he shoved me down the stairs and led me into Adan's private office. I nearly lost my balance when the goon finally let go of me.

Coming face to face with Adan, I noticed his expression was as serious as a prison warden's. "Take a seat. We need to talk," Adan ordered in a powerful voice.

"I'm not impressed with your welcome," I muttered. I heard the door close behind me, but I already knew I was a captive audience. I took a seat in the black leather chair across from Adan's polished wooden desk.

"My superiors are concerned about our business agreement, Otto. In your last correspondence, you indicated a desire to end our association due to your retirement. They have too much at stake to let that happen." Adan's cold, penetrating stare made me squirm in my chair.

"Hasn't our agreement made us rich enough men already, Adan? The onset of the war has increased shoreline security. It is a great risk to continue this arrangement." My clasped hands were damp with sweat.

"My comrades know of these changes. Unfortunately, they have a different view. If you refuse to continue," Adan paused, "my orders are to kill you." Without warning, the rear door crashed open, and two soldiers with machine guns surrounded me. "Your contract was sealed when you accepted the money I and my associates offered you, Otto. You have twenty-four hours to rethink your decision."

Adan gave orders to the men in his native tongue, and in seconds, the butt of one of their weapons slammed into my face with the force of a baseball bat. Blood spurted out of my nose and I slumped to the floor, rolling in pain.

The territorial soldiers proceeded to drag me down a hall while I desperately kicked and screamed. "Get your fucking hands off me!" I demanded.

They dropped me in an empty room with no windows. My whole body shivered as the door locked behind them. With trembling hands, I reached inside my pants pocket and pulled out my hanky to wipe the dripping blood from my chin.

"You bastards!" I shouted. This is how they treat me for making them rich, I thought.

My anger mellowed in the silence as time ticked by and the seriousness of the situation sank in. These people meant business and the threat on my life was real. It had been an even bigger mistake than I'd imagined to get involved with these people.

How the hell was I going to get out of this?

Hours passed as hunger and thirst added pressure to the gnawing question.

"Damn it!" I cursed. I don't want to die in this hellhole, I thought.

Yet with each passing hour, a solution was no closer to hand. If I retired, how could I continue their agreement? I knew I had the Preston family trust and my will in place, in case of my death. My family would be taken care of.

My body was getting weaker and my eyes were growing heavy. I wondered if this would be the end. The city would have a big funeral, but who would truly miss me? Only one person came to mind: Cynthia. Could she be the answer?

I looked at my watch in the dim light to see there were only fifteen minutes left to come up with a solution. With my stomach growling from hunger and my tongue feeling paste-dry, I tried to think clearly. Cynthia was the one person I knew would never deny me anything. Her trust was unquestionable. If he asked her, she would undoubtedly do anything to save my life.

Slamming my fists on the door, I hollered, "I'm ready to talk." My head was pounding as the guard opened the door and pressed his gun hard into my side. We again headed toward Adan's office.

My legs were shaking and once we arrived, I fell to my knees before my tormentor. "I can continue with our agreement," I blurted out. "I'll arrange for my daughter Cynthia to take over."

My words seemed to linger in the air as Adan pondered them.

"Otto, you do understand that if you try to weasel out of the deal, your life and hers will be forfeit," Adan warned.

"I understand," I lowered my head.

"Very well. My superiors will be pleased to receive your answer." My captor shouted, "Release him."

The uniformed thugs returned and helped me to my feet.

"It is time for food and drink. Now you will be shown the hospitality you deserve." Adan stood up from his desk and Zamer appeared. "Let my guest clean up and escort him down to our dining room," Adan instructed.

As fast as my nightmare began, it soon transformed into a dream of abundance. Back in my room, Zamer presented me with my own mandarin-colored silk suit. The servant washed my wound and dressed my feet in silk slippers.

Beautiful, exotic women brought mouthwatering trays of food to our table downstairs. Some of the ladies stopped to cool my swollen face with ice packs. Overflowing bowls of fruit, fresh steamed fish and spicy hot dishes were brought in. When we finished our meal, I rested on a blanket of soft pillows to watch exotic belly dancers sway their hips to the rhythm of flutes and tambourines.

Adan offered me a taste of pleasure from his water pipe. "This will ease your pain, my friend," he coaxed me.

I couldn't refuse. I breathed in the sweet aroma of fresh opium. The cool smoke invaded my body with a blissful feeling unlike anything I'd ever experienced before. Stumbling into a dreamlike state, I surrendered to young beauties that began to undress me. What followed was an exotic orgy of physical sin.

The next morning, I awoke in bed without a stitch of clothes on. I got dressed and was relieved to find my door unlocked. I headed downstairs, where Adan was already waiting for me.

Talking business immediately, he said, "The cartel will send the deliveries to your country in another method. It has been confirmed that they accept your offer."

After a light breakfast, my partner handed me an envelope and a small package. "These are presents. A small token of appreciation for your continued business," he smiled.

We walked out to the courtyard together where the limo was waiting.

When I arrived safely back home in Santa Barbara, I opened the package. Inside, I found a small water pipe with a sealed jar filled with opium.

My next challenge would be to figure out how I would inform Cynthia of her new role. She would surely be grateful to know that she had saved my life.

As my retirement ceremony approached, there was just one final task I had to complete before leaving office. With the long-range Santa Barbara Planning Commission manuals open on my desk, I corrected the parcel numbers and returned the government's money to the city coffer. With that complete, I felt ready to step down from my post.

I gave my retirement speech on a clear sunny afternoon with Elizabeth, Cynthia and Barbara at my side. My four young grandchildren watched in the stands as they sat with their nannies. "I stand here knowing my years of service and accomplishment will benefit this great city and its citizens for years to come. I thank all those who helped me along the way."

I looked out at the large audience and was pleased to see W.R. and Marion and in the distance, I recognized Tony Marcello with Stella by his side. I wished Gordon and my mother could have been there to see what I'd achieved.

I took a moment in my speech to acknowledge Elizabeth, who had supported me. I was grateful for her help in securing the Preston legacy. Internally, I acknowledged Stella for her personal maintenance.

As I left the county courthouse, I didn't look back. I was proud of myself. No one knew of my secret, personal desires. I managed to keep them in the closet all these years. I had finally quieted the voice of failure. I played my life with the skill of a good chess game. Now it was time to pass the game board on to the next generation.

In the coming months, I would continue to guide Cynthia into the political arena and encourage her to follow in my footsteps. This would ensure her ability to fulfill the overseas contract.

Chapter Nineteen
The Preston Heritage

1950
Santa Barbara, California
Cynthia Preston McDaniel

Three months after retirement, my father died suddenly of a heart attack. Losing Papa shattered my world like a broken mirror. A dark cloud of shock, grief and anger filled my heart. I never had the chance to say goodbye or let him know just how much I truly loved him.

The city marked his passing with a full-page obituary and photograph with him standing in front of the courthouse.

Mr. Preston's career and tenure as Chairman of the Board of Supervisors was remarkable not just in length, but also in accomplishments. In his nearly three decades of service, he championed public works projects, including roads and dams that will greatly benefit county residents for years to come. An engraved gold plaque will grace the hall of the county courthouse in honor of his dedicated service.

It was a cold, rainy winter day when they laid Papa to rest. Mr. Blaine gave a beautiful speech, as did Mr. William Randolph Hearst. Mr. Tony Marcello spoke a few kind words. It all brought comfort to me.

I stood at his grave site, tightly holding my umbrella while Jack's body supported mine. My tears blended with the rain, but Mother and Barbara shed very few.

Afterward the line of attendees who came to pay their respects seemed endless. It was overwhelming how many people shook my hand to offer condolences and brought Mother flowers. I didn't know most of them, but one woman who accompanied Mr. Marcello bent down, lowered her dark glasses, and seemed to recognize Jack.

When Mr. Hearst paid his respects, he told me, "You will never know how indebted I am to your father. If there is anything I can ever do for you, please let me know."

The city mayor approached me and offered some encouraging words, "Cynthia, your father expressed that he would be thrilled if you would follow in his political footsteps."

"I'd like that, too," I said. "Just last month Papa took me to the county courthouse and introduced me to many of his political colleagues."

"A seat on the board will be vacant soon. I will support you if you decide to enter the political arena," he added before leaving.

The following week, Mother notified Barbara and me that an appointment was scheduled for that Friday at 1:00 PM at the law offices of Mitchell and Blaine for the reading of Papa's will. None of us really knew the extent of our family's wealth, as Papa had kept it to himself. There was an unspoken guarantee that he would take care of all of us, yet I was anxious to hear the directives of his last wishes.

I nervously sat fidgeting in my chair as Mr. Blaine detailed the valuable agricultural property of over two thousand acres, the downtown real estate and the stocks held in the Preston estate. Then the lawyer began describing my father's final requests. When the name Stella Barnes was read, I watched my mother's face blush red.

When Mr. Blaine announced that a $1500-monthly endowment would be paid to that woman until her death, Mother immediately leaped from her seat. She slammed down her foot and shouted, "That dirty bastard! How could he do this to me?"

"Elizabeth, I'm sorry, but I'm only reading the provisions your husband wrote." Mr. Blaine took mother's hand and helped her back into her seat.

A heavy silence followed as the painful knowledge of Papa's secret mistress penetrated the air.

After a few moments of heavy silence, Mother sprang up from her seat, cleared her throat, and with her head held high, addressed us. "The existence of this woman must never be made public. I will do whatever it takes to erase her name from our lives." Her eyes widened with anger as she took a deep breath to regain her composure. "Cynthia and Barbara, your father's infidelity denied me the one thing I longed for: true love." Mother's body straightened and her voice quivered as she defiantly stated, "Now, to ensure my dignity, I demand that this woman's name never be mentioned again."

My throat caught while Barbara and I agreed. Mr. Blaine started reading from a document that outlined mother's inheritance, which included the contents of a safe deposit box that no one knew existed.

"Mr. Preston left instructions that upon his death this box be opened and its contents distributed as indicated," Mr. Blaine declared as he handed the key and long metal container to my mother.

Her head bent downward as she slowly lifted the lid and carefully removed three large velvet drawstring bags from inside. "There is one for each of us," she frowned.

Mr. Blaine carried the tokens over for Barbara and me to open. Tucked inside mine was a hand written note from Papa, and when I looked around, it was obvious that he'd written something to each of us.

I silently read the letter.

> *Princess,*
>
> *I could always count on you. I'm proud of the beautiful woman you have become. My hope is that one day you walk in my political footsteps. I've enclosed a small token of that love. The Preston legacy is now in your hands. I do have one favor to ask. Please contact Mr. Adan Shariff in Bangkok, Thailand. He will disclose an affiliation I made long ago. You will one day know the true meaning of this favor. Princess, I have always loved you.*
>
> *Papa*

Tears ran down my cheeks as I noticed another enclosed small pouch. When I opened it, my heart skipped a beat as I saw a handful of sparkling loose diamonds inside. My heavy burden was lightened when I realized the worth of our relationship. Not a word was spoken between us.

I do not know to this day what the others found inside their pouches.

It was clear that Papa had chosen me to take charge of what he'd left behind. I wondered about the favor he'd asked. Would it be another test of my undying love? It didn't matter. I felt proud that he knew I would never deny his request.

The following day I sent a telegram to Adan Shariff, notifying him of Papa's death. Later, in Adan's return correspondence, I received two airlines tickets to Thailand for Jack and me. He said our meeting was urgent and would be in our best interest.

I knew that Papa would not ask for this favor if it weren't important. So Jack and I asked Mother to care for Sandy, Clark and Claire. I told her, "We need some time away." She agreed it would be good for both of us.

Mother told me off-handedly in the same conversation, "I've instructed Mr. Blaine to make a settlement with Stella Barnes to leave the city and never return."

No doubt that cost a bundle.

Papa's inheritance greatly improved each of our financial situations, and before leaving overseas, Jack went on a spending spree. He brought new farm equipment, a brand new Cadillac and a small plane. Mother advised us that it was time to send Sandy, Clark and Claire to a private boarding school for a proper education. She offered to make these arrangements before we returned. When we were ready to leave, I felt everything was nearly under control. (Except, of course, Jack's drinking problem. But then I had never expected to get that under control.)

We took a train to San Francisco where our international Pan Am flight departed for Bangkok to meet Mr. Shariff. From the moment we landed, it felt like we were on a different planet. Our ivory skin, modern dress and American mannerisms stood out from all those around us. Seeing armed military guards at every gate brought fear and an element of danger to our trip.

Two Asian men who were built like Sumo wrestlers greeted us. "Welcome, Mr. and Mrs. McDaniel. Your host, Mr. Shariff, was sorry to hear about your father's passing."

Jack whispered, "Thank God they speak English." The husky men retrieved our luggage and the pair escorted us to a private car.

In the back of the limousine, Jack turned toward me and announced, "I really didn't want to come, Cynthia. I have a bad feeling about this."

"Stop it, Jack. Remember, we are his guests." I gazed out the window at this very foreign land with crowded outdoor markets, wooden carts drawn by oxen and many inhabitants dressed like beggars. I felt like such an outsider.

After we passed through the city, Jack shook his head. "What has your father gotten us into?"

I remained silent as the same thought ran through my mind. Yet once out of the city, miles of rice-paddy fields zoomed by with the beautiful backdrop of lush green hills.

We entered through a wide iron gate with several armed guards. In the distance, the sky highlighted a silhouette of a golden temple. We stopped in front of a courtyard with a flowing fountain and several Buddha statues surrounded by a lush bamboo garden. Three barefoot men playing flutes bowed in greeting at the massive double doors.

Once inside, I felt nervous about meeting our unknown host. A charge of excitement flared within me when the tall, handsomely tanned stranger appeared and bowed before us. His intriguing dark eyes, thinly trimmed mustache and foreign mystique caused a lump in my throat. "Welcome to my humble home, Cynthia. I offer my deepest sympathy for the loss of your father."

"Thank you, Mr. Shariff. It is a pleasure to meet you."

"Please call me Adan. Your father and I were business partners. We will speak more about that later." He raised my hand and pressed his moist lips gently against it. I felt my face blush like a young schoolgirl.

I couldn't take my eyes off his striking face and impeccable white silk suit. In my romance novels, that would have reflected his goodness as a hero. Adan's sophisticated manner, in-charge voice and salt-and-pepper hair, like Papa's, stirred a desire in me to discover more of the man.

I had forgotten all about my husband until Jack pushed his hand forward, nearly knocking me over. "I'm Cynthia's husband, Jack," he loudly announced. Watching the two shake hands, I instantly regretted his presence on the trip.

"Please let my staff make you feel at home. You will have time to rest until dinner." Adan waved his hand and a teenaged boy picked up our luggage.

We followed the boy up a nearby marble staircase. As we walked along the hallway to our room, we passed many small alcoves displaying golden-jeweled antique treasures. The spicy scent of incense filled the air. When the servant opened the door to the guest room, a giant bouquet of parrot-green, daisy-yellow and bright-red flowers warmly greeted us. I walked over to the fireplace mantel to get a closer look. "These are so different than the ones in Mother's garden."

Before leaving, the barefoot houseboy brightly smiled, saying, "My name's Zamer. Please let me know if there is anything else I can get you."

"No, thank you," I answered, wondering, how could things be more perfect?

"I need a nap," Jack sprawled out on the king-sized bed.

"Go ahead," I advised, but I had the inclination to explore every inch of the room and grounds. My fingers traced the gold design on the fireplace tiles and touched the woven tapestries that accented the Asian décor. Inside the fully mirrored bathroom, a walk-in shower and step-up sunken tub awaited our comfort.

I wondered, how do you suppose this man acquired this kind of wealth? Deep inside, something told me I didn't want to know. Suddenly, a sinking feeling overwhelmed me. Few types of businesses supported that kind of lifestyle. How did Papa fit into the picture?

One thing was certain: Jack and I were already involved way over our heads. Everything around me screamed, *run for your life*! Yet how could I? Papa had trusted me to follow in his footsteps. Still, a dagger of danger plunged fear into my heart. I wondered what Father's commitment might entail.

I slipped beneath the covers and molded my body to Jack's, as if he could shield me and keep me safe. It wasn't long before he was loudly snoring beside me. I couldn't fall asleep and worried about what sacrifice I might have to make for Papa. In time, pure exhaustion made me doze off. Hours later, a hard knock blasted from our door.

"Dinner will be served in thirty minutes," Zamer's voice echoed.

Jack and I quickly showered, changed clothes and prepared ourselves to face the music of my father's past. Zamer arrived and escorted us downstairs.

In the dining room before us, several large glass oil lamps hung down from the high ceiling. Three empty chairs rested before a long wooden table accented by candlelight. In the far corner, the familiar flute players played their instruments; filling the room with a sweet rhythm.

We watched a line of exotic women—bodies draped with multi-colored silk scarves—shake their shimmering beads and bangles as they carried overstuffed platters of vegetables, meat, fruit and wine into the room.

From a side doorway, the sleek vision of the wealthy sultan appeared. He took his place at the head of the table and waved for us to be seated. "I hope the accommodations were to your satisfaction," he dipped his head to the side.

"Your hospitality is more than gracious, Adan," I answered while neatly folding my simple black dress beneath me. "Jack and I look forward to better understanding your association with my father."

"I considered him an excellent partner and intend to explain our connection. First, I want you and Jack to enjoy the fruitfulness of our success," he clapped his hands and within moments, the costumed servers reappeared. They swayed their belly-dancing hips to a faster, gyrating beat.

The entertainment mixed nicely with the piquant food, and our wine glasses never emptied. Jack's eyes widened when one of the veiled beauties closely brushed against him.

"Jack, I understand you appreciate the taste of fine liquor. I have a world-class cellar and invite you to explore it," Adan offered.

"That would be a pleasure," Jack eagerly answered.

I wasn't pleased by the invitation, and so it didn't surprise me when a harem of shapely young women appeared and my husband was whisked out of the room.

As I sat alone with the stranger's intense stare, a shiver ran down my spine.

"Your father never revealed that he had such a beautiful daughter."

"I'd never heard your name mentioned until I read Father's final letter to me. It said that you would explain everything after we arrived."

"The last time your father was here, he told me that you were the one that he could always count on."

"Yes. Papa trusted me," I sighed, feeling some effect from the alcoholic beverage.

"He did so with his life," Adan said and paused briefly. The foreign businessman's hypnotizing voice held my attention as he further explained, "Many years ago, I was a client of your father's law firm. At that time, your country suffered a devastating stock market crash that put him under great financial distress. It was then that our original trade contract commenced." Adan reached out to touch my hand, but I withdrew it.

I tried to stay focused on the circumstances that had brought me to that distant place, but a dream-like euphoria filled my veins. "This news is unsettling, Adan. Please tell me more."

"I understand, but my international business partners seek a guarantee that you will continue his agreement. I'll give you some time, but I will need your answer before you leave."

My heart pounded as the truth of Papa's past commitment touched my life with the pain of a fresh wound.

Just then Jack returned. I noticed his eyes looked bloodshot, and his shirt was disheveled. It bothered me, but I ignored him, my other concerns pressing on my mind.

Another entertaining line of servants carried in a flaming dessert. More questions ran through my mind about Adan's and my father's affiliation, but I remained silent, as it seemed that Adan wanted to confront me directly with the proposal.

We were served after-dinner liqueur while the dancers continued another impressive performance. Jack didn't take his eyes off one young girl with a buxom figure. She invited him to dance with her. I was disgusted when he made embarrassing gestures and acted like a complete fool.

"Would you like to join me on the terrace for some fresh air, Cynthia?" Adan invited me.

I accepted his moment of chivalry, and we escaped the revolting scene. Breathing in the cool evening air, I had the sinking feeling that my host knew a lot more about me than I did about him. We stood side-by-side outside on the balcony beneath a starlit sky. As the nearby palm trees swayed, he whispered in my ear, "I'm very honored by your presence."

"Tell me, Adan, what are the risks associated with this partnership venture?" I stepped back, but pressed forward for more information.

"Your father's contract involved a cartel of traders who seek the safe delivery of their goods to your native shore."

I walked away, then turned around and faced him, "What if I choose not to continue with this contract?"

"The compliance and continuation of this association was guaranteed with your father's life." He paused. "And yours." Adan stepped toward me.

My body shivered with a chill. Wanting to escape the scene, I turned and headed inside.

Adan's strong hand grabbed my wrist, stopping me. "I need to explain something to you. Please stay."

Right then, I felt dizzy and nearly lost my balance. Adan drew me close and offered his body for balance. Alarmed at my actions, I tried to straighten up. Only then, I realized that I was not in full control of myself. I wondered if Adan had slipped something into my drink. Anger welled up inside of me and I tried to push him away.

"Don't fight this Cynthia. It's a game you can't win," his strong arms held me close.

My eyes closed in fear, trying to block out the words I didn't want to hear.

"Oh, my God. How could Papa do this to me?" I sobbed and rested against his strong shoulders.

Adan gently lifted my chin and our eyes met. In an instant his lips met mine in a heart-pounding kiss. Then he pulled back. "Forgive me, Cynthia. I got carried away. I know you have a husband."

At that moment, I wasn't thinking about Jack. My whole body was consumed by a searing heat of passion stronger than anything I'd felt before. Every cell in my body screamed for more. I faced him and said, "I didn't want you to stop." My voice was weak, but my words were strong with truth.

The next scene was right out of one of my romance novels. I surrendered to my fantasized Harlequin stranger, under a blanket of stars in this far away exotic land. Papa had covered his own addiction well. Even though I had never tasted the white powder that came from this place, I recognized its effects on me.

Taking a deep breath, my head whirled with the depth of Papa's involvement in the escapade. The truth was, I'd already lost Papa, and this was the first sacrifice I didn't mind making.

Adan lifted me off my feet and carried me inside. Jack was nowhere to be found. With my head spinning with elevated euphoria, we entered his bedroom. The next few hours were a fog where I remained in a complete state of ecstasy. Flashes of our naked bodies, sweat and the sweet taste of physical satisfaction engulfed my senses. In this dream-like state, all the fantasies of my novels came to life. With Adan's handsome face above me, we pulsated together through the night like the young lovers in my books.

When I awoke the next morning, I was alone. The aftermath of the night before was confirmed when I saw the remnants of the white heroin powder that remained on the nearby table. The satin sheets beneath me couldn't cool the anger that began to rage through my veins. Jumping out of bed, I grabbed the silk robe resting on a nearby chair.

"What have I done?" I screamed out loud. For the first time I wondered what happened to Jack.

I found my black dress hanging over a painted wooden screen and quickly slipped it on. When I reached for the door handle and found it locked, I got mad as hell. I banged on the door until a man's voice ordered, "You are not allowed to leave this room."

"Where is my husband?" I hollered.

"He is on his way here. You must wait."

I nervously paced the floor, feeling like I might lose my mind. Suddenly the door swung open and Jack staggered inside. His clothes were wrinkled, his eyes glassy and his words slurred as he grinned, "Boy, do these people know how to party." Then he tripped and fell to the floor.

"My God. What happened to you?" I exclaimed.

There was a smirk on his face as he lifted his head and said, "Looks like you had an interesting night yourself."

"Jack, this was a set up. These people my father got involved with are tied to organized crime. What are we going to do?"

Jack slowly picked himself up and pulled out a small box from his pant pocket. There was a note attached and he handed it to me. "I was instructed to give this to you."

"I don't want anything from him!" I shouted, tossing the package onto the nearby bed.

"Honey, I don't think you understand who you are dealing with. Yeah, they set us up. Let's face it; they also have the upper hand."

"You are pitiful, Jack. If we go along with them, they will own us for the rest of our lives."

"I don't know about you, but I could get used to this kind of lifestyle," Jack grinned.

"This means more tracks I'd have to cover up. If any of this ever went public, Papa's reputation and our lives would be ruined."

"Can't you look at this as our opportunity to live a life most people only dream about?"

"We can't be stupid about it." Yet the more he talked, I realized there wasn't a choice. Finally, I reached over and retrieved the note attached to the small black box.

Cynthia,

You gave me a breathtaking memory, which I do not regret. I know we live in two different worlds, but I'm grateful to the man who brought you into my life. I hope last night makes your choice easier. Please accept this gift, which shows how much our time together meant.

Adan

I lifted the lid and inside was a magnificent set of three-karat dangling diamond earrings.

While I sat at the edge of the bed, something Papa once told me crossed my mind: *Cynthia, life is like a game of chess; it's all about the strategy of your moves.*

Right then I knew it was my move. The picture was clear. Years ago, Papa did what he had to do or it would have cost him his life. If I didn't do the same, it would cost me mine. With it, he offered us a tool to help wash away the pain.

Banging on the door, I told the guard we needed to meet with Adan. I was grateful that we were taken to our room to freshen up first. As we walked down the steps toward his office, Jack took my hand. "We're in this together."

The whole trip seemed like a nightmare as we sat and listened to Adan outlining the details of the deal he'd made with my father—now our deal. "International racketeering is big business. The cargo is drugs, diamonds and guns. My job is to monitor distribution routes. With your inside help, these shipments can easily slip by authorities." When Adan addressed me, my heart pounded wildly. "You will find this agreement to be fruitful, but know any breach puts all our lives in danger."

I took a deep breath and somberly answered, "Yes, I understand."

"Your limousine is waiting." He motioned us to follow him. After Jack was inside, I stood for a moment with Adan. "We'll make good business partners," I smiled.

"I'm indebted to you and your father." Adan gently kissed my hand and slipped a small piece of paper into my purse. We quickly embraced.

Later when I was alone I read it.

> *Dear Cynthia,*
>
> *Your father would be proud. I hope we shared something more than our business contract. I look forward to our continued partnership.*
>
> *Adan*

Chapter Twenty
Mothers, Daughters and Sons

1950-1960
Santa Barbara, California
Cynthia Preston McDaniel

During our trip home, Jack and I discovered a new bond in our tattered relationship. His words, "We're in this together," glued his name to my promised commitment. I soon found out this came with other costs.

Even before we arrived home, Jack indulged himself. In San Francisco, he purchased several pieces of rare art and a premium set of golf clubs. He also secured stock investments in oil.

I made the decision to use some of the unexpected financial windfall to help start my own political career. Surely Papa would have approved of that. Once home, I knew our finances would be better controlled by me.

While we were away, my Mother arranged for our children, Sandy, Clark and Claire to attend boarding school back East. My first political ambition was to be elected to the Board of Supervisors.

Jack kept busy with all his new toys, including a larger boat and a private jet. When Barbara gave birth to her new baby boy, Joel, Jack took a special interest in him.

I focused on reconnecting with Papa's old cronies to let them know I'd started my own political career. When I made out my application for a city council position, I decided to use my maiden name, because Cynthia Preston would be better recognized in the community.

It was a pleasant surprise how many people decided to support me who had known Papa. The mayor quickly became my ally when the large contributions I made to his campaign enhanced his own reelection.

In time, I put in a call to Mr. Hearst, and he invited me up to his home in San Simeon. Riding along Highway 101, the sun gleamed like diamonds off the ocean, creating a panoramic view. I thought about Papa, who often had made this trip during his lifetime. He seldom spoke about their long friendship, but at Papa's funeral, the speech Mr. Hearst gave expressed a sincere gratitude for their trusted relationship.

I found the location of his residence ideal. It wasn't far from the city, secluded on a hilltop and similar in size to some medieval castles I'd seen in the travel brochures Jack brought home. There was a chill in the air as I followed his butler down the dim corridor to Mr. Hearst's private office.

Mr. Hearst stood up as I entered the room. "Welcome, Cynthia. How are you?" he beamed.

His eyes looked tired as he leaned back into his chair and I explained the reason for my visit. "I've decided to join the political arena. My first step is to achieve a seat on the city council."

"I'll support you and your new political career any way I can," he promised, straightening his posture.

Moments later, there was a knock at the door. A petite blond, close to my mother's age, entered with a glass of water in her hand. "It is time for your pills, Pops," she smiled.

"Cynthia, you know Marion, my personal caretaker."

"You're Otto's daughter!" she squealed. "How about when you're done, I show you around?"

"Good idea," W.R. confirmed. "Your father was a good man and he helped me more than you'll ever know. I guarantee my personal endorsement," he added as I got up to join Marion.

Acting like two school-girls, we chatted about some of the misadventures tied to the historic site. Before I left, she requested, "Please come back and visit soon, Cynthia." I sensed a lonely sadness in the tone of her voice.

Two weeks before my election, a favorable article appeared in the *Mariposa Daily* where Mr. Hearst personally praised me by stating, "Cynthia Preston is worthy of walking in her father's footsteps."

Although I was elected, I did not win by a landslide. It made me realize that not everyone worshipped the ground my father had walked on. I was nonetheless confident that with unlimited funds on my side, I could win over any opposition.

My first city meeting brought unexpected confrontation. It was over the Santa Barbara Planning Commission manuals that my father had created before his death. Several private citizens had raised a safety question regarding the proposed location of a new high school.

"As a concerned parent, I believe it is critical to guarantee our children's safety. An investigation needs to be made regarding the toxic waste site located nearby," a female citizen requested.

Never having read the Santa Barbara Planning Commission manuals penned by my father, I kept quiet. I knew they listed the location of the nearby nuclear waste site, but was unsure where it was. Fred Olson, the new chairman of the board of supervisors, assured her that a public disclosure would be made.

After the meeting adjourned, I spoke to Fred about it. "What was the reason my father allowed a toxic dumping site be designated within city limits?"

"When the dam projects began years back, Otto made a deal with the federal government to secure funds with the stipulation that land would be set aside for a nuclear waste site."

"Where are the records for this transaction?" I inquired.

"They are stored in the archives at the Santa Barbara municipal records building."

"Will you let me handle this investigation?" I requested.

Fred agreed.

I had a nagging suspicion deep inside me that something was amiss. I had to obtain those records to see for myself what had transpired.

The next day, I made the trip. It was an all-day project to locate the records, but I finally found a box marked "Federal Nuclear Waste Pit." I checked out the contents and promised to return them the next day.

Once back in my newly remodeled home office on our ranch, I told Jack, "There is some city business I have to take care of tonight."

Before I had closed the door, he said, "I'll head over to your sister's house and be out of your way." Jack was spending way too much time at

Bernie and Barbara's, but at least it kept him out of my hair.

Opening the lid of the cardboard file, I spread the papers out across my desk. With each stack, I found more questions than answers. The unorganized documentation made it hard to figure things out. In one file, it stated the government had required fourteen acres for a toxic dumping site to be set aside. Yet in another, the parcel listed consisted of twenty-five acres. When I checked the city map, I was concerned when certain parcel numbers did not line up with their location.

Finding the original documents, my heart sank. It appeared that the parcel numbers had been altered. A chill passed through me as I wondered if anyone really knew exactly where the toxic dump was located.

I hastily searched out a recent city map. When I pinpointed the parcel of land proposed for the new high school, I was relieved that the toxic dump parcel was listed as being over five miles away.

As I put the papers back and documented my findings, fear trickled down my spine. Were the parcel numbers changed? Why?

If they had been changed, it could open up an ugly can of worms for me. After double-checking my findings, I decided to present the documentation stating the nuclear waste site was far enough away from the school location that it was not a threat to anyone. Once I presented my findings, all questions were dropped. I was relieved to know that my position on the board of supervisors remained secure.

The years passed quickly. Sandy, Clark and Claire remained in boarding school and returned home only for holiday visits or vacations. One year when my reelection campaign was approaching, I received a disturbing letter from the school chancellor stating that Sandy and Clark were noted to have excessive class truancies. The personal letter from the headmaster stated that the children were on probation for three months and faced expulsion if their actions continued.

That same year, Barbara insisted on having our annual Hanukkah family dinner take place at her new suburban tract home. I didn't have the patience or desire to address Sandy's continued rebellious behavior or Barbara's competitive conduct. Not to mention Jack had grown distant with me again, and his constant visits to my sister's house annoyed me.

When he offered to help her move into their new home, I scolded him. "God, Jack. You spend more time at Barb's house than ours anymore."

"Well you're never home even when you're home," he shouted back.

It was a cool blustery day when Jack and I went to pick up Sandy, Clark and Claire from the train station. In the car on the way there, I brought up the headmaster's letter. "Jack, we need to address Sandy's and Clark's recent behavior."

"Don't worry, Cynthia. They're just being kids."

"As parents, we can't allow them to do whatever they want."

"Well, aren't we two good examples for great behavior!" he frowned.

I blurted out, "What kind of father are you, anyway?"

"One who remains at your side for all the wrong reasons."

My husband's words felt like a slap in the face. "I see. All you really care about is that the money keeps coming in. Don't worry. I'll take care of things myself."

The tension between us permeated the air as we pulled up to the train station. A loud whistle could be heard in the distance.

We stood on the wooden platform with a crowd of anxious people waiting for the return of their loved ones. As the train wheels halted and the doors swung open, I scanned the cars to find our children.

I caught sight of Sandy's long blond hair, tied back in a ponytail with her favorite hot pink scarf. She joyfully pulled off her rhinestone, cat-eye sunglasses, crazily waving to us. Right behind her, Clark, in his leather bomber jacket, waved his arm high in the air to acknowledge our presence. Claire came running toward us.

As they approached, I chuckled, thinking my older children's attire mimicked today's teen idols Diana Dors and James Dean. Claire remained the clean cut adolescent.

"Kids today are sure different than when we were young." Jack's words substantiated my very thoughts.

"Good of you to pick us up." Sandy mischievously grinned as she fought the wind to keep her poodle skirt down.

Clark looked over at Sandy when I didn't greet them with open arms. "I feel a chill in the air."

"The two of you have some explaining to do," I coolly announced.

"You can't be that upset, mother," Sandy began. "Tell me you never skipped a class in boarding school."

"You watch your words, young lady. We knew better than that. Clark, what is your excuse for getting involved?"

"Brotherly love," he smartly replied.

"Well, for this behavior, I'm going to cut your usual holiday allowance in half."

"Mother! That means there'll be no fruitcake for Grandma." Sandy smirked.

"Worse yet, I won't be able to buy the new Elvis album," Clark chimed in.

"Cut it out, you two," I demanded. "You better be on your best behavior tomorrow night at my sister's house, or your New Year's allowance will be cut, too," I threatened.

"That's right. Why are we doing our family dinner at Aunt Barbara's this year, anyway?" Sandy questioned.

"She wants to show off her new house," I bluntly responded, slamming the car door behind me.

"You both know how your mother and her sister are always trying to outdo each other," Jack added.

"Shut up, Jack. You seem to enjoy spending more time at their home than ours."

Clark cringed. "Dad, please turn up the radio. We didn't come all this way to hear you two bicker."

"I have a mind to pull you both out of school. If education wasn't so important, I would," I loudly threatened.

"I vote for a holiday truce," Sandy piped up.

"Fine with me," Jack agreed.

Once we arrived home, Sandy turned toward me. "Watching Claire and Joel open presents is always the best part of the holidays, anyway."

As we headed down our long driveway, I thought to myself, the one thing I could thank Mother for was her help in raising my very well-mannered, quiet and musically refined younger daughter. Every time Claire gracefully played the piano or accordion, it made me proud.

I slipped into my office to do some work. Later that evening, Claire gave a special holiday performance of "*Oh, Hanukkah*" for Clark and Sandy.

Just as the music ended, Jack stood up and announced, "Claire and Joel will be doing a duet tomorrow night."

This was the first I'd heard about it and the thought infuriated me. "What are you talking about, Jack?"

"It was supposed to be a surprise, but I thought maybe you should know about it."

"Why tell me now? This is something I should already have known about."

"Well, Cynthia, this is one thing your sister and I didn't want your permission for."

I threw my hands in the air and shook my head. "So that is what you have been up to behind my back."

"Mother, get over it. Dad just wanted to do something on his own for a change," Sandy interjected.

"What do you mean by that comment, young lady?" I scowled.

"You run a tight ship, Mother, with your hands clenching the purse strings. Maybe this will make him feel more like a man," Clark spoke up.

"That's enough from you two," I ordered.

"Time to call it a night, folks," my husband announced loudly.

I glared at Jack and stormed upstairs. His lack of interest in the bedroom, excessive time at Barbara's and outspoken comments made me wonder why I stayed married to him. But I knew it would be impossible to find another partner who would accept or condone our overseas arrangement.

The next morning, Jack took Claire over to Barbara's early to practice with Joel. I heard Clark and Sandy in the kitchen laughing as they made homemade cookies to bring for our meal that night.

"I like the chocolate chip ones," Clark told Sandy.

"No, let's make pecan snowballs," Sandy argued.

"Make them both," I called out.

The delicious aroma of fresh baked goods still filled the house as we got ready to leave for Barbara's.

As I stared out the car window on that star-filled evening, I wondered what dreadful comment my Mother would make to spoil it. On many of these family occasions, she confronted me about my extravagant lifestyle. She didn't approve of my political position, and last Thanksgiving, she had told me, "Cynthia, your outspoken, aggressive and frank behavior doesn't fit into my social circle."

I kept quiet because I needed the votes of her stuffy rich friends, but I did not choose to socialize with them. The political arena was comfortable to me, and I fit well in Papa's position. I knew he would be proud of the job I'd done. Being in my political position of power had lent me accessibility to bribe, payoff, or use my clout to fulfill our overseas commitments.

As we approached Barbara's trendy neighborhood, many of the Spanish stucco houses were decorated in Christmas lights. It was easy to pick out my sister's, because it was decorated in solid blue lights with a large menorah on the lawn. As we carried armloads of Hanukkah gifts inside, I was surprised to discover her interior design had an Asian theme. It reminded me of the classic styling of Adan's palace.

Before our meal, we sat in her open-beam living room. Claire began to play her black lacquer grand piano while Joel followed along with his violin. They chose the song, "*If I Were a Rich Man*," from *Fiddler on the Roof*. The performance brought forth the gaiety of the season.

Looking over at Jack, my anger subsided as I realized it was his forethought that had made the concert possible.

Mother clapped the loudest and hugged the grandchildren as she told them, "Double dessert for both of you tonight."

While Barbara, Mother and I stood together working on dinner preparations in my sister's custom-built kitchen, my mother turned toward me and asked out of the blue, "Will Jack present Sandra at next years debutante ball?"

In the still air, I watched Barbara's face drain white.

"Mother, Sandy is still young and we have time to decide that," I answered, feeling tension moving down my spine.

Mother's body straightened, "Every young woman should be properly introduced into the society in which they belong."

Barbara turned her face away, took a deep breath and continued filling a ceramic bowl with mashed potatoes. "Drop it, Mother. You have no idea how your social requirements have impacted my life." Barbara's sharp words cut through the air like the sound of Bernie's electric knife cutting the turkey.

Mother began washing her hands in the sink. "I've tried my best to give you girls a proper upbringing, but now I see that each of you has chosen to discard it."

"What exactly do you mean by that?" I set the dishrag I'd been using to dry dishes on the counter.

"Mother, you can't begin to imagine what has been done to keep any dirt off your hands," Barbara seethed.

I turned toward her and demanded silence with a stern look.

"Cynthia, do you think I am blind to the reprehensible and eccentric lifestyle you lead?" Mother's accusation whirled at me.

"Who are you to judge my lifestyle? You have no idea the sacrifices I've made so you can keep yours." My angry words spilled like venom from my lips.

"How dare you to speak to me that way!" Mother banged a basket of rye bread down on the tile countertop. "Your disrespect makes me lose my appetite. I cannot tolerate this kind of conversation."

Barbara and I stood speechless as we watched Mother bolt from the room.

Jack entered the kitchen and asked, "Is something wrong with your mother? She seemed really upset."

I explained to him that she had brought up something very personal that we disagreed on.

He shook his head, "Women. I'll never understand them. Please let us know when dinner is ready."

At the large, formally set dining room table, tension permeated the room. Mother's cold stare irritated me as she doted on the plans and dreams of my children and completely ignored me. I overheard her tell them, "I'll always make sure you are well cared for."

I wondered just what she meant by that.

At the end of the evening, we watched the children open their presents. I yearned to leave, but stayed to help clean up.

Barbara took me aside. "Thank you, Cynthia, for handling Mother's comments earlier."

"We have to keep the past buried, Barbara. It is our burden."

"Well, sometimes I think there is too much dirt between us that can never be washed away."

Our eyes locked with emotions that reflected the weight of the hidden secrets we carried between us.

Just then, Jack walked in. To my surprise, he handed Barbara and I each a small wrapped box. "I know we said no adult presents, but I wanted to do something special for both of you."

As we unwrapped the small packages, I realized they were identical.

Inside each box was a sparkling diamond brooch that spelled out the word, Peace. "My hope is that you can find this feeling between the two of you." Jack smiled.

The fact that he would give my sister and me the same present was unsettling. It wasn't his business to interfere with our relationship. It insulted me when Barbara kissed Jack on the lips right in front of me.

"You're so thoughtful, Jack," she chortled.

The whole thing bothered me. Jack knew my relationship with my sister remained rocky and competitive. It felt like another slap in the face. It showed he didn't care about my feelings. Maybe Jack wasn't the only one staying together for all the wrong reasons; I certainly wasn't with him for the right one. But even so, Jack wasn't to blame for those reasons. Papa had left me without a choice in the matter.

At the end of the evening, I watched Claire and Joel say goodbye to one another. As they stood side by side, the thought that they looked more like brother and sister pierced my heart.

Chapter Twenty-One
The Pain of Justice

1950-1959
Santa Barbara, California
Elizabeth Preston

When my husband suddenly died of a heart attack, it signaled a time for change. For so many years I felt the only identity I had was as Otto Preston's wife. To the outside world, he left a fine legacy as a philanthropist, political pioneer and successful lawyer. Even though his will provided financial comfort for his family, the underlying pain and suffering he left behind can never be washed away.

I wondered if Otto really ever loved me—like he did my daughter, Cynthia. I believed she knew I was jealous of their relationship. It angered me that she probably had knowledge of his mistress, but never spoke a word about it to me. Now, she lived a political lifestyle like my husband's. Her extravagant jewelry, wasteful spending and I suspect, her notorious personal habits are shocking and repulsive to me.

As a widow, my social status remained intact, but my personal relationships now took on a greater meaning. The time I spend with my four grandchildren, Sandra, Clark, Claire and Joel has brought me the most joy. I so looked forward to visiting with them this holiday before they returned to school.

With the pleasant weather we are having for this time of year, I thought we would all have lunch together out on the patio that overlooked my English garden.

Barbara arrived first with Joel, my youngest grandchild.

"We can't stay too long, Mother." My daughter immediately announced, "Joel has a violin lesson later this afternoon."

I hugged Joel and handed him a birthday envelope as he had just turned seven a few days ago. "I really enjoyed your duet with Claire the other night." I expressed my sentiments.

His smile warmed my heart and I told him he could watch television until his cousins arrived.

"How is Bernie?" I asked Barbara as we headed outside to the patio.

"The same boring man I married."

"Just because he doesn't fly you all around, like Jack, doesn't make him boring," I commented.

"Let's not go there, Mother. I know you don't approve of the time Jack and I spend together."

"It does seem excessive. Are you going out of your way, just to make your sister jealous?" I asked.

"Cynthia and I live in two different worlds. Father's favoritism made sure of that. Jack freely offers me a taste of their lifestyle."

"Maybe you should try to be satisfied with your own," I advised. Just then the doorbell rang and I left to answer it.

Cynthia looked stunning in her Givenchy, tan, silk skirt-suit with matching brown hat, shoes and purse. Of course her outfit was accessorized with her signature diamond jewelry. Sandra, Clark and Claire strolled in behind her and offered warm kisses and hugs to me.

Clark saw Joel in the living room and quickly joined him, while Sandy and Claire stayed by my side. As we walked by the boys I told them, "Lunch will be ready soon. I expect you to come on my first call."

"Sandy you look so pretty today." I told her admiring her pale pink cotton dress with a strawberry sash cummerbund.

"Thank you grandma. Can we go sit out by the garden?" she questioned.

"Yes," I answered knowing this was our usual special spot to chat together. "Cynthia, Maria will get you and Claire something to drink."

Sandy and I walked together outside and sat down on the iron bench beside the garden entrance. I was closest with her since she was my very first grandchild and at twelve-years-old she seemed so different than my own daughters. Sandy always had a smile on her face and looked at life with wonder. I loved her adventurous spirit. She was always open to trying new foods, games or meeting new people.

"Grandma, I couldn't wait to tell you about something that I've decided while I was at school."

"What is it, sweetheart?" I wondered.

"My school counselor asked each of us to think about what we would like to do most, after we graduate. I knew right away what I wanted to be."

"Don't keep me in suspense, Sandy. Please tell me your plan."

"I want to become a nurse and help people."

"How did you come to decide that?" I asked.

"If you promise not to tell my mother, I will tell you."

"Ok, I promise," my curiosity was raised.

"I came across a set of medical books stored up in our attic. Inside, the pages were filled with the most fascinating pictures I'd ever seen."

I was certain my husband bought those books, years ago, when Cynthia thought she might become a nurse and later changed her mind. All I could say was, "That would make me very proud."

Maria announced that lunch was ready and we all gathered on the patio and sat down at the table.

Before long the bickering between my daughters began.

"Please, Cynthia and Barbara, I don't feel your differences should be discussed in front of the children."

"You're right mother. Family secrets must remain hush, hush. Heaven knows what would happen if an ugly word was ever spoken against our Father," Barbara's voice lashed out in anger.

"Please don't fight," Clark spoke up.

"This is none of your business, son," Cynthia scolded.

"Clark was only trying to help," Sandy defended.

"Both of you will be grounded until you return to school. No outside activities at all," Cynthia ordered.

"Lets finish this meal in peace, please," I suggested.

Underneath the table, since she sat next to me, I squeezed Sandy's hand with reassurance. I purposely changed the conversation and asked if either of the girls had watched last nights Ed Sullivan show. "He showcased a wonderful singer named Dinah Shore."

"She has a great voice," Barbara agreed.

"I like her style," Cynthia added.

For the rest of the lunch we remained civil to one another and I was relieved the meal ended on a lighter note.

After my family left I thought about how the inheritance that Otto had left made my children's lives more complicated. Since I didn't approve of their self-indulgent lifestyles I decided that I would change our Preston living trust.

I had Mitchell and Blaine draw up the addendum as follows: my children would only be entitled to money received from the leases on the real estate and agricultural land held within the trust. I instructed that all assets be transferred equally to my four grandchildren. It was suggested that I add this provision. A sale of land may take place in the event of a death in the family and with all heirs' approval.

Now, only the passage of time would reveal the final legacy Otto left behind.

Chapter Twenty-Two
The Stage is Set

1951-1967
Santa Barbara, California
Cynthia Preston McDaniel

As my reelection approached, I visited Marion and W.R.'s ranch, sometimes spending the night. We swam, played tennis and watched old movies in the theater. I admired her loyalty as W.R.'s caretaker as the aged magnate's health deteriorated. My favorite pastime was hearing Marion tell stories about Papa's younger days. Later that year, I heard the sad news that the legendary giant, Mr. Hearst, passed away.

The next seven years passed quickly. The time finally came for Sandy and Clark to graduate from boarding school. Even though Clark was a semester behind, he had accumulated enough credit to join Sandy's graduating class. Mother accompanied Jack, Claire and me when we flew out to the East Coast to attend their commencement ceremony. We all loudly applauded as their names were read.

Mother's eyes filled with tears. Her dream realized: Clark and Sandy had completed a proper education.

That evening during our celebration, Mother asked the kids, "What plans do you have for your future?"

Sandy looked directly at me and said, "I want to move to Los Angeles and become a nurse."

"I will make sure that happens," Mother promised as she handed Sandy a sealed envelope that I'm sure was stuffed with cash.

"My plans are to become an agricultural engineer," Clark set down his fork and faced Jack.

"What a perfect choice, son," I confirmed.

"You did always love to get dirt on your hands. At least now something will become of it." Jack smiled and handed Clark an envelope, as did my mother.

"Wow, flying lessons! Thank you, Dad. This means a great deal to me. Thank you too, Grandmother."

Sandy turned to Claire, "How about you? Do you have an idea what you might want to be when you grow up?"

"I want to be just like Grandma."

We all laughed as they hugged each other.

During our plane ride back home, we became alarmed when Mother suddenly felt ill. She was coughing, complained of being dizzy and had difficulty catching her breath. By the time we landed, she was completely disoriented. Jack and I decided to rush her to the hospital.

When the doctor came out to speak with us, we were informed that mother had suffered a stroke. The news was hard to believe, since she was seldom sick. I wondered how my vibrant, headstrong mother could be so close to death.

For the next few days, we all watched and waited as she slipped in and out of a coma. Mother barely moved from her fetal position in her hospital bed. Sandy and Clark wept by her side. When Barbara arrived, she became hysterical and had to be medicated.

I had to leave the room when Sandy bent down and whispered to her, "Grandma, thank you for loving us for all these years."

Jack and Bernie stood vigil, too, but all the sadness was too much for me and I wished it would be over quickly. The overpowering smell of medicine, the heavy emotions and the feelings of helplessness made the hours drag by.

It was the first time I had ever seen Jack and Clark break down and sob. At home, I watched Claire tightly hold the porcelain doll Mother had given her for her last birthday. I tried to get some city business done, but the whirlwind of events of the recent days had blocked my mind.

On the third morning as I prepared to leave for the hospital, I got a call from Jack that my mother had passed away during the night. For me, it was a relief, but for those around me, the world seemed to be falling apart.

Jack distanced himself and gave me cold, blank stares. Clark and Sandy tried to console each other and reached out to Claire, who was withdrawn. Barbara called to tell me about the funeral arrangements and asked if I wanted to speak at her service. It was the hardest speech I'd ever written, but I knew fulfilling the social expectation would bring political praise.

The number of people that arrived at Mother's memorial service from our relatively small town impressed me. Several hundred members from her high-society organizations attended. After speaking, I listened to many testimonials and learned more about my mother's life than I had ever known. Her contributions to women's rights were commendable, and her financial support to many institutions remarkable. I wondered if they were speaking about the same woman who had raised me.

Several weeks later, Barbara informed me Mother's will was soon to be read at the law offices of Mitchell and Blaine. She gave me the date and time.

Nothing had prepared me for the news I received that day. I was not surprised when Mr. Blaine stated, "The appointed trustees of Elizabeth Preston's estate are Cynthia Preston McDaniel and Barbara Preston Baumgartner," but his following announcement brought me to the edge of my seat. "Elizabeth Preston added an addendum to the original trust. It is as follows: all two thousand acres of agricultural preserve must remain as leased land. The trustees are entitled to the proceeds of these leases as their income, but cannot touch the principal. Any sale of land may only take place upon the death of an immediate family member. All other properties contained in the living trust of Otto Preston are left to Elizabeth's grandchildren: Sandy McDaniel, Clark McDaniel, Claire McDaniel and Joel Baumgartner."

"That bitch!" I screamed. "How could she deny us the legacy our father worked so hard for?"

"Why would she do that?" Barbara cried out.

"We can contest this," I insisted. "Can't we, Mr. Blaine? My mother was out of her mind."

"Yes, but the process is long and costly with no guarantee that you will win," he answered.

"Cynthia, calm down," Barbara commanded, seeing my growing disdain. "Maybe we should accept Mother's condition. Bernie and I can use the money from the leases."

"This isn't about the money, Barbara. It's the idea that Papa would have wanted you and me to inherit the empire he built. Not that it be passed by us and all given to the grandchildren."

"Let's be realistic. Mother resented your relationship with Father and always harshly judged our choices. I believe she didn't trust us to be fair."

"Fair! She never knew how fair we were. Besides, this is about Papa's wishes, not hers. I just can't let this slide."

"For now, Cynthia and Barbara, these terms will stand," Mr. Blaine spoke up. "All property listed in the living trust of Otto Preston will now be deeded to Elizabeth's grandchildren."

I faced Mr. Blaine and Barbara. Holding my head high, I said, "This may stand, but I vow to teach these children that a life of status and money comes with a high personal price."

Part Three

Sandy McDaniel
Clark McDaniel
Amber McDaniel
1970-1997

Chapter Twenty-Three
The Legacy Continues: One

1971
Los Angeles, California
Sandy Preston McDaniel

Standing before a full-length mirror, I carefully examined every detail of my crisp, cotton nurse's uniform. My cap was carefully tucked down and securely pinned over my ponytail. I held my head still while I straightened my new name tag: *Sandy McDaniel, RN.* Grandmother would be so proud if she could only see me now, I thought. Grandmother had told me, *I'm so glad you're becoming a nurse, because your mother never did.*

My mind wandered as I recalled my favorite memories of her. I loved our many afternoons sitting together talking on the iron bench in front of her English garden. Bright yellow marigolds, fragrant cornflowers and dainty forget-me-nots offered us the sweetness of fine candy. She once told me, *life is fragile like the petals on my flowers, Sandy. When nourished, they will flourish. When neglected, they will wither and die.*

Looking back, I believe this reflected her life. Grandmother had always contained a deep sadness within her that I only caught in small glimpses. The reason I became a nurse was my desire to help those who were hurting like I always knew she was. Life had been lonely without her these past years. Grandmother offered me what my own mother never had to give. She listened to me, and I always knew she deeply cared about me.

After her death, Clark and my best friend, Amber, were the only ones I could truly count on. Amber Branson and I met in nursing school. She was the smartest student in the class and had an inquisitive mind like Clark. Being French-Cherokee, a poet and a dreamer, she always had interesting thoughts and feelings about life and love. I loved to listen to her talk about them.

At first, we would just hang around together. After my first year, we became roommates. Amber shared her chaotic childhood with me. Her parents had divorced when she was just two years old. Each of us knew that having family didn't guarantee that you wouldn't be lonely. When we were together, our striking shoulder-length blond hair turned heads everywhere we went.

During my second year of school, my spirits rose when I learned that my brother Clark had decided to attend Cal Poly nearby. When I introduced him to Amber, they hit it right off. We all loved to rent horses and go riding together. I quickly noticed a special look in Amber's eyes whenever she was with Clark.

As graduation approached, I began feeling apprehensive. Mother, Father, Claire, Aunt Barbara, Bernie and Joel would all be flying in for the ceremony on Saturday. The jealousy, underlying competitiveness and mistrust between Mother and Aunt Barbara still caused many uncomfortable family confrontations. For years, I'd suspected the tension between them was caused by a terrible secret in the past that was never spoken about, but I couldn't confirm it.

To get things off my mind, I decided it was time for some fun. Amber, Clark, my new boyfriend, John, and I decided to head to the beach for a small class party. The warm June weather, some beer and a reason to party always brought out the playful part of me. Before our beaus arrived, Amber and I gave each other a last minute check.

"I love your gypsy skirt," Amber complimented as we put on tube tops with our string bikinis underneath.

It was just like Clark to arrive with a dozen long-stemmed red roses for each of us. I was a little disappointed when my handsome surfer dude, John, showed up empty-handed. We headed out in Clark's pale-yellow Malibu convertible with our hair blowing in the wind. I scooted away from John when his crystal blue eyes kept snooping down my chest.

With the radio blasting and my brother and best friend in the front seat, it was easy to ignore John's crude advances. But by the time we arrived at the bash and we'd popped a few beers, his behavior was getting out of hand. I'm one for having a good time and not wanting to ruin the evening, so I playfully kept pushing him away.

For a while, we all sang around the bright campfire, and slowly couples separated into the darkness. John was a great kisser, but as we lay together on a beach towel behind a large rock, his hands kept pushing beyond my set boundaries. When he untied my bathing suit top and yanked it down to my waist, I realized his passion was out of control.

"John, stop!" I demanded as the weight of his body pushed on top of mine. In the darkness, panic filled my shaking body. Without warning, he pinned my hands down behind me. I could feel his aroused manhood, making its way up my skirt and I tried to use all my strength to push him off. He wouldn't budge. My voice rang out in terror as I screamed for help.

Suddenly, John's weight was yanked off me. In horror, I watched Clark swing a punch to his face. John's body reeled backwards, and blood spurted from his nose. Amber quickly helped me to my feet. I scrambled to fix my top as Clark shouted, "Keep your damn hands off my sister!"

"Are you all right?" Amber asked.

"Yes, I think so. I'm shaken, but safe with your help."

"Find your own way home, John, and think about how you should treat a lady," Clark ordered.

As we were walking away, Clark asked, "Are you sure you're okay, Sandy?" He put his arm around me.

"Thank you for the rescue," I sighed.

"Sandy, this was our night to celebrate. I'm so sorry this happened." Amber comforted me and insisted that I sit up front with them on the way home.

"John is such a jerk. I don't have good taste in men, Amber. I'm so glad you do."

"Well, I guess this is as good a time as any to tell you about our plans, Sandy. Amber and I want to get married." Clark beamed as we arrived at our apartment.

"We thought you should be the first to know," Amber added.

"I'm so happy for you," I smiled.

"My only fear is telling Mother. She is so critical of anything we do," Clark voice quivered.

"Why don't you guys elope and then tell her afterward," I suggested.

"We will wait a while to break the news so we don't spoil your special moment."

I headed into the bathroom and took a long shower while the two lovers said goodnight. Amber was so lucky to find her knight in shining armor. I feared my mother's reaction, especially since Amber wasn't Jewish.

I loved Clark and wanted him to be happy. His intelligence, warmth and great sense of humor had been my salvation during most of my life. I knew he would make a great agricultural engineer and husband.

Funny how we are so different. He finds peace while flying his airplane, while I find it in loud music, smoking a joint and living life on the edge.

On Saturday morning, Clark drove us to the airport to pick up our parents and family members. Amber's parents rented a car at the airport, and mine took a limousine to the nearby Sheraton Universal Hotel.

My father, Claire, Aunt Barbara, Uncle Bernie and Joel were happy to see us. Mother commented, "I have so much work waiting for me at home. You're just lucky I fit this into my busy schedule."

With graduation, my life was finally taking direction. It was a beautiful sunny June day when Amber and I stood with our classmates dressed in full uniform and accepted our nursing degrees. Loud applause rang out when our names were called and we were handed our nursing certificates.

There was an obvious contrast between my parents and Amber's.

Her mother and father were humble farmers, kind and simple, while the flamboyant lifestyle my parents lived was visibly over the top, by their standards.

Mother had booked a private room at the hotel for a dinner celebration. Champagne and a large bouquet of balloons decorated the table when we arrived. Mother made sure everyone knew the occasion was her treat. The food was wonderful and the spirits helped me forget my family's shortcomings for a while.

At the end of our meal, my mother swaggered up from her seat and said she wanted to make a toast. Her blood-shot eyes and slurred voice were embarrassing. "I toast these two young women." She slowly turned her face toward us. "They've reached a milestone I never did. Well, for God's sake, someone had to heal the world." She quickly slumped back down into her chair.

I bit my lip and shook my head at her disgraceful performance. To my delight, my father who usually was the one who was smashed, stood up with dignity, "I'd like to add a few words. Sandy and Amber, I commend you for this remarkable and honorable accomplishment. I'm so proud of both of you."

I thought I saw a sparkle of tear in his eye.

Then my brother raised his glass, "Amber and Sandy, don't let anyone or anything stand in your way of success. I'm proud of you too, Sis," he finished his toast with a wink and an ear-to-ear smile.

"Me, too," Claire added.

The toasts continued across the table. Amber's parents also said a few comforting words, but their reserved demeanor and conservative ways were evident by their early departure.

Just before leaving, Aunt Barbara told my mother she would like to contribute to the bill.

Mother's response was "No, thank you. I can better afford to take care of this."

"The question is how you can, Cynthia," my aunt said with sarcasm. "We both received equal amounts of Father's trust, yet it seems you have acquired tenfold what Bernie and I have."

"Does every argument have to revolve around money, Barbara? Are you jealous of my success?" Mother physically leaned on my dad. "Check with your sweet husband, Bernie. He'll tell you where every penny goes."

My father took her arm and led her out of the room.

Bernie looked over at us. "This is not the time or place for this discussion. Let's drop it," he demanded.

Like many other heated conversations over the last several years, nothing was settled between them. Mother had gone to court and had tried to change my grandmother's will, but her objections were thrown out. No doubt she was still furious over it.

I'd learned that having too much money sometimes can make people do terrible things. The greed, gluttony and excess offered them multiple possibilities to mask the guilt of their behavior, which included alcohol and drugs. It was no doubt that my parents were products of this very existence. As far as I was concerned, I would have no part of it.

When Clark dropped me home, he smiled at me, "Somehow we survived our childhood. Thank goodness it hasn't killed us yet."

His words stung with the power of truth.

Chapter Twenty-Four
Breaking News

1972
Los Angeles, California
Sandy Preston McDaniel

One night six months later, after working a double shift at the emergency room, Amber told me we needed to talk.

"What's wrong?" I asked, taking a seat in the living room of our apartment.

"I think I'm pregnant, Sandy," she broke down.

I wrapped my arms around her. "Everything will work out. Clark loves you. I know he'll do the right thing."

"This messes up our plans," she sobbed. "I'm torn about what to do."

"Babies are blessings, no matter when or how they arrive. You have to tell Clark and trust that he'll be there for you."

Amber took the next day off from work.

That evening when I returned home, she revealed, "Clark wants to elope in Las Vegas, and we both would like you to be there."

I was excited even though I knew Mother would be livid about it. I believed it would be the best approach to their unexpected situation.

On a cloudy winter day, we left Los Angeles and set off for our weekend trip to Las Vegas. During our four and one-half hour drive, loud music fueled our spirits. We were adults handling a situation the best way we knew how. Any fears we had evaporated into the brightness of the Las Vegas neon lights.

Clark prearranged a wedding at the *Little Chapel of the Flowers*, a place he'd found in the Yellow Pages. They supplied everything. All we had to do was stop at the courthouse and obtain a marriage license. We checked into the *Thunderbird Hotel*, and as a surprise, I reserved the honeymoon suite for them.

"Thank you for being here," Amber told me while I pinned baby roses into her up-swept hair.

"It means the world to me and I wouldn't have it any other way," I said. "I'm so excited. I'll be an aunt soon enough."

Later that day, Amber was a beautiful blushing bride as she stood in front of the lily-covered altar. My brother looked so handsome in his cream-colored suit, with his tanned skin, trimmed beard and boyish smile. Chills flashed through me when they said I do and kissed. It was a quick and simple, but lovely ceremony.

That evening while sitting in their valentine-pink colored suite, I raised my champagne glass to toast the newlyweds. "May you always feel about each other the way you do today. I hope every dream within your hearts comes true."

Once we returned home, I volunteered for extra work. It helped pay the additional expenses of the apartment, since Amber had moved in with Clark. I agreed to accompany them when they headed up to Santa Barbara to give our parents the news. It rained all the way there.

Clark suggested we go directly to the courthouse where my mother would be less likely to go into a mad rage. We parked on the street in front of the new *Sambo's* restaurant. The adobe walls of the courthouse loomed before us like the ramparts of a castle. This was once my grandfather's political fortress and now it was my mother's. We climbed the front steps and I shivered crossing from the hazy sunlight into the building's shadow. How would Mother react to this defiant act? My heart raced, thinking about what the bitch might say.

We passed the leather-covered, brass-studded double doors of the board of supervisors' assembly room where my grandfather Otto Preston had ruled the city so long ago. I remember mother deeply grieving over his death. Grandpa was always kind and generous. I only knew him as a highly respected political figure that Clark and I looked up to.

Clark took Amber's hand as we climbed up the staircase to Mother's second-story office. Earlier, we had phoned her secretary to be sure she would be in.

Just before we entered the door, I heard the courthouse clock tower chime. Her secretary announced our arrival, and Mother immediately stood up from her polished desk when she saw us, "To what do I owe this surprise visit?" Her face was pale with alarm.

"We have something to tell you," Clark began.

"Would you like to sit down?" she asked as her eyes flickered from Amber to Clark.

"Mother, I think you should sit down, too," Clark requested, but she didn't move.

I swallowed hard, knowing how tough this was for my brother.

He slowly put his arm around my beautiful friend, took a deep breath and poured out the news, "I want you to meet my new wife."

"What?" Her voice echoed, "What are you talking about?" She angrily folded her arms in front of her.

"Mother, give him a chance to tell you his story," I interjected.

"Clark, surely you are kidding. You wouldn't do this without informing me first." Her eyes flared with disbelief and her face distorted with emotion.

"Let me explain, Mother," Clark pleaded. "When Amber discovered she was pregnant, we eloped to Las Vegas."

"How could you do this, Clark?" she groaned and slammed her fist down on the table. "No!" she shouted. "Clark, you're a fool! If you had spoken to me first about this, it never would have happened."

"No, Mother, you're wrong. I love Amber and had asked her to be my wife before I got her pregnant, anyway."

"Young man, I'm owed some respect for supporting you all these years. How did you expect me to react?"

"Congratulations would be nice," Clark grinned.

"She's probably just after your money, Clark!" Mother yelled out, looking at Amber, "We can still get this annulled and have it all taken care of."

"Not a chance, Mother. No threats or amount of money will change my mind." Clark body straightened and he tightly held Amber's hand.

"Mrs. McDaniel, I love Clark," Amber finally spoke up. "I'm sorry we've upset you. I could not care less about your money. I just want us to be happy."

"If you loved him, you wouldn't have gotten him into this mess," she snapped. "This could have been prevented."

"Mother, stop!" I raised my voice. "Can't you accept anything graciously?"

"Sandy, maintaining the status of the Preston-McDaniel name is my responsibility. I do not support this. The mark of a bastard child cannot be allowed to tarnish our family name." Mother's voice broke as her personal sentiments came through.

"No matter what you say or do, Mother, this marriage will stand. I agreed to give Amber our name and I'm proud of it." Clark stood up, looked at me and said, "It's time to leave."

Clark and Amber turned and walked out of the room.

I stood before my mother. "Amber and Clark truly love each other. Something you can't possibly understand." I turned and stomped out the door.

Outside we waited for a moment by the car while Clark spoke to Amber. "I'm so sorry, honey. My mother has tried to control us all our lives." He gave her a hug. "I'm done with that, now."

"I'm the one who should be sorry, Clark. Some of her words were true. Maybe this was a big mistake. What if your mother disowns you?"

"I expected this of her. Mother has a fit when things don't go just as she'd planned. We'll let her cool down and give her some time to think it over. We'll get a hotel for the night."

"He's right, Amber. She will speak with my father, figure out a plan and propose her way of doing things. You'll see," I agreed.

"I've never met such a headstrong woman," Amber sighed.

"Don't let her intimidate you. She's been a bitch all her life. We're just used to it."

We all laughed.

"Mother and money have always been synonymous in our family. She used her financial strings to maneuver us like puppets. Through the years, Sandy and I have grown to tolerate her drill sergeant orders, expectations and demands." Clark opened the car door and turned toward us, "Don't worry, somehow we'll work through this. I promise."

"I don't think she'll ever like me, Clark," Amber shook her head.

"The only thing that really matters is that we love each other." Clark started the car and we put Mother's harsh words behind us.

After arriving at the Biltmore Hotel nearby, Clark decided to preempt the inevitable and call our father. He relayed the conversation to Amber and me. "Mother wants to meet with us tonight."

We all agreed to meet them at 7:00 o'clock that evening in the hotel's restaurant. Somehow I knew my parents would come up with some plan of saving grace for everyone. Still, I dreaded hearing about it.

After a short nap, I dressed in a bright yellow skirt, a white top and a shawl to lift my spirits for the coming news. Clark, Amber and I sat down to wait for my parents. I immediately ordered a tequila sunrise to calm my nerves.

Mother arrived wearing her signature three-karat diamond earrings, dressed like a model from a high-end boutique on Rodeo Drive.

"You smell great, Mother," I commented, noticing the pleasant scent of her spicy perfume. "Is that a new perfume you're wearing?"

"Yes, thank you. It's Christian Dior."

"Tell her the name of it," my father smirked.

Mother gave him a sharp look as she answered, "Poison, but it has a lovely scent."

I couldn't help but snicker. The name of the perfume fit her perfectly.

Once we were all settled, Mother cleared her throat and declared, "Your father and I have come here with an offer."

In the quiet of the secluded table, she set down her rules, "This situation must be handled delicately. I feel there is an appropriate solution to this situation. I will plan a small wedding ceremony for you two so that Claire and the outside world need never know of your accident. Afterwards, the two of you will leave on an extended trip to the Orient as our wedding gift. This will delude any questions or speculation of the date your child was conceived."

Her agenda was a mouthful to digest.

Clark turned to Amber, "Her offer is generous..."

"Wait. There are a few more things I have to say," Mother insisted.

"It figures," I heard Clark say under his breath.

"I also want you and Sandy to meet my business associate in Thailand. His name is Adan Shariff, and he will give you a package for me."

"What do you think about it, Amber and Sandy?"

"It sounds very fair to me," Amber confirmed. "I've heard Thailand is beautiful."

"Such a trip would take me away from my job. I'm not sure I should tag along on their honeymoon, either," I told Mother.

"Sandy, I insist that you go with them. I promise you will be graciously compensated," Mother assured me.

"I believe your mother's offer is in your best interest," Dad intervened.

"Thailand is a great place for you and Amber to honeymoon, and for Sandy it could be an adventure of a lifetime."

Something told me there was more to Mother's plans than she was willing to reveal. But a free trip overseas sounded appealing. It would be a chance to get away and clear my mind. I knew going with Clark and Amber would be fun.

So with some hesitation, we all agreed with Mother's proposal.

"I'll take care of all the wedding plans. I'll arrange tickets from Portland and accommodations for your parents for the wedding," she said.

What followed was another round of offers. Clark could manage one of the leased agricultural properties here in Santa Barbara and would receive a generous salary. Mentioning this, my mother concluded by looking over at my sister-in-law. "Amber, there is one more thing I need to make clear: you will never be entitled to a red cent of the Preston family trust."

For a moment, there was dead silence. Clark turned to his wife and, with a slight grin, told her, "Honey, welcome into the Preston family."

Chapter Twenty-Five
Thailand Journey

1973
Bangkok, Thailand
Sandy Preston McDaniel

We were timely informed by mail of the dates, details and directives related to Clark and Amber's upcoming wedding ceremony and our trip to Asia. Their nuptials would take place the first Sunday in May, and our airline tickets showed us leaving the following morning on a nonstop flight to Tokyo, Japan. We would have a four-day layover there to rest and see some sights. Then we'd fly to Bangkok, Thailand.

Amber asked me to be her maid of honor, Claire was a bridesmaid and Joel, a groomsman. Roger, an old roommate of Clark, would be his best man. Our long-time conservative rabbi agreed to perform a small synagogue service, even though Amber wasn't Jewish, after Mother gave a large donation to the temple.

Since my brother and new sister-in-law were moving back to Santa Barbara, I decided to relocate, too. Mother offered grandmother's old house for them to live in until a lease was available on one of my parents' agricultural farms. I'd rent an apartment in town and take a job at the county hospital upon my return.

Several weeks before their wedding, Amber appeared at my bedroom door. I could tell she'd been crying. "What's wrong?" I inquired.

"Our whole wedding. Your mother's even picked out my wedding dress."

"I'm so sorry, Amber."

"She chose the invitations, cake and colors. It may as well be her wedding." She sank down on the sofa.

"Mother is a control freak and is used to having everything her way," I flatly stated.

Amber sighed, "When my own mother called to ask how I was doing with the wedding plans, I broke down and apologized that she had no say in them. It's just so wrong."

"It's normal for us, Amber. Mother has manipulating ways."

"Normal? Not where I come from. A wedding is usually planned by a mother and her daughter. I realize our circumstances are different, but I can't understand why she treats me like I don't exist."

"You are marrying into a dysfunctional family. You may as well know now that a life as a McDaniel comes at a high price."

"Sandy, you know I love Clark. I can deal with it for him, but it's our child I'm concerned about."

"Things can work out, Amber. Remember, Clark is your husband and you can minimize your interaction with my mother."

"I hope so," she answered.

I changed the focus of our conversation to our upcoming trip, hoping to distract my friend.

On the final days before the wedding, the tension between Mother and Amber lessened. She loved her dress, the cake and the beautiful white lilies Mother ordered for decoration.

Walking into the synagogue, I admired the elaborately decorated lattice archway waiting for the bride and groom. When I opened the door to the bride's dressing room, I stopped in my tracks seeing both Amber and her mother with tears in their eyes.

"Don't worry, Sandy. They are tears of joy, mostly," Amber assured me. "Mother was just telling me she thinks Clark will make a wonderful husband, but she was also expressed some concern regarding Cynthia."

"It was a nice offer for your mother to pay for our tickets and hotel, but when I declined, she went and took care of them, anyway. That isn't how we do things at home." Grace, Amber's mother, squeezed her daughter's hand, "All we want is for Amber to be happy."

We helped my best friend put on her veil and I quickly changed into my pink satin bridesmaid's dress. I loved seeing Claire in a satin formal dress and Joel in his custom tuxedo and bow tie.

The pews were filled with Mother's high-society guests. Mother held her head high, watching the spectacle she had created.

Clark stood proudly waiting in his white tux for his new bride. My brother beamed with joy as he stood anticipating Amber's grand entrance. Goose bumps broke out over my entire body as the bride's march began. There was a radiant glow on Amber's face as she walked down the rose-petaled aisle with her stepfather. The custom-made, multi-layered, pearl bodice gown graciously covered up her swelling belly. Listening to committed love sealed by the rabbi's ceremony, I wondered if I would ever find the man of my dreams.

After the ceremony, a dinner reception followed in the temple hall. Tables with candle centerpieces, a full orchestra and glasses filled with champagne offered a romantic mood. After Roger gave his toast, I stood up and faced the bride and groom. "To the most wonderful brother and my best friend, I wish you a love that lasts forever and raise my glass to your promising future." Others made toasts, and music and dancing followed.

Before leaving, Clark and Amber stood and faced the guests, "We appreciate all of you sharing this special day with us."

That night as I drifted off to sleep, I wondered if I'd ever have a wedding or meet the man of my dreams. I had a bad history of picking the wrong kind of guys. Would I ever meet Mr. Right?

Clark and Amber picked me up early the next morning and we headed toward Los Angeles International Airport. The hours on the plane seemed endless as I watched Amber fall asleep on Clark shoulder. Staring out the window, my mind wandered until my eyes slowly closed. What will I discover in this exotic place? I thought. Who is this Asian business associate Mother knows, and is there a secret between them waiting to be found? My eyes popped open upon hearing the announcement of our arrival in Tokyo.

During our four days there, we explored lush Japanese gardens, tall pagodas and several museums filled with historic treasures. We ate sushi, tried exotic dishes and drank lots of tea.

The most memorable moment in Tokyo was when we stopped at a local curio shop. As Clark opened the door, the pungent smell of scented oils filled the air. A young, pretty Japanese girl with long, black, silky hair pulled back in a bun greeted us. I admired her stunning, white-tunic jacket with a fire-breathing dragon embroidered on it. We followed her around the store as she described her many art treasures from the orient.

"Clark, look at this three-piece set of carved ivory figurines. I just love their native clothes and form," I heard Amber say.

"They're beautiful," Clark agreed.

"These pieces were once a part of a collection that belonged to a royal dynasty," the young girl elaborated.

"Worth a small fortune, I bet," Clark commented.

"If you really like them, I can give you a good price," she offered.

When Clark and Amber walked away, I decided to buy the set for them. When the woman handed the gift to Amber, the expression on her face was priceless.

"Sandy, you shouldn't have."

Then the sales lady kindly told each of us to pick out a small bottle of perfumed oil as a complimentary souvenir.

"You are the best friend and sister-in-law ever!"

We hugged.

We then enjoyed walking around one of the crowded outdoor markets. There were strange fish, exotic flowers and beautifully painted ceramics.

The long days together with them were so happy, but sadness crept in when I was alone in my room at night. I so envied the heated spark the young lovers shared.

Upon arriving in Bangkok, I immediately felt the mood was electrifying.

It looked like a hot spot for world travelers, businessmen and tourists. The streets were filled with men in suits, exotic dressed women and local beggars. The city had a diverse population equal to Haight-Ashbury in San Francisco. We quickly settled in at our hotel and decided to go for a walk. The crowded foreign city had a primal feel with its native culture, friendly people and colorful atmosphere. I felt an instant bond to the exotic place. The hot, sunny weather, the fast pace of the city and the wildly scented cuisine raised my spirits.

Clark notified Mother's business contact, Adan Shariff, of our arrival the second day we were there. Mr. Shariff invited us to his residence for dinner. For the occasion, I decided to wear the silk, teal-and-gold-bordered sari I had purchased the day before. Amber helped wrap it tightly around my body so I wouldn't worry about it coming undone. She wore an off-the-shoulder, emerald green, silk blouse, a long silk skirt and a matching scarf. Clark dressed up in his custom-made new silk suit and cabana hat. We hoped to look like locals.

Mr. Shariff's limousine pulled up to our hotel. Once inside, we asked the driver to roll down the windows and let in the warm summer breeze. I looked over at Clark and asked, "What do you know about this man, Adan Shariff?"

"Mother didn't tell me any more than you: it's important we meet with him and that he'll have a package for her."

"Well, the evening should be interesting," Amber exclaimed as our car entered through a wide wrought-iron gate with armed guards.

I gasped seeing the elaborate oasis that appeared. Bamboo trees swayed in the breeze in the oriental garden at the entrance with a large mosaic fountain. Stepping out from our vehicle, Mr. Shariff's residence resembled a scene out of the old movie, *The Thief of Bagdad*. A glistening temple stretched before us highlighted with several giant Buddha statues. As the sun faded from the twilight sky, Clark clasped both our arms and we entered the magical golden fortress. My heart skipped a beat, seeing the handsome young man that stood by the side of a man my father's age.

"Welcome. I'm Adan, and this is my son, Kaseem." They both bowed while nearby barefoot men played flutes.

My brother greeted them with his outstretched hand. "I'm Clark, Cynthia's son. This is my wife, Amber and sister, Sandy."

I felt warmth fill my face as the young foreigner took my hand and gently pressed his lips to it. Something deep inside me stirred.

As we waited in the domed hallway, I breathed in Kaseem's cologne. It smelled like sweet peaches and cinnamon. As we walked inside, he moved with the sophistication of my favorite actor, Sean Connery.

Our host, looking the part of a sultan in his white turban and full beard, welcomed us, "It is a great pleasure to meet Cynthia's children and Otto's grandchildren."

Father and son escorted us into a candle-lit dining room with giant hanging oil lamps overhead.

Kaseem came to stand by my side. "You hold the beauty that my father speaks about your mother having." He guided me to sit in the chair next to his.

A trio of men playing flutes appeared. Servants carried in overflowing trays and bowls of food that were set before us. We enjoyed a pleasant meal of lemon grass-coconut noodle soup, Pad Thai, seafood curry and sticky rice with mango.

I intently listened to Kaseem describe his homeland with words and eyes that held the charm of a great storyteller. "If you like to swim, Sandy, tomorrow we can take out my father's private yacht," he offered.

His invitation was enticing. Kaseem described his adventures as a deep-sea diver and expert horseman. I couldn't help but notice he hadn't taken his eyes off me. After our meal and several glasses of wine, Kaseem asked me to join him out on the terrace.

The palms waved in the breeze. With the flute music playing in the background, he asked me to dance under the starlit sky. We swayed together, bathed in the reflection of the full moon. Just when I thought he might kiss me, Clark appeared.

"Sandy, it's getting late, and Amber's tired."

Kaseem politely released me. "Until tomorrow," he whispered.

"I'll have to check with Clark," I told him.

On our way home, I told my brother about Kaseem's offer.

"We already made arrangements to return tomorrow to pick up Mother's package. Adan also invited us to take a sightseeing tour in his private plane. How can we pass up an invitation like that?"

"Would it be alright for me to spend the day with Kaseem while you and Amber go on your plane ride?"

"I'm not completely comfortable with that, Sandy."

"Don't worry, Clark," Amber interjected. "I heard Adan say that Kaseem has a bodyguard that goes with him everywhere."

"Please. Please," I pleaded.

Clark finally agreed.

The next morning I awoke to a knock on my door. Opening it, I was overwhelmed with a giant bouquet of yellow lilies. The card attached read, *the brilliance of your beauty shines like the sun above.* It was signed, *Kaseem.*

We were all picked up early and headed back to Adan's grand estate. Clark and Amber were whisked off by Adan in his limo while Kaseem ushered me outside, took my hand, and asked if I wanted to take his motorbike down to the dock. Agreeing, I slipped my hands around his trim waist and laughed as I looked back and saw an entourage of cars following us.

"Don't mind them, Sandy," he warned. "They will be mulling around all day. My father is a powerful man and bodyguards watch over me every minute."

"Every minute?" I asked him.

"I'm used to it—and if we really want to be alone, I have my ways." Kaseem picked up speed and it felt like we were flying in the wind.

A bright yellow sun penetrated a cloudless powder-blue sky. The aqua-colored sea, rolling waves and sandy coastline appeared before us. It was right out of a romantic Caribbean movie. Arriving at the dock, Kaseem's servants, bodyguards and workers prepared the elegant ship for launch. When we boarded the ninety-eight foot boat, it was hard to imagine that we were the only guests.

After a short tour of the magnificent vessel with built-in lawn chairs, a full bar and sleeping quarters below, we stood close together at the bow. Breathing in the fresh, salt-water air and the Indian Ocean's magnificence, I turned toward my host and smiled widely. "Your country is so beautiful, Kaseem. I'm glad I came here and met you."

"It is my blessing to have you here. My father has spoken highly of your family and the partnership they share."

This was the first time I'd heard anything about a partnership with his family. I felt it too early in our relationship to ask any questions. But I was very curious. We went below to change into our bathing suits, and for the next few hours we tanned our bikinied bodies in the hot Eastern sun. While I sipped a tequila sunrise to cool my thirst, my growing hunger was not for food, but for the tantalizing stud that lay beside me.

Later on that afternoon, Kaseem outfitted me with a full set of diving gear. He taught me about the fascinating underwater world as we swam side by side. The colorful creatures, strange formations and serenity captivated me.

With the concern of a patient teacher, Kaseem never let me out of his sight. On board the ship I told him, "Thank you for showing me that beautiful underwater world. I just loved it."

"It is not comparable to your beauty, Sandy," he kissed my hand.

I blushed and disappeared below to a private room to shower and change before dinner. Topside, I was greeted by a breathtaking apricot-colored sunset as I headed toward the polished wooden bar. Our wine glasses were filled, and Kaseem made a toast, "To a lasting friendship."

Kaseem smiled. "I have never met anyone like you, Sandy. You are so full of life. American women are different from those in my country."

"In the United States, women have a lot of freedom," I explained as he held my hand.

"I would like to spend more time with you. Is there any way you can stay longer?" He moved closer to me.

"That might be difficult," I said. "As you know, I am traveling with Clark and Amber on their honeymoon."

"I have an idea. What if I could act as the guide for all of you for the rest of the trip?"

"I'm not sure, Kaseem. Though I love that idea, I would have to speak with Clark and Amber first."

"I will speak with them as soon as we return this evening," he anxiously announced. "I promise if they say yes, I will show you an unforgettable time."

While savoring the idea, Kaseem slipped his hand across the back of my neck and drew his lips to mine.

When he pulled away, I said, "Please don't stop."

Chapter Twenty-Six
A Trip to Remember

1973
Bangkok, Thailand
Sandy Preston McDaniel

That evening when we arrived back at the palace, Clark and Amber were waiting. They gave us a few details about their excursion. "We followed this long river inland, and Adan swept down low for us to get a good look. We saw herds of elephants, Asian buffalo and wild cats." Amber's voice was filled with excitement.

Clark's face had an ear-to-ear grin, "Adan even let me take the controls for a while."

"Kaseem and I went scuba diving and had a great time," I told him.

I looked over at Kaseem, who was talking with his father. The pair came to join us, and Adan said, "My son has suggested we extend our hospitality to you. If you agree, he is willing to be your personal guide for the rest of your trip."

"Well, the invitation is very kind," Clark responded, "but you've been more than generous already."

"I think a personal guide would be great. I'm sure Sandy would appreciate the company," Amber chimed in.

Clark hesitated.

"It certainly would make me happy if you agreed," I encouraged.

For a moment, he looked over at Amber, who nodded her head. "All right, I approve it."

"Oh, I can't forget, I have something for your Mother," Adan clapped his hands as we prepared to leave. One of his servants appeared with a brown, wrapped box the size of a coffee pot. He handed it to Clark.

"Please make sure your mother gets this, and give her my best regards," Adan instructed. "I know Kaseem will show you all a great time."

Even though we were curious about the box's contents, we didn't ask any questions.

Before saying goodnight, Amber gave me a hug. "I think Kaseem is smitten with you."

I acknowledged her comment with a sassy smile.

For the next three weeks, we traveled the countryside. There were visits to several traditional Siamese villages. We shared time with Thai natives and went on an elephant ride. Some friendly farmers shared their homeland culture with us. There were many Buddhist temples along the way filled with giant golden statues and monks in humble attire who bowed before us. Sometimes we stayed in luxury hotels only steps away from the starving and homeless.

Clark commented, "This country seems like a mixed confluence of human desires, with a dose of raw corruption."

I didn't have much sadness to spare for the locals, though. I was too happy to be spending time with Kaseem. Whether we were at the open marketplace or viewing a religious spectacle, Kaseem held my hand with pride. As our guide, he gave touching humane descriptions about the people and country he loved. At every turn, Kaseem was buying me gifts: a stone amulet, perfume, silk clothes. I loved to model for him.

Dinner was always a banquet of local food with tangy new tastes. We sampled snake and scorpion wine. Kaseem even gave us lessons in the Thai language.

As our time together came to a close, I started feeling restless. How could I become so attached to someone in such a short time? I wondered if I could possibly be falling in love with Kaseem.

On our last night, I whispered in his ear, "Come to my hotel room tonight."

I had candles and incense burning when his knock came at my door. He said, "I'm alone." With the passion of young lovers, we made our way toward my bed, casting aside each other's clothes on the way. Kaseem's gentle touch, heated body and succulent lips slowly partook of every part of me. He understood a woman's needs. His pace and control were calculated and matched mine to perfection.

It was a long night of fulfilling and continued pleasure. By its end, all the beauty of his country he spoke to me about, I felt in him. I'd never felt safer in anyone else's arms. But as the morning light trickled through my window, we both knew it was time for him to leave.

It was hard to restrain my feelings when Clark, Amber and I joined him for breakfast the next morning. "How can our time together be over?" I asked him as we finished our meal.

Amber thanked him with a hug, "Goodbyes are always difficult."

"Kaseem, you showed us a great time. We won't forget it. Thank you," Clark shook his hand.

"I'll never forget you, or this trip." Kaseem's eyes met mine, "I want to see you again, Sandy." Kaseem was choked up. He swept me up in his arms without thinking. At that moment, I didn't care if Clark or Amber suspected that we'd been lovers.

He walked us toward our waiting car. Kaseem whispered in my ear, "If you can't return, I promise to travel to the United States."

In the car on our way toward the airport, I broke down in tears. "I didn't want to say goodbye."

"You had a thing for him," Clark looked directly at me, "didn't you?"

"Yes," I sobbed.

"I just want to warn you that Mother would not approve."

"Maybe she'd be happy for me. They are business partners."

"That remains to be seen," Clark shook his head and didn't say another word about it.

After we arrived home, I waited a few days to tell Mother about my feelings for Kaseem. She had invited me to dinner and I decided to tell her about it then. Before our meal, I sat chatting with my father in the living room. Then mother came in and sat down.

Mother crossed her legs and lit a cigarette. "Did you enjoy your trip, Sandy?"

"It was wonderful. Thank you."

"I heard from Clark that Adan's son Kaseem offered to be your guide."

"That's right. Actually, we hit if off quite well and I hope to see him again."

"What do you mean, Sandy?"

"I think I'm in love with him."

"You might be in love with the lifestyle he leads, but it is absolutely forbidden to get involved with someone outside your culture."

"Mother, I understand you are somehow involved with his family business. He never disclosed the relationship, but he did indicate a strong friendship between you and his father."

My father abruptly got up and left the room without a word.

Mother continued, "We do have a long-term business association that has nothing to do with you or Kaseem. Nothing can interfere with that."

"You don't own my feelings or me, Mother. If I want to see him again, I will."

"Not without consequences," she warned and added, "That's final." She got up and left the room in a huff.

I found my father in the other room. "I sometimes wonder why you've stayed married to her all these years."

He downed a drink from the shot glass in his hand and answered, "Sometimes you do things for the wrong reason, sweetheart. I hope you don't make the same mistake."

I wasn't sure what my father meant.

"Be careful, honey. She's a viper in bed with a nest of snakes," he poured himself another glass. "I know if you see Kaseem again, she'll cut you off financially—or worse."

"I hate her!" I shouted and knew she probably heard me. I grabbed my purse and scrambled out the door.

At home, I called Amber to vent my anger. "She doesn't own me. I can survive without her support. Mother thinks she knows me, but her saying I can't see Kaseem just strengthens my resolve to be with him."

"Sandy, calm down. Long distance romances can be difficult. There must be a good reason why she is doing this. Maybe Kaseem can answer why."

After we hung up, I decided to call Kaseem. He told me I could call him collect anytime. Just hearing his voice calmed me down.

"Sandy, I will be traveling to the States to see you in two weeks. You must not tell anyone about this visit. It could be dangerous. I'll explain more upon my arrival."

Dangerous, I thought. What is mother hiding? Why would she be so hostile and negative about this? Thank God I didn't tell her we were lovers.

Over the next week, we talked often, but Kaseem would never answer any questions regarding the danger of our parents' involvement.

I was scared and excited about Kaseem's coming. What would Mother do if she found out? The suspense of not knowing the true reason for my mother's reaction weighed heavily on me. After several sleepless nights, I decided to call Amber and ask for her help.

Chapter Twenty-Seven
Digging Too Deep

1975
Santa Barbara, California
Sandy Preston McDaniel

I made Amber promise not to tell Clark about Kaseem.

"I'm not sure this is a good idea, Sandy," she said, "but because you say you love Kaseem, I will help you."

Together we drove to City Hall to check public records and see if the name Adan Shariff came up. This failed to offer any answers until, while searching microfiche records, we found a court case from 1932 in which Adan Shariff had been the defendant. My grandfather had represented him on behalf of Mitchell and Blaine. No details other than their names were provided.

I asked Amber, who had become good friends with my Aunt Barbara and Uncle Bernie, to ask them if she knew anything about it. It totally backfired. "Barbara didn't want us to poke our noses into their business," Amber told me.

With little else to go on, I confronted Kaseem in our next conversation. "I don't understand what's going on. What does your father say about us?"

"When I approached him about this trip, he warned me not to see you again, Sandy. He told me that I was overstepping confidentiality. When I pressed him further, he got angry and ordered, 'I don't want to hear any more about it.'"

My heart sank when I thought that I might never see the love of my life again.

"Don't be sad. I have come up with a plan. Father is leaving on business next week, and I can secretly arrange a trip to New York. If I buy you a ticket, will you meet me there?"

"Yes. Yes. Yes. Just tell me where and when to meet you."

"You can't tell anyone about this."

"Promise."

"They say love can conquer anything, Sandy. I hope it's true for us," Kaseem confided.

I sensed some hesitation in his voice, but tried to ignore it.

When we hung up the phone, my heart told me my mother was the one to blame for keeping us apart. I vowed that she would not stop me from being happy.

We planned our secret meeting in New York and I didn't tell a soul. Our plan was to arrive in separate taxis. Kaseem booked our rooms under fictitious names.

I waited by the hotel phone for his call. As the minutes ticked by, my heart began to race. What if something had happened and his father had discovered our plan? I had been careful and told Amber that an old friend from high school had invited me to her wedding out of town and that I didn't want to miss it, so no one should have discovered me...but what of Kaseem?

I began pacing the floor. I called room service and ordered a tequila sunrise to calm my nerves. Hearing a knock at my door, I opened it to find Kaseem standing with open arms, gloriously alone.

"Nancy Reed, I've missed you," he smiled, calling me by the name I'd registered under. I didn't want to let him go once enfolded in his arms. We never left the room that night and stayed in our own world of pleasure where no one could interfere with our hearts' desires.

In the morning, as I watched him sleep, there was no doubt I always wanted him to be by my side.

When he awoke, I sat up in bed and asked, "How are we going to be together, Kaseem?"

"My father and your mother are powerful people, Sandy. I found out they have an agreement neither can back out of without very dangerous consequences. I believe they fear our involvement puts all of us in jeopardy,"

I watched my lover's body tense with apprehension. "What agreement? What kind of people are they involved with?"

"My father told me few details about it and made me swear not to tell you anything. It can only bring harm to all concerned."

"No, we can't let them do this. We have a right to make our own choices," I demanded.

"We are innocent victims. Our families sold out to the demons of the world and we are held hostage by their agreement."

"There has to be something we can do. I'm willing to confront my mother."

"No, Sandy." Kaseem reached into the pocket of his leather jacket resting on the night stand. He pulled out a small black box and handed it to me. "I'd already bought this to give to you before I spoke with my father."

I opened the box and reeled back, my whole body trembling with excitement upon seeing the five-karat diamond ring inside. My hands were trembling as I put it on.

"You see, I wanted to ask you to marry me, Sandy, but now I think that it might not be possible."

"No! We have to work this out," I yelled and jumped up from the bed.

Kaseem walked over and wrapped his arms around me, "Sandy, I love you. But after my father told me the truth about his connection with your mother, believe me, there is little hope for our future."

I pulled away, tears streaming down my face. "I hate my mother for this. She is evil and doesn't know how to love. She has ruined the only thing that made my life worthwhile. I wish that she were dead."

"Sandy, this is something we cannot change. I came here instead to say goodbye."

"I can't do that. I won't. Please, Kaseem, I don't want you to ever leave," I buried my face into his shoulder.

"I can try to contact you when I can, but if we continue, our lives will be in danger," he wiped my tears.

"I'm willing to take that risk, Kaseem. Isn't true love worth dying for?"

Chapter Twenty-Eight
Not So Happy Endings

1976
Santa Barbara, California
Sandy Preston McDaniel

Nothing was going to stop me from being with Kaseem. I certainly would not let it be my mother. I was so happy that Kaseem wanted to marry me! It could be my only chance for true love. Leaving New York, I knew it was time to confront my mother and get to the bottom of things. Before we said goodbye, Kaseem and I had mutually agreed to confront our parents, no matter what the outcome.

Back in Santa Barbara, I put in some overtime at the emergency room where I was working nights so that I could have the next day off. That Sunday morning, Mother and Jack would be at home in Cayuma to relax on the farm.

I got dressed, left my apartment and drove out of the city. The long ride and empty highway offered me time to think. I needed to be clear, to the point and unwavering in getting the information I wanted. My

parents guarded their privacy like watchdogs. Father was an alcoholic—
that was evident, but my mother's secrets were hidden deep and well. I
wouldn't leave until I got some answers.

Through the years, I've never understood her or felt close to her in
any way. We were always so different in our actions and ways of thinking.
She seems angry all the time. Her vile, negative and belittling comments
spilled like poison over Clark and me throughout our childhood. Though
I have to admit, she seldom cursed Claire the way she did us.

Mother purposely set our lives up so that she could control us with
her purse strings. She always threatened to take away our generous
allowances if we didn't follow her rules. But I wasn't going to take
any more.

At that moment, driving to the Cayuma dairy farm, thinking
about Kaseem, I didn't care what happened afterward. Even if she
threatened to disown me, nothing she could say was going stop me from
marrying Kaseem.

Even so, as I pulled into the driveway and headed toward the farmhouse,
I dreaded the confrontation. I climbed the steps of the wrap around
porch and took a deep breath before knocking on the front door.

"Come on in, sweetheart," my father told me from inside.

"I have to talk with Mother," I revealed as we walked into the downstairs
living room.

"She is still upstairs, but I can go get her." Dad smiled after he took a
sip of his morning drink.

There was already the scent of liquor on his breath as he left to go
get her.

I sat down on the leather couch and waited.

"What brings you out here on this early Sunday morning?" Mother addressed, having reached the bottom of the stairs.

"We need to talk, Mother," my eyes starkly focused on her.

"I'll be in the other room," Father graciously exited.

Mother sat down in the side chair that faced toward me.

"I am here to tell you that I plan to marry Kaseem. We are in love and I am willing to uproot my whole life to be with him."

"Over my dead body will that ever happen."

Anger pounded through my heart as I yelled, "I won't let you stop me!"

Mother's jaw tightened with anger, "This is just a stupid passing romance. You're young and will get over it." Mother gritted her teeth.

I jumped up from the sofa and faced her. "Why do you have such a problem with it?" I shook my head.

"This relationship of yours would create dangerous consequences for me. Due to an involvement that I am not at liberty to disclose, your relationship could put our entire family in danger."

"Kaseem told me that too." I raised my voice, "I demand to know exactly what you are talking about."

"You'd better sit down, Sandy. You are not going to like what I have to say."

I stayed standing. "Mother, I'm tired of you running my life. Nothing you say can change my mind."

"You know nothing about my life or the burdens I've carried to ensure your welfare," she stood up to face me.

"Maybe not," I raised my head defiantly. "All I know is that I will not make the same bad choices you have."

In a flash, she slapped me across the face.

Suddenly, I lost control of all the hate and anger I had built up through the years. The next thing I knew, I had reached my hands around Mother's neck, I squeezed it hard, with all my might.

Mother let out a loud shriek.

Within moments, I felt my father's strong grasp on my shoulders as he came between us and pulled me away.

I slipped down onto the couch, finally getting control of myself.

My father aided my mother and helped her get to the nearby chair. She was gagging and coughing for breath.

A wild rage filled my mother's eyes as she stood up and faced me, "You will never lay a hand on me again. Now get out of this house!"

"Sandy, your behavior was over the top," my father said as he walked me to the door.

"I want her gone now. Consider yourself out of my life, Sandra," Mother shouted out to me.

"Does she really think I care what she does to me?" I asked him before leaving.

It was an ugly scene, but one I did not regret. I was free from her strings and couldn't wait to tell Kaseem.

Chapter Twenty-Nine
Consequences

1976
Santa Barbara, California
Cynthia Preston McDaniel

After my confrontation with Sandy, I knew I had to call Adan. I was always worried about who would carry on the overseas contract after my death. Jack wasn't capable. Sandy or Clark would never agree to it. I knew Claire would be the right choice.

I could introduce her into politics like my father had done for me... teach her about the advantages of power. She would accept and not fight the heavy responsibility that came with the Preston name: she would accept it.

Sandy's relationship with Kaseem complicated things because if it became widely known, it might potentially lead back to the illegal ties my father had made so long ago. I vowed to keep the Preston name clean. My father would have expected that. Oh Papa, if only you knew the sacrifices I've made for you. I've accepted the fact that a life of status and money comes with sacrifice.

Jack approached me as I picked up the phone to make the call to Adan.

"What are you going to do, Cynthia?" he asked.

"What ever it takes to secure our lives," I answered flatly.

"I'll never understand why you are so indifferent to the pain and suffering of others. We are guilty of our own sins," Jack accused.

"I can't believe I married such a loser. Let me take care of this," I retorted, already starting to dial. After a few moments, Adan answered.

"Cynthia, I'm glad you called. We need to discuss the matter of your daughter and my son."

"A marriage is not acceptable. I understand that this puts all our lives in jeopardy. How do you think it should be handled?"

"We have no choice, but to take serious steps."

"I understand and will take care of it," I answered.

"Cynthia, I will do the same," Adan somberly agreed.

As I prepared to make my next call I asked Jack to leave the room. This was family business that only I could take care of.

Chapter Thirty
A Love Worth Dying For

1976-1980
Santa Barbara, California
Amber McDaniel

It was 12:30 PM and I was worried. Sandy was supposed to meet me for lunch at *Marcello's* at noon, but did not show up. I tried her home phone, but got no answer. She'd always been on time; this was so unlike her. I called Clark. He hadn't heard from her, either. At 1:30 PM, I frantically left the restaurant and immediately drove to her apartment.

On my way, I remembered her saying that, after lunch, we would go shopping for baby clothes. Since Sandy returned from New York one week ago she remained distant; I had tried to find out if something was wrong, but she had never said a word. I loved that woman dearly, not just for introducing Clark to me, but as my best friend. We'd had so much fun together in nursing school and I felt so lucky to have her for my sister-in-law.

I repeatedly rang her doorbell and then knocked hard. When there was no answer, an adrenalin-induced panic flashed through me. I dashed toward the manager's office and begged for a key.

I unlocked the door and seeing her coffee table tilted over on its side, instantly a chill of fear ran down my spine. The kitchen light was on, so I called out her name, hoping for an answer. I noticed the bathroom door was partially closed, so I headed that direction. When I pushed open the bathroom door, I gasped in horror as my eyes took in the unmistakable spatters of blood that filled the wall above the bathtub.

I took one more step and fell to my knees. Sandy's pale face stared up from the murky tub water. My nursing skills automatically kicked in. I raised her head and frantically checked for a pulse. With her skin cold as ice and her blue lips, I couldn't deny the fact that my beautiful friend was gone.

"No!" I let out a gut-wrenching howl that echoed through the small room.

I tightly held Sandy's head above the water, not wanting anything to ever hurt her again. My body trembled as I wailed, "God, why did this have to happen?"

My foot slid on the wet tile floor and when I looked down, I jumped back seeing a handgun resting near my shoe. My mind fought the idea that Sandy didn't drown, that my friend's life had come to a very violent end. Wails of agony followed, issuing forth from me as though not my own.

The apartment manager must have heard my screams. "The police are on their way!" he called out in a terrorized voice.

I refused to move until they arrived and took her from my arms.

They asked me many questions that I had few answers for, except that the gun was not mine. All I wanted to do was call Clark. When I finally got to the phone and it started to ring, I struggled to find the words to tell him this tragic news. When he answered, my voice cracked and all I could say was "Please come quick, Clark. Something terrible's happened. It's your sister ..." And I burst into tears, telling him she was dead.

"What?" he yelled, and I repeated my words. "Oh my God, not Sandy." He quickly added, "Amber, I'll be right there."

The next few hours are a blur. I was numb with disbelief when the police told us she died from a self-inflicted gunshot to the head. I never knew she owned a gun. Clark remained in a daze and kept saying over again, "I just can't understand how something like this could happen."

When Cynthia showed up, I was appalled that no tears flowed from her eyes. She was more concerned with talking to the police about what the newspaper might print. In the confusion, a detective discovered a typewritten suicide note. It was unsigned.

To those I love,

If you are reading this, I have done the unthinkable. My sadness overwhelms me and I've lost faith in life. Please forgive me and know I am at peace.

The letter didn't resonate with me as words Sandy would have written. I thought it odd that she didn't sign her note.

I wasn't sure if I should say anything about her relationship with Kaseem. No one else knew about it but me. She'd told me they were no longer in touch with one another. Though something deep inside me, refused to believe it. If she'd been that depressed, I wondered why she didn't share those feelings with me, her best friend.

Now it was Clark who I was worried about. He looked like a lost child. It was Cynthia who took over the scene and made us go home. "I will handle this," she ordered.

In the next few days, we learned Sandy's death was listed as a suicide. Cynthia scheduled her body for cremation. A small memorial service was quickly put together and Clark and I prepared to attend.

The morning of her funeral, I spoke for the first time about my hidden suspicions. "Clark, something's bothering me about Sandy's death. Her note seemed odd. She never let on something was wrong. She loved life too much, enjoyed helping others and was against guns and violence. I just can't bring myself to believe she ended her own life. Do you think there could be more to her story?"

"It is hard to believe she's really gone, Amber. My mother said she was with her the night before and she was very depressed. Besides, who would want to hurt her?" His shoulders slumped.

Clark was still in such pain that I decided not to go further. My body cringed when I saw her beautiful picture at the memorial. The more recent image of her still tormented my mind. Jack, Aunt Barbara, Claire and I said a few special words, but Cynthia declined to speak.

I experienced a special personal moment while giving Sandy's eulogy. It was the first time I felt my baby move inside me.

After Sandy's funeral, time seemed to pass quickly, ignoring the life that had been lost. We prepared for the move into Otto and Elizabeth's old house. Clark's grandparents' home, built in 1930, was located just off Main Street. I loved the antique stained-glass door entry, exquisite hand-scraped hardwood floors and the unique multicolored stone fireplace that filled the downstairs living room wall. Cynthia and Barbara agreed never to sell it. All we had to do was clean out the cobwebs, take off the sheets that covered their antique furniture and open the windows to let out the stale air that remained inside.

The seven-bedroom, three-story home looked like an old relic suspended in time. I was comfortable not changing a thing, but sometimes I had the strange feeling that Elizabeth still watched over her home. My favorite place to read was out in her beautiful garden while I sat on an old iron bench.

Some days, I studied the black and white photographs of Clark's grandparents and relatives that lined the wooden stairway. They made me curious about my husband's family tree. One of the hanging pictures was Otto and Elizabeth's wedding portrait where they looked so happy, yet in a later picture I noticed more serious expressions. They were so good-looking and their children's resemblance to them was quite evident.

Over the following months, my stomach grew quickly. I dreaded going downstairs to the basement to do laundry. It was cold and damp and the smell took my breath away. The lights flickered curiously on and off several times while I worked down there.

One day, I was surprised to find Elizabeth's usually closed bedroom door ajar. An inner feeling prompted me to go inside. Immediately, I breathed in the scent of roses, even though the ceramic vase on her antique dressing table was empty. Next to the fireplace, a tall bookcase overflowed with leather and paperback novels. In the far corner, a full-length wooden mirror stood like a soldier waiting for final inspection. As I stepped further inside, I tripped slightly over a small frilly fabric basket with a miniature book inside. Picking it up, I opened the yellowed pages to an entry that was dated March 5, 1939.

> *I'm alone again. Otto is off somewhere on the political battlefield. Many would say I have nothing to complain about. Although I do enjoy my high-society life and have many lady friends to share tea with and my children are off at boarding school, my passion for life has dulled and my inner spirit feels like a wilted flower craving water.*
>
> *These thoughts drain me, but I have to mask the misery of being the wife of Otto Preston: a man who serves the community yet leaves his wife to her empty bed.*

I thought of Sandy, who like her grandmother, had been sad, but had hidden the pain from the outside world. Clark and I recently spoke about how much we missed her. I heard Clark come in downstairs, quickly put the book down and closed the door behind me.

Lately, Clark had been working late on plans to take over one of the family's alfalfa ranches belonging to the Preston family trust. It had seven hundred acres of agricultural land located just outside Santa Maria. I was excited to get back to my wholesome farming roots. My mother agreed to come and help us when the baby arrived, so we could be sure to devote enough energy to the land.

On a cool winter day in February while carrying a load of laundry to the basement, my water broke. I barely made it back up the stairs to call Clark. He was at the courthouse with his mother and promised to rush home. I called my doctor, who said he would meet me at the hospital. I then dragged my suitcase downstairs and waited.

By the time Clark arrived, my contractions were five minutes apart. "We better hurry," I said.

Clark held my hand on the way to the hospital. I'd begun to have unrelenting pain. It took my breath away.

At the hospital, they ushered me into a room as I screamed out, "The baby's coming!"

The child came so quickly, they didn't have time to get me into the delivery room. The doctor rushed in just in time to deliver our perfect eight-pound baby boy. When the nurse set our healthy newborn upon my chest for me to see, I realized Clark had witnessed his birth while standing in the corner. His eyes were wet with tears.

Later when I woke up from my exhaustion-induced nap, my husband was standing by my side. "Brian has your hair, my eyes and cries louder than all the babies in the nursery," he said, taking my hand.

I laughed.

Cynthia sent balloons and flowers, but didn't come by until the next day. Barbara, Bernie and Jack were there for all the visiting hours. Clark picked up my mother from the airport and then me on the day I was released from the hospital. I felt comfortable knowing her strong Cherokee work ethic, deep caring heart and healing hands were there to help me.

One month later, Cynthia called and asked if she could come over to talk. While the baby slept, we sat together in her mother's living room. "Amber, I want to be sure you're clear about things," she began. "As you know, Clark is named as an heir to the Preston family trust and spouses are excluded—"

"Cynthia, I've told you before: I love Clark for who he is, not for his money." Even though her assumptions rubbed me wrong, I held my tongue.

"It was reflected in my mother's written will that she cared more about her grandchildren than her own flesh and blood. She was a cold, hard, unhappy woman who was jealous of the close relationship I had with my father."

"Sandy never spoke about her in that way," I defended.

"Well, for your information, Brian will be listed as a beneficiary. It is a privilege given to those who carry on the Preston bloodline."

"Clark and I understand that."

"Also, I came here to tell you that Barbara and I have decided to remodel the farmhouse on the property you will be leasing. When Sandy died, we were able to sell a portion of the land held by the trust to the Santa Barbara school district. We'll be using the funds from the sale to finance the remodel."

"What exactly are you trying to tell me, Cynthia?"

"You will have to wait longer to move onto the farm or take a small guesthouse nearby for now."

"I'll speak to Clark about it," I told her, turning my head to where I heard the baby stirring in the other room.

"Before I go, one more thing. I'm going to make sure this child is brought up worthy of his Preston heritage." With the last word, she left.

"How dare she start to try and run our lives already," I slammed my fist on the kitchen table. If anyone was a "cold, hard, unhappy woman," it was she. It made me wonder how such a warm and sensitive man like Clark came from such an insensitive woman.

That night I shared the details of the conversation with Clark.

"Mother always has to feel her power, honey. Don't let her get under your sweet skin." He gave me a warm hug and asked, "How's our little guy?"

"Growing by the minute."

"Well, Mother already informed me that the farm remodel was funded by a sale of property that belonged to the Preston trust. She needed my signature on that deed of sale."

"What do you think about moving into the guesthouse earlier?" I asked Clark.

"It sounds like a good idea. It will get us farther away from my mother. I can handle getting the shabby shack ready and you can start packing up here."

"It's time we had a place all our own."

That night as the cold March wind danced around the dead of night, I felt Clark's hungry eyes watching me undress.

"I'm so lucky to have you all to myself. Come here," he beckoned. "I want to taste every part of you."

Sometimes, just a certain look from Clark made the windows of my mind fog with passion. He reached for me and ran his fingers through my hair, knowing that was one of my weak spots. Soon the delight of his warm breath in my ear made my head tilt back in surrender. His moist lips pressed against my neck as they made their way downward. I'd learned his weak spots, too. My hands surrounded his manhood to satisfy both our needs. "I love to love you," he sighed. Several hours later, in complete exhaustion, we fell asleep.

Over the next few weeks, we got ready for our move outside the city.

One afternoon, while Brian napped, I decided to walk the property one last time. It had rained heavily the night before and I noticed something sticking out of the ground near the back of the fence. Walking over to it, I realized it was the top portion of an iron hanger. When I dug it out, I was surprised to discover it looked like it had been purposefully shaped into the letter P. As I stood there for a moment, I heard the phone ring in the distance and ran inside. It was Barbara on the other end.

"Heard you were moving this weekend and wanted to see if you needed some help," she said.

"Sure, that is really nice of you."

"Jack is taking Claire and Joel to the movies. I'll come over afterwards."

"We can always use an extra pair of hands, Barbara."

I didn't say anything about the hanger and put it away down in the basement.

On moving day, Cynthia showed up and surprised us with a new Ford pickup truck to use on the farm. "I leased it for you," she explained. "I'm sure you'll make good use of it."

It was great for loading most of the baby furniture and some of our clothes. Clark was grateful, but I wondered what Cynthia's real motive was. Barbara arrived and helped me with the kitchen and I asked Cynthia to go downstairs in the basement and get a few more boxes. When she returned, her face was white as a ghost.

"Where did this come from?" she barely got the words out as she held the bent hanger in her hand.

"I was walking around outside and saw it sticking out of the ground," I answered and glanced at Barbara, whose mouth was wide open. I tried not to stare at her and turned back to look at Cynthia. "It seemed strange someone made it into a shape. Have you seen it before?"

"A long time ago," Barbara responded and I sensed a tension between the sisters and wondered why. "I think something like that should stay buried in the past," Barbara sighed.

Just then Clark walked in and everyone got quiet. "Something wrong here?"

"We're just finishing up and are ready to go," I broke the silence.

We all helped closing the house back up. Walking away, a feeling of sadness overwhelmed me, but I couldn't pinpoint a reason for it. Barbara followed us out to the farm, but Cynthia did not. She seemed upset when she learned that Jack was with Claire and Joel.

It didn't take long to fix up the tiny, two-bedroom cottage. That evening, Clark and I sat in a pair of old wooden rocking chairs on the wrap-around porch. As we gazed over the open agricultural field, I finally felt at home.

Through the winter months, Clark returned every night from the field covered with dirt from head to toe, but he always had a wide smile on his handsome face. It was the happiest I'd been in a long time, too. I loved to look out of our kitchen window and see the view of nature's bounty. It fed my soul.

Shortly after getting settled, we met our neighbors, Emily and John Carlson. They grew beans, peas, corn and they raised—of all things—ostriches. They told us they had heard rumors that the famous pop singer, Michael Jackson, had bought the land to the back of ours. We enjoyed speculating with them what he would do with it.

I welcomed spring by planting a small garden. The remodel of the ranch house moved forward at a snail's pace. Brian took his first steps right after the first buds of alfalfa sprang from the earth.

By midsummer, I discovered that I was pregnant again. Clark and I were very excited about welcoming another child. One evening, Cynthia and Jack invited us out to dinner and we decided to break the news. I was a little nervous to face Cynthia because of her unpredictable nature, but Clark said he would handle it.

We met for dinner at 7:00 o'clock that evening and Jack was already there. "My wife will be late as usual. She got tied up in a business meeting."

Jack and Clark talked about the ranch and my mind wandered, thinking about my very strange mother-in-law. To the community, she looked flawless. Her model figure, designer clothes and porcelain-pale skin reflected an image found on the cover of fashion magazines. With her jaw-dropping, wavy, blond, shoulder-length hair defined by her striking widow's peak, she made heads turn. Her sensuous, crystal-green bedroom eyes held the power to seduce at will. I'd watched her use those assets well in the political arena. Clark boasted that her social circle read like an invitation list to the governor's ball. But even her dazzling diamonds couldn't hide the dark side I'd seen so many times before.

We all turned toward the door when Cynthia made her entrance. She looked stunning in a beige, two-piece Ralph Lauren suit accented with a brown-and-cream-colored silk scarf and diamond brooch. Her signature perfume filled the air as she sat down next to Jack. "I apologize for being late. City business is demanding."

After ordering our food, Clark looked at her and announced, "We have something to tell you. We're expecting."

"What? Again? This soon?" she responded, a disgruntled look on her face.

"Brian will be one year old next month, Mother. Can't you just be happy for us?" Clark shook his head.

My eyes met Jack's as he frowned as if in agreement with Clark, but neither of us said a word.

"Clark, you have a lot of responsibility on your hands right now. Not to mention the time commitment to the land. I'm not sure you're capable of taking care of your family and the property that I'm allowing you to run."

"Give me a chance, Mother," Clark held my hand in support.

"The new baby won't interfere with Clark's work, Cynthia. I'll make sure of that," I quickly backed up my husband.

"If you're unhappy with the job I'm doing, Mother, just say so." Clark looked over at me, stood and said, "Maybe we should leave."

After a tense moment, Cynthia commanded, "Sit down, Clark. There is no need for you to go anywhere. Just keep your priorities straight and remember this farm lease arrangement is for the benefit of all of us."

When our food arrived, Jack suggested a congratulatory toast. Throughout dinner, Cynthia only said a few words to me and I felt her underlying displeasure of our news.

As soon as we were home on the alfalfa ranch, away from the city, Cynthia and family issues were put behind us. Cynthia did pay us well for running the ranch. The long, hot summer days were filled with family barbecues, beer feasts and tractor rides through our growing fields.

Clark and I each decided to buy our own horse. I named mine Juliet. He called his Romeo. Jack came by often with Claire and Joel in tow.

They all loved to feed and take care of the horses.

Soon the leaves began to turn as harvest time drew near. The remodel was finally complete and we moved into the larger ranch house. It had five bedrooms, a maid's quarters, a large study, an updated kitchen and a separate dining area.

I was only eight months along when suddenly I felt a sharp pain in my abdomen. "I think I had my first contraction," I told Clark with some disbelief.

He stood up with concern. "Isn't it too early for that?"

"Yes." I squirmed in my seat as another intense pain followed.

When the pains continued, I went inside to call my doctor. Within moments, we were leaving for the hospital. We had recently hired a live-in housekeeper named Carmen Flores who watched Brian.

Inside the pickup, right after we left, I felt a strong pain. "Oh, God!" I yelled. "My water just broke."

The seat beneath me was wet and I was numb with disbelief when I saw it was also filled with blood. "Something's wrong, Clark. Get there as fast as you can," I begged.

He wouldn't let go of my hand as he made his way toward the emergency room entrance. My medical training told me the severe pain and excessive blood were signs of trouble, but I didn't share the information with Clark. I didn't want to scare him. I clenched my teeth and moaned, refusing to let the wild scream of raging pain pass my lips. A rush of hands helped me onto a gurney, but somewhere deep inside, I knew a fight for survival had just begun.

Distantly, I heard Clark's desperate voice shout, "Hold on, Amber. I love you."

Then everything went black.

Waking up, I felt weak and dizzy. I became aware of a constant pain in my lower abdomen. "We almost lost you." Clark touched my cheek. "Honey, you started hemorrhaging and they had to do a caesarean," he explained.

I had no memory of what had happened. Raising my head from the pillow, I asked, "What about the baby?"

He held my hand tightly before speaking. "There is a fifty-fifty chance our son, Paul, won't make it through the night."

I listened to Clark's words with disbelief. "No! No!" I sobbed. "That can't be."

My husband's serious expression reflected the slim possibilities for our newborn. "Honey, they have him under an ultraviolet light in a tangle of tubes and wires. I've prayed to God that you both would survive."

I saw a tear trickle down Clark's cheek and silently added my prayers to those in higher hands. In my mind, I surrounded our new blessing in love.

I was deeply grateful when he did in fact make it through the night.

Clark brought me flowers every day. With agony in our hearts, we watched and waited. I was sent home from the hospital without Paul, but slowly he gained an ounce of weight here and an ounce of strength there. He was a month old before we could finally hold him in our arms. Two weeks later, we brought Paul home to meet his brother, Brian. The ordeal brought us all together, but left us with a mountain of hospital bills.

The stress of harvest time dropped like a bomb on us. Clark worked from dawn until dusk. His hands were bloodied, blistered and calloused, his body worn to the bone. Clark never complained about the injury to his left shoulder from an earlier car accident, which left him unable to lift his arm higher than his shoulder.

I tried to help by taking over feeding the animals, which now consisted of three horses, several chickens and two pigs. In the twilight hours, I sat with Paul in my arms and Brian at my feet watching Clark bale. One night as darkness was approaching, I saw him walking toward me in his dusty overalls with a wide grin across his face. "We did it. The harvest is done."

He looked back at the field and stood tall with a blade of hay between his teeth. I was so proud of him that tears of joy filled my eyes.

"Amber, I love you."

"I love you too, Clark," I said, patting him on the butt.

Over the next few years, we watched our family grow and our land flourish. Clark handled all our financial affairs, including any correspondence with Mitchell and Blaine. Clark's mother, Cynthia, rarely came by, since Clark brought all the records to her in the city. He shared stories with me about Cynthia's and Barbara's constant bickering over money that disrupted many family occasions.

Two years later at Thanksgiving, I decided to have a family dinner at our ranch. Cynthia and Jack had just returned from an overseas trip. I'd heard from Clark that Barbara and Bernie wanted to adopt a child, since she had trouble conceiving a second time. She remained jealous of the fact that her sister Cynthia had three children and she only one.

Just before dinner, I was at the sink looking out the window and saw Claire, Paul and Brian preparing to go horseback riding. Our golden retriever, Lumbaugh, was running circles around them and Jack. Bernie and Clark were carrying cold beers out to the barn for some guy time.

Suddenly, my attention was drawn to loud voices coming from the living room. I quickly made my way there.

Cynthia's back was turned away from Barbara as she cursed, "It's none of your damn business."

"What's going on?" I inquired.

"I asked my sister how she affords all her diamond jewelry, expensive overseas trips and high-profile life, when we both get the same allowance from our father's trust."

"I believe that is a private matter," I said, even though that same question had occurred to me.

"Well, it seems strange when we both receive equal money. Bernie tells me that Cynthia's net worth is ten times ours!"

Cynthia's eyes darted between Barbara and I. "Are you accusing me of taking money from the trust?" her voice trembled.

"No," Barbara blushed. "I just want to know if Father left you something he didn't leave me."

Cynthia let out a loud, strange laugh, but no words.

Moments later, Jack, Clark and Bernie appeared with the children right behind them.

"Dinner is almost ready, so let's gather at the table and all give thanks for each of our good fortunes." I suggested and turned to Barbara asking her to join me in the kitchen.

While we stood by the kitchen counter filling a plate of green beans, Barbara apologized. "I don't want to upset anyone. It's just, when we were young, Cynthia was our father's favorite, and since his death, her fortune has ballooned beyond belief."

"You can't help but notice the diamond jewelry," I agreed.

"What do you think, Amber? Is my sister hiding something?"

"I don't know. Maybe there is a logical answer, but I've never met a more controlling, stubborn woman in my life," I shared.

"Ever since Father died, she's taken over his seat of power. If it were up to me, I'd like to see her fairy-tale life come tumbling down."

I had never before realized the extent of jealousy between the two sisters, but her remark brought a shiver down my spine. There was an uneasy atmosphere throughout dinner. Nagging mental questions about their strained relationship encouraged me to dig deep into Clark's family's past.

Chapter Thirty-One
Family Secrets and Lies

1980-1985
Santa Barbara, California
Amber McDaniel

The following week, I got a call from Barbara asking me out to lunch. We agreed to meet in town at *Marcello's* while the kids were in school. When Barbara arrived, I couldn't help but notice her eyes were red. It looked like she'd been crying.

"What's wrong?" I questioned.

As tears streamed down her cheeks, she blurted out, "I think Bernie is having an affair."

I sat and listened while she told me her story, "Recently, he has been coming home late and I recognized the scent of perfume on his clothes."

"Have you confronted him?" I inquired.

Barbara's eyes widened. "Not yet. It's complicated, Amber. I think the other woman is Cynthia."

The news hit me with the speed of a lightning bolt. I was stunned speechless.

Just then our waiter appeared to take our order. I asked him to give us a moment and handed Barbara a tissue to dry her eyes. "I'm so sorry you have to deal with this," I said.

"The whole situation is already ugly," she looked down at the table.

"Are you sure it's Cynthia? Do you have any other proof?"

"Well, I can't deny I recognize her perfume."

"It is a popular brand, Barbara. Do you have any other proof?"

"Years ago, Bernie admitted to me he'd slept with her."

I sat stunned, thinking what an unforgivable betrayal that must have been. "Maybe you should hire a detective to be sure," I suggested.

When our server returned, I ordered a bottle of wine and told her, "My advice is to think any action through."

As our glasses emptied during lunch, Barbara started talking about her past, "I was the sickly ugly duckling of our family." She set her fork down near her salad. "My father never showed me any attention and Mother was too busy socially. Cynthia and I were close early on, but after high school, our relationship changed," Barbara's voice cracked with emotion.

"What happened that made your relationship change?"

She cleared her throat and threw down her napkin. Her body stiffened. "That bitch ruined my life. Recently, my gynecologist told me that the reason I can't conceive anymore children was due to what Cynthia did to me years ago."

I drew back with surprise. "What are you talking about? How? Did she hurt you?"

"I've never told anyone before. Not Bernie. Not my mother. No one."

Silently, I waited while Barbara squirmed in her chair before revealing her deep secret.

"The hanger you found marked the grave where Cynthia buried my dead baby in the backyard of my parent's house. For years, I've been plagued by kidney and bladder infections, and now I'll never be able to conceive again." Her impassioned words flowed across the table like ink across a page.

When she finished the cruel description of her childhood nightmare, the painful details cut into my heart with the sharpness of a scalpel. "Oh, Barbara, what a terrible thing to happen. I will be here to support you for whatever you need."

Heading home, my mind tried to digest Barbara's shocking story and suspicions. As the distasteful facts and accusations were recapped, I had a horrible realization: What if my mother-in-law was a mad woman who, at all costs, took things into her own hands? What could she be capable of?

Sandy's death zoomed into the forefront of my mind. What if it wasn't suicide?

Chapter Thirty-Two
The Plot Thickens

1980
Santa Barbara, California
Amber McDaniel

When I got home, I was torn about whether or not to tell Clark about my suspicions. Ever since he became treasurer of the Santa Maria County Water Reclamation Board, he had been withdrawn. I'd felt a distance growing between us. I believed the added stress of his new job and its pressure were the reasons for his recent curt voice and somber mood. He'd taken the job because of the proposed pipeline project that would run through our property and this weighed heavy on his mind. I decided not to say anything to him until I gathered more information.

I wasn't sure if what Barbara had told me was true. What if she wanted to acquire me as an ally against her sister? It was time to investigate on my own to get a better picture of the dynamics of Clark's family.

The next morning, with Brian and Paul at their Montessori private school all day, I had time to do some investigating. I wasn't sure where to begin, but I knew Clark's grandfather, Otto Preston, must have set the stage for some of the drama that followed. Cynthia was so protective of the family name that she offered few details about the past. So I decided to look for any information that might help me understand the Preston family tree.

I went into town and headed for the municipal public records office. It had the feel of a library. I could access microfiche to look up names, dates, or documents. My search was disappointing. Though the records offered a detailed timeline of birth, marriage and death for each of the Preston family members, no intimate personal information was available.

Starving, I stopped by *Marcello's* for a bite to eat. My eyes widened as I spotted Cynthia having lunch with Bernie. I hesitated, but walked over to them. "What a small world. Do you mind if I join you?"

"We're just finishing up some business," Cynthia's face flushed.

Bernie didn't look me in the eye.

"What are you doing in town?" Cynthia squirmed in her chair.

"I was at the county clerk's office checking on something for Clark."

The whole scene was awkward. I told them that I had another meeting to get to. I went to the counter, ordered a sandwich and left as fast as I could. Even though my original objective wasn't met, the chance encounter spoke volumes. If Barbara was telling the truth, Clark's family tree definitely grew seeds of evil.

In the evening, while Clark and I sat on our porch watching the sun go down, I turned to him. "Honey, you seldom talk about your childhood. What was it like?"

"My patriarch mother ruled by the standard: do as I say, not as I do."

"What exactly do you mean?"

"Mother projected a flawless image to the outside world, while at home she drank, swore and verbally abused us. Using her purse strings to control us, she demanded that we hold a high standard of social behavior worthy of the Preston name."

"How was her relationship with Sandy?"

"They never got along. As you know, Sandy was a rebel. We always covered each other's back. Even so, if we got in trouble and Mother found out, she'd find a way to make our lives miserable."

"She hasn't changed much."

"I'll never understand her," Clark sighed.

"I know how much you miss your sister, Honey. I miss her, too. You've been under a lot of stress lately. I'd like to plan some time off soon and get away."

"Amber, I can't right now. There are too many pressing matters that need my personal attention on the pipeline project."

"Is there anything I can do to help you?"

"No, just be who you are, the most loving wife a man could ask for." Clark held my hand as the twilight sky faded into darkness. In that moment, I felt a reconnection with the man I loved.

That Sunday, our whole family headed toward town in our Suburban to attend church. On our way home, Brian and Paul were busy listening to their cassette player headsets. In the quiet moment, I reflected on our pastor's message about surviving our struggles through the power of faith. I recalled him saying, *yesterday's battles teach us to appreciate today's blessings.*

It brought back memories of my own childhood. We lived in Los Angeles when my parents divorced. Even though I was small, the pain and fear of abandonment stayed with me. Years later, my mother remarried and we moved to Portland, Oregon, near my grandfather's berry farm. Later my stepfather's married daughter bought the farm next to ours. I was glad to see my mother happy again.

Back then, I was a loner and loved to work outside and get dirt on my hands. I hoped the man of my dreams would love nature and the Earth as much as me. When I met Clark, I knew he was everything I had longed for. Many times he told me, "Amber, you are the other half that makes me whole." He came from a totally dysfunctional family and survived. Looking over at my husband, I realized how much we were blessed to have found a special love we both can count on.

Then without warning, a deafening scream of exploding glass thundered inside our moving vehicle. Windshield fragments rained over me and my eyes clamped shut.

Clark's terrified voice shouted, "Get down!"

With the panic of an emergency room crisis, I ducked below the dashboard. My heart beat wildly as the sound of screeching brakes and burning rubber filled the air. In the darkness, my body trembled with fear as one thought filled my mind. *Oh my God, the children!*

Clark held onto my hand so hard it hurt while he got the car to an abrupt halt. Then my husband hollered, "Is everyone okay?'

From the backseat, Brian's shaky voice piped up, "We're okay back here and we got down right away. What the heck happened?"

When I looked up, I gasped in horror seeing Clark pale face spattered with blood. My nursing skills instantly kicked in, and I quickly checked him and the boys for injuries.

I was so grateful that Brian and Paul were only shaken. Then I saw a stream of blood drip down onto Clark's crisp white shirt. There was a one-inch gash on the left side of his forehead. No spurting. No arteries cut. I grabbed his handkerchief and pressed hard against his wound to stop the bleeding.

"We hit something, or something hit us," Clark pointed to the broken windshield.

There was a golf-ball sized gaping hole on the driver's side. Just then, Clark looked down and picked up the cause of our disaster. When he opened his palm, my body filled with terror seeing the shiny bullet casing inside.

Clark grabbed his mobile phone, dialed 911 and then jumped out of the car. He kept a distance from our vehicle, so as not to upset the children with his conversation. Moments later, his voice still shaken, he informed us, "The sheriff is on his way."

Clark's face was tense as he paced outside. I didn't want to alarm the boys and told them, "Everything is fine. Go back to listening to your music."

Standing several feet from our car, Clark's searching eyes checked all around us. An uneasy feeling overwhelmed me as I watched him. I was trying to understand why he was so upset. Wasn't this an unfortunate accident? Yet seeing beads of sweat appear across my husband's forehead made me worry that it was something more.

I stepped outside and walked over to him, "Are you okay?"

He pulled away, dropped his head and with his eyes wide with fear told me, "I think someone just tried to kill us! My God, Amber, we were sitting ducks."

"What are you talking about?" I shook my head and tried to remain calm. "Who would want to hurt us?"

"I'll handle this, Amber," Clark ordered with a cold stare.

Before the officers arrived, I questioned him once more, but never got a straight answer.

Finally a sheriff's patrol car pulled up next to us. "A tow truck is on the way," one of the officers informed us.

They asked if we needed an ambulance, but Clark refused any treatment.

Then came a barrage of questions. "What direction did the shot come from?"..."Were there any other cars or trucks in the vicinity when this occurred?"..."Did you see anyone or anything suspicious before it happened?"

With each question, Clark became more agitated. His answers were loud and abrupt. Finally, he threw his hands in the air and shouted, "Can't you see? Someone out there tried to kill us!"

"Mr. McDaniel, calm down. We're just trying to get the facts. Without a suspect, we have to report this as a random incident," the sheriff explained.

"Isn't it your job to protect us?" Clark shook his head.

"Mr. McDaniel, we need you to keep your composure," the other officer ordered.

"Wait a minute. Someone just shot at my family. That's attempted murder in my book." Clark kicked the dirt.

"Honey, we're lucky none of us were seriously hurt," I tried to encourage my irate husband to control himself.

"I want this documented as attempted murder," Clark demanded again.

"Hold on, Mr. McDaniel," one of the lawmen grabbed Clark's shoulder. "The shot might have been from a careless hunter's rifle or a young kid doing target practice. Accidents like this are rare, but they do happen."

"This was no accident," Clark insisted, but refused to say anymore.

"Unless you have an idea as to who might be responsible, the only thing we can do is complete a report and list this as an accidental gunshot."

"The children are getting restless, dear. Please cooperate for their sake."

As the report was being taken, a tow truck and our ranch foreman, Bruce, showed up.

While heading back to the ranch, Clark put his arm around me and said, "Amber, you, Brian and Paul are the most important things in my life. It is my job to protect you."

"Clark, this wasn't your fault," I assured him, but my words didn't seem to lighten the burden he carried.

Then at home, to my disappointment, Clark headed toward the bedroom and shut the door behind him. I figured he needed to be alone and told Brian and Paul, "Your father's been working very hard lately and has a lot on his mind."

Still my stomach churned with emotion from the day's events. Until a month ago, Clark had never kept secrets from me. Something was definitely bothering him, and I knew I had to get to the bottom of it.

Later, he refused to come to dinner. So I got the children to bed early and headed directly to our bedroom to get some answers.

I flipped on the light and studied him for a moment. His skin looked yellow like old newspaper, his cheeks were sunken, and his innocent green eyes glistened as though he burned with fever. Clark had curled up his six-foot frame, which normally reached the end of our bed, into a fetal position. Despite my medical knowledge as a registered nurse, I felt helpless. It seemed like something dark lay between us, growing larger with every moment. Each attempt I'd made to get him to name it had failed, but I had to try once more.

"Clark?" my stomach clenched. "Are you okay?"

Silence.

"Are you?" I repeated.

"Yes." His voice sounded thin, distant, as if he were miles away. I reached out and touched his arm. His muscles were rigid beneath skin much colder than mine.

"Are you sure?" I laid my hand on his forehead. His chilled skin was stretched taut across the bone.

He pushed my hand away. "I'm fine. Just can't sleep, that's all."

"You've barely slept in weeks."

"I'm fine, Amber. I have a lot on my mind."

"Tell me, Clark. Something's wrong." Looking deep into his eyes, I saw pain where there once was only innocent optimism. "Clark, please tell me what's bothering you."

"Nothing is bothering me," he turned away and curled back into the covers. "You're just imagining things."

"I'm not," I answered, sliding closer and molding my body to his. A trickle of fear slid down my back. Was he trying to shield and protect me? I shuddered and fought the desire to turn off the light and let him be. "When I married you, I promised to love and care for you, and you promised to do the same. If you truly love me, then you'll tell me what's going on."

I heard Clark's breath catch in his throat and felt his heart kick against my hand, but for long moments, he said nothing. Then he lifted his head off the pillow. "You won't believe me."

"Why? You've never lied to me before." I gently kissed his cheek. "Of course I'll believe you."

He shivered in my arms, straightened, and turned toward me. "I think my mother and some of her political cronies are involved in a plot to kill me."

"What?" I wailed. "That's not possible. Where did you get an idea like that?" I pulled away. "Clark, you've been working too hard lately."

"You've got to believe me, Amber," Clark threw back the covers, jumped out of bed and began pacing the floor.

I swallowed hard against the lump in my throat and recalled the many times I'd watched my mother-in-law treat Clark with the callousness of a dictator. Sitting up, I asked, "Are you sure?"

He stopped in his tracks, faced me, and with his brow tense with fear, said, "Two weeks ago while researching land records regarding the new water pipeline, I stumbled across something." He paused and took a deep breath. "I found a deed of sale in the amount of $14 million for property that belonged to our family's trust. I knew nothing about this."

"Oh, Clark. What did you do?" I asked.

"I tried to locate the bank records for these funds, but instead uncovered another document that reconveyed this same property back to our trust. Amber, that's what people do when they're money laundering."

Clark's words stunned me like an electric shock.

His eyes widened as he hollered, "I couldn't believe that my own mother's signature and members of her political machine approved all the documents."

"Oh, my God!" I cried, feeling the color drain from my face.

I opened my arms to soothe the pain of my wounded partner. His hands gently stroked the arch of my back while pictures flashed through my mind of his parent's lavish lifestyle. Where did those shiny diamond rings and pendants really come from?

"Damn it all! How can this be happening to us?" I cupped my hands over my shivering lips.

Clark suddenly stood back and shuddered. "I was tired of being a worm. I decided to stand up to my mother."

"What happened?"

"She denied everything and called me a worthless fool. Tore up the papers I'd shown her and threatened, 'If you take this information public, you'll regret it. You know that I have the power and money to ruin you and your family.'"

"That bitch," I shook my head as I faced Clark. "Honey, I'm so proud of you for standing up to her."

For a while, we held each other, not saying a word, as our minds were caught in fear's choking grasp. What could Cynthia be capable of to prevent her fairy-tale kingdom from tumbling down?

Chapter Thirty-Three
The Nightmare Begins

1985
Santa Barbara, California
Amber McDaniel

Later that night I offered Clark a sleeping pill. He looked emotionally exhausted, but couldn't fall asleep. My body molded to his while I listened to the strong steady beat of his heart.

Questions filled my mind about the day's events. What was Cynthia hiding? Could it be a political cover-up? Had Sandy discovered the same secret? What kind of mother would ever think of harming her own children? How was Barbara involved in all this?

Unable to sleep, I struggled to make sense of it. My mind drifted to the past. Right after we were married, Clark sat me down and explained the details of the Preston family trust. I recalled his words: "My mother and her sister are the designated trustees. The family trust owns commercial buildings, real estate and over two thousand acres of farmland held in a designated agricultural preserve. The heirs include me, Sandy, Claire and Joel—the four grandchildren." He made sure I understood that spouses had no entitlement to those assets. I had no problem with that and had told as much to Cynthia every time she reminded me of it.

After Clark's grandmother died, he'd told me about a stipulation she had added that he thought was odd. He even read it to me.

> *During the lifetime of the trustees, they may only receive income through leases or rental of the land within the agricultural preserve. They cannot touch the principal. Any sale of property can only take place upon a death in the family and would have to be approved by all heirs.*

Clark never understood his grandmother's purpose for this, but told me, "Grandmother never approved of my mother's lifestyle, and she wanted to be sure her grandchildren were well taken care of."

More questions continued piling up like yesterday's trash. Did Cynthia find a way to filter undisclosed income through their family trust, or could she be involved in something even bigger? Was my mother-in-law a bitch from hell the outside world knew nothing about? She often hid her bad side behind the mask of sparkling diamonds she wore. The answers eluded me for now, but I vowed to find them as I drifted off to sleep.

The next morning, Clark sat up in bed. "It's time the world sees my mother for who she really is. I'm going to make sure the truth comes out."

"I support you, Clark. Let me know what else I can do."

"Call your parents today in Oregon and let them know we will be moving there to set up an organic farm." His stunning announcement bore witness to the depth of urgency the crisis called for. He felt we would have to leave to avoid Cynthia's wrath.

A searing panic quickly drove me out of bed to get things in order.

At breakfast, I broke the news to the boys. "Your father and I have decided to move to Oregon. School will finish on Friday, and we will leave immediately."

"What? Why?" Brian looked up from his cereal bowl.

"We'll be staying at your grandparent's house until we get settled and find our own organic farm. Dad has been under too much stress here and we need to make a change."

"Do we have to? Can I take my horse?" Paul asked.

"We'll talk more about it after school," I told them as they scurried off to catch the bus.

Watching them through the kitchen window, I felt a sense of guilt about making such a quick, dramatic change to their lives, but I feared what might happen if we stayed.

I called and left my parents a brief message. I wasn't sure what to tell them. Throughout the early morning, I prepared a list of things I'd need to get done. Just before noon, I heard the garage door open and my heart skipped a beat. I knew something was wrong. Clark never returned at such an early hour.

Walking toward our side garage door entrance, I saw Clark enter the house. There was a large discolored bruise on his cheek. "What happened?" I gasped.

"My mother went ballistic when I told her my plan to expose all those involved in illegal deeds. I said that she couldn't scare or buy me from telling the truth. When I turned to walk out of her office, she swore and threw a paper weight at me."

"What should we do?" I questioned, getting some ice from the refrigerator to put on his swollen wound.

"I've got a plan," Clark said with a childish smirk on his face.

I placed the cool compress against his skin and he gave me an encouraging wink. "You're scaring me, Clark. What do you have up your sleeve?"

"I stole a copy of the Santa Barbara Planning Commission's manuals. It holds all the proof we need to convict my mother and her accomplices. I believe she used our living trust to launder drug money. I think it's possible Sandy found out and Mother had her killed. Now she's after me."

A riptide of emotion paralyzed me. My mouth opened, but no words sprang from my lips. Feeling like prey trapped in a web, I struggled to accept the shocking revelation of unspeakable crimes. My mind couldn't imagine what kind of craziness would make a mother murder her own flesh and blood.

Clark grabbed me by the shoulders. "Honey, you've got to believe me. This is so big it will scare you to death! The sheriffs are involved, and it goes all the way to the top of the local political ladder."

I began to tremble as anger filled my veins. How could Cynthia do this?

Suddenly I burst into tears.

Clark wrapped his arms around me. He repeated, "Don't worry. Everything will be all right."

Still, my heart sank, feeling the world crashing in around us.

"Amber, we are in grave danger once I let out this information. Our only hope is to leave this life behind as fast as we can."

"You're right. I understand."

We decided not to tell our children or my parents about the horror story until after we'd moved. We then directed all our attention to the preparation for our relocation. We had five days.

Two days later, I answered the phone and a threatening man's voice blared, "If your husband says a word to anyone, we'll kill all of you!"

In a gut-wrenching scream, I yelled, "You son of a bitch!" Then I slammed down the phone and shaking, ran to tell Clark.

"Their threats don't scare me, but Saturday won't come too soon," he shook his head.

That night before we drifted off to sleep, he whispered, "Amber, I love you. Don't worry, honey. Our love can conquer anything."

The alarm sounded at 5:30 AM Friday morning. Instantly, I panicked when I realized that Clark was not in bed. Did he wake up early to work on the plans for our upcoming trip?

Heading toward the kitchen, I passed the library and saw the TV on. My throat tightened seeing Clark's recliner empty with the footrest still up. Why was his robe belt resting on the carpet? I yelled out his name. Shaking in fear, I tried to calm myself; I knew that when he couldn't sleep he would go into the library and watch TV.

"Clark?" I called out.

With no answer, I hurried to the garage to see if our Suburban was inside. I flipped on the light switch. The bulb was out and it took me a few seconds for my eyes to adjust to the dim light. It was a relief to see our vehicle, but that faded when I caught sight of a dark liquid spreading across the cement floor. My eyes traced its origin to Clark's crumpled body resting near the rear tire of our car. I ran to Clark and realized that my beloved husband's skin was pale, his lips blue and his eyes dilated and open; a confirmation that he was gone.

I felt my own blood drain from my face. My knees buckled, and I braced myself against the wall. Shock and disbelief stabbed at my heart, desperately wanting to erase the picture before me. I dropped to my knees and started CPR, hoping somehow I could breathe life back into his body. Only pure exhaustion stopped me.

I sat there frozen for how long I'm still not sure. I lay my head upon his shoulder as I'd done so many times before. My heartbeat was the only sound I heard. If I could have stopped time, I'd still be by his side.

I took a deep breath and caught a glimpse of an object lying a few feet away from Clark's head. I raised up to get a closer look and recognized it as one of my son's baseball bats. It was covered with blood. This sight awakened me to the real nightmare that was just beginning. Rage filled my veins as the first thought of a perpetrator came to mind. I raced inside and called 911.

"I've just found my husband murdered," I shrieked into the phone.

The operator instructed me, "Calm down and give me as many details as you can."

"He is dead. Someone killed him," I sobbed.

"Don't touch anything," she ordered. "Give me your name and address."

I rattled it off and told her, "I think he was beaten because there is a bloody bat nearby."

"A sheriff is on the way. Are you alone in the house?"

In a shuddering whisper, I answered, "Yes, except my children are sleeping."

Then suddenly I remembered what Clark had said about the sheriffs the day before. Terror seized my heart, and I hung up the phone. Even though I longed to return to the garage and hold my beloved, I was unable to move.

Thinking on the children again, I caught my breath and ran to check on them. It was a blessing that they remained asleep. How would I ever find the right words to tell them their father was dead?

The deputies arrived with guns pulled. I was shaking, scared and still in my bathrobe when they told me I had to go outside while they searched the grounds for an intruder. They were careful not to wake and scare the children.

When the search was complete, one of the lawmen informed me that Clark's own revolver was found under the Suburban and that a single bullet had been fired. He sat me down and said, "Mrs. McDaniel, we have found no evidence of foul play. Your husband's death looks like suicide."

"No!" I screamed. "No, he was murdered."

Nothing prepared me for the scenario that was about to unfold. Even though I insisted they must keep looking for the person responsible, I was ignored. I explained to them that Clark had been in an auto accident ten years ago, and his injuries prevented him from lifting his left arm above his chest. He couldn't have physically shot himself. Nobody listened!

When I asked about the bloody bat, the policemen said it never was found. During the continued investigation, I felt like a zombie as I watched county authorities stand around talking in the shadows.

Things remained a blur until Cynthia and Barbara arrived. Barbara immediately helped with the children, but Cynthia never shed a single tear. Nor was a comforting touch exchanged between us. In time, the staged events slowly made me realize that Clark was not the only victim. A conspiracy surrounded me.

The authorities made it look good and played their part well. The deputies questioning me had even made me feel as though I had something to do with it. They asked if I'd found a suicide note and even checked my hands for gunpowder. Clark had warned me, but only the events that followed would confirm my greatest fears.

As time passed, I slowly grasped my desperate situation. I remember the sadness and tears and how Brian and Paul hung on to me as I told them the news. They were ten and twelve years old, too young to grasp the impact it would have. I'll never forget my mother's primal cry on the phone when I told her about Clark.

I was shocked when I found out that Cynthia had, without my consent, arranged to have Clark's body cremated, just like she had Sandy's. No matter who I spoke with or tried to convince that Clark's death was a murder and not a suicide, no one believed me.

My mother and stepfather came down for the funeral, but couldn't stay long. Three weeks after Clark's funeral, I received a letter from Mr. Blaine, Cynthia's attorney, requesting my appearance at his office. I had hired a few farmhands to help with keeping up the ranch, but I felt depression and exhaustion setting in as I walked up the steps to the offices of Mitchell and Blaine.

Cynthia was already there. As I sat beside her, I felt like an old dish in a China cabinet. She wore a diamond-studded, tailored, cream suit while

I was in jeans and a sweater. Even though hatred and anger ran through my veins, I did my best to hold these feelings in check.

I acknowledged her presence and then pushed myself back into the soft leather armchair.

Mr. Blaine's son David, who had recently taken over his father's practice, handed me a bundle of papers and said, "This is a formality. With the event of Clark's death, your lease for the Preston property is terminated. This is your thirty-day notice to vacate the property."

My mouth dropped. The unexpected news felt like a one-two punch. I turned to Cynthia. "You bitch. You killed my husband, and now you plan to throw the children and me to the wolves. How could you?" I leapt up from my chair and went after her. My instinct was to pull her hair out and slam her to the ground, but my anguished hands were forcibly restrained.

"Keep your dirty hands off me. You said you didn't marry Clark for his money. It is my right to have you evicted from the farm. If you ever come at me again, I'll file charges."

I turned and bolted for the door. First she took my husband and then she was kicking me out of the home where Clark and I had worked and loved together. I aimlessly walked down the main street for quite a while before entering *Marcello's* for a drink to calm my nerves.

As soon as I sat down, the tears began to fall. The owner, Tony, came by. "Hey the world isn't ending," he said as he sat down beside me.

For the next twenty minutes, I poured my heart out to him. Tony was about the same age as my own father and said he knew Clark's grandfather, Otto. "I'm sorry for you, kid," he said.

"Oh, Tony, I'm afraid no one can help me. I want to get justice for Clark, but I can't prove he was murdered. I'm worried about my own safety and that of my children. I'm so lost right now and don't know what to do."

Tony left the table for a moment and came back and handed me a business card. "He is a good private detective and a friend of mine. Give him a call."

By the time I left the restaurant, some hope had returned to my spirit. I vowed to continue to fight Cynthia—for Clark, for the truth and in the name of the love we shared.

Chapter Thirty-Four
Trials and Tribulations

1986
Portland, Oregon
Amber McDaniel

It felt like yesterday, but it had been five months since Clark's death. The eviction notices kept coming, but I ignored them and threw the papers in the garbage. My parents lent me some money so I could hire the private detective, George Paulson that Tony had referred me to. Unfortunately, he was still working the case when I saw the first sheriff's car come up the driveway.

I had some boxes packed, knowing that day would come, but even after they showed me the court order, I still refused to leave. Luckily earlier I had taken Brian and Paul to Miko's house. She had been Clark's private secretary and was the nicest Asian lady. Clark described her as all business on the outside, but sweet as cotton candy inside. We'd kept in touch, and after Clark's death, she confided to me that she suspected he had some trouble, but he hadn't given her any details about it.

The two armed officers escorted me out of the house. As a wave of grief ripped through me, I took one final look back before driving away. The next few nights, we stayed at Miko's. Lately, I'd been scared of a suspicious car following me, so I called George the detective Tony had referred me to. We met at *Marcello's* for coffee.

"Do you have any idea how powerful the people are that you are up against?" George began.

"Yes. I know they have unlimited financial and political assets."

"My advice is stop digging, if you value your life," George recommended before he left.

In fear and desperation, I called Miko, who offered us to hide at her family's cabin. "I know you will be safe there for at least the next few weeks." She handed me the key.

I was grateful to the young woman who had worked with Clark and who believed me.

She revealed, "I never saw Clark as worried as he was in those last days before he died. Something was terribly wrong, but he must have felt that he couldn't get me involved." She handed me a map of the San Joaquin Mountains, where her hideaway was located.

After driving several hours on the forest roads, I was relieved to find there were no cars behind us. A narrow dirt road led up to the cabin. It was the real McCoy—a square box of logs stacked on top of each other, notched where they met at the corners, stripped of bark and weathered a pearly gray by years of sun and wind. Inside an enormous stone fireplace presided over a drop-leaf table and chairs. Bunk beds covered with quilts, stitched from scraps the colors of all the flowers in Elizabeth's garden, would keep the boys and I warm at night.

Yes, we'd be safe there for a time. Miko had told me it didn't have a phone. I was glad that no one could reach us. I pulled back the denim drapes and opened a window to get out the musty smell. It was obvious that the place hadn't been used for some time. I gripped the windowsill, which looked out over a wide, green valley below. Taking a deep breath, I thought, If only I had wings, I could soar across it like an eagle.

We brought our own provisions that included cards and board games that would keep us busy. During the day, we went on hikes, while at night we read books before a roaring fire.

"I wish Dad could be here with us," Brian sighed.

"I miss him, Mom," Paul curled up in my lap.

It was hard to hide my tears from the boys, let alone the anger and frustration I was feeling. How was I going to care for them without their father to help me?

As I headed down the mountain, I knew what I had to do. I called my parents and announced, "We are coming to live in Oregon as soon as possible."

Clark's death had completely changed my life. I was a widow now, alone and longing for a feeling of home. I hoped the Pacific Northwest would be a healing place for us to adjust, and I dearly wanted my boys to feel like they had family again.

My parents welcomed us at the Portland airport with open arms. For a while, I focused on the future and put the past history on hold. It felt good to get settled in a place where I could reexamine the past few months of my life. Perhaps it was the Cherokee ancestry of my parents that made me feel so at home with the beauty of green forests, majestic mountains and bountiful rivers. All my life, I'd embraced nature and the earth with a spiritual reverence. In no place had my heart felt so joyous than my teenage years spent on our family's raspberry farm in Troutdale.

Brian and Paul slipped into the farm life with the ease of wearing an old pair of shoes. They helped with the horses, fed the chickens and picked berries in early summer. My chores were to drive the tractor, collect the eggs and help tend the garden.

Miko arranged to have my furniture shipped up to us. It was covered and stored in the barn. For a long time, I still checked over my shoulder to make sure no one followed me.

In my upstairs bedroom of our two-story, old fashioned, white farmhouse, I set up a computer to keep track of my personal investigation. I wasn't ready to give up the fight to find justice for Clark and Sandy, even though now I was over eight hundred miles away. At night, tears often stained my pillow when my family couldn't see.

Enjoying a cup of coffee at a local cafe one morning, a naturally pretty woman with long, straight, dark hair and bright pony-brown eyes handed me a flyer. Immediately, I noticed the rows of dangling beads that hung from her neck. She tossed her fringed shawl over her shoulder, and with a warm smile and slight accent, she introduced herself, "I'm Donna Graham. I've just moved here from Columbia and am offering an introductory class in Reiki."

"I'm not sure exactly what that is," I revealed while reading the flyer.

"Reiki is a Japanese technique for stress reduction and relaxation that promotes healing." Donna pressed her hand to mine.

"It sounds like something I need." I smiled back at her and promised to attend.

After I returned home, I noticed my aging father working on his John

Deere tractor with the barn door open. We nicknamed my stepfather Merlin because he magically repaired everything and anything that broke on the farm. As I got closer, he asked, "How you doing today, dear?"

"I'm okay." I meekly smiled.

"Keep your spirits up, darling." His head lowered, "I wish this was something I knew how to fix."

My frail, gray-haired mother appeared at the back screen door wearing her worn, checked apron. "Amber, I can use some help in the garden."

"Sure," I nodded. I was grateful to be staying with them. Both my parents were nearing seventy. Dad's memory was failing, and my mother had recently recuperated from breast cancer.

On that cool yet sunny spring day, I gladly joined her outside. Silently we tore away the weeds while resting on our knees side by side.

Mom turned to me, "Amber, sometimes the best part of something is finishing it." She had a slight smile on her weathered lips.

They had supported me through my trials without judgment. I don't know what I would have done without them. I told her about meeting Donna and the Reiki workshop, and she said, "It probably is a good way for you to get your mind off things."

Sunday after church, I headed toward Multnomah Village where the workshop was being held in the healing center. I passed through the quaint neighborhood of specialty shops, galleries and small, locally owned cafes. On a side street in an older neighborhood, a three-story, dark green house with shutters displayed a wooden sign that read *Wholeness Center*. I parked nearby and walked through the rickety picket fence with peeling paint. Ahead, the soothing sound of bellowing wind chimes welcomed me.

There was a large basket filled with shoes by the front door and I removed mine. When I stepped inside, the open living room with a roaring fireplace and mantel filled with glowing candles embraced me like a cozy blanket.

Donna greeted me with a huge hug and introduced me to the other six women and two men who sat in a circle on the area rug resting over the shiny hardwood floors. She explained that she had worked with the indigenous people in South America where she was from. They had taught her the ancient practice of hands-on healing.

For the next hour, the experience of gentle human touch brought tears to my eyes. It made me realize how much I missed Clark. His hugs, his kisses and the warmth of his loving arms. Donna calmed my sobs and said she understood.

Afterwards, I made another appointment with her, and she invited me to lunch. Two days later, as we sat together in a small wooden booth at *O'Connor's* restaurant, I decided to share my story with her. We discovered there were many similarities in our lives.

She was familiar with loss and had walked away from her husband and jungle hacienda in South America, after she discovered his infidelity. She encouraged me to not give up my quest for justice.

"Amber, should you decide to further pursue justice, I would be willing to go with you to the FBI office here in Portland," she offered.

The next day, I phoned the Federal Bureau of Investigation in Portland. They referred me to a woman named Linda Langdon who handled all the out-of-state cases.

I set an appointment and one week later, picked up Donna. She was wearing her usual native attire. She put her arm through mine as we entered the glass, double-door entry of the federal building. We waited what seemed like an eternity before my name was finally called. A petite brunette wearing dark-framed glasses and dressed in a navy blue business suit, stretched out her hand, "I'm agent Linda Langdon. I'll be taking your report."

We walked to her office where she closed the door behind us. Donna squeezed my hand as we sat down.

"Please be as specific as possible and offer detailed facts. I also need full names and dates of all events with those involved. Your statements will be taped and kept on file for other agents to review later."

For the next two hours, I talked into a microphone and recalled the events leading to Clark's and Sandy's deaths. I also included the information about other connections I discovered through my research. Connections with the Orange County school system bankruptcy, the smuggling of diamonds through the shipment of ostrich eggs, and several names of victims shot execution style, behind the left ear, like both Clark and Sandy.

Throughout this exhausting experience, Donna never left my side. At the conclusion, I told Linda, "My husband brought home a copy of the Santa Barbara Planning Commission manuals. He told me that all the evidence to convict his mother was there. Unfortunately, with over two thousand pages, I haven't been able to make good sense of it."

"Right now, Amber, we need to document the facts. Your statements are all we have to go on. I can subpoena any other information later that we feel may be necessary in your case."

As we prepared to leave, Donna patted me on the back, "You did a good job, Amber. I'd like to give you the name of someone who also might be able to help you." She set a business card in my hand for a spiritual advisor she trusted.

Later that night after dinner, my mother told me about a German woman in her late eighties, named Mary, that needed nursing care at home. She asked me if I would be interested in working for her. We met and I liked her right away. There was no doubt it was time for me to get back to work, so I took the part-time offer.

Two weeks passed without a word from Linda. Finally, one morning as I prepared to leave for work, I heard my mother call from upstairs, "Someone from the Bureau is on the phone for you."

Instantly, I recognized Linda Langdon's serious voice on the line. She informed me that the legal documents she subpoenaed from the Santa Barbara Courthouse were reported to have been destroyed, by an accidental fire just weeks earlier.

The news took my breath away, as fast as the evidence that vanished. No doubt it was an inside job with money well spent by guilty parties.

I asked, "What should I do now, Linda?"

For a moment, she was silent. She finally spoke. "Amber, I've learned the cliché to often be true that power corrupts, and absolute power corrupts absolutely. I'm sorry, but all I can do now is forward your information to the appropriate local authorities. I will include the death threats that were previously made against you and your children."

I hung up the phone and cried out with the pain of a beaten victim. A wave of despair washed over me. The power of money had again destroyed my hope for justice. Clark was gone, and everything we'd worked for had been washed away like the blood from his gunshot wound on the garage floor. Clark's final words echoed in my mind. It really was so big that it scared me to death.

Only then did I truly understand just how big the conspiracy Cynthia had involved herself with was. The sheriff's department was in on the cover-up and had labeled Clark's death as suicide. Cynthia had ordered Clark's body cremated and the county coroner had done it without my permission. Even the courts had been influenced, leaving me and my two boys without a home. Then those bastards had made ashes of my evidence, just as they had done to Clark. It was another stinging defeat.

Feeling the weight of the injustice, I wondered if it was time to give up. With money and power on their side, I struggled to find the strength to go on. I had to, for Clark and Sandy, because I didn't want the powers of evil to win.

Chapter Thirty-Five
Clues in a Dream

1987
Portland, Oregon
Amber McDaniel

I woke up in a flash as the emotional remnants of my dream surged through my veins with the speed of adrenalin. I quickly fumbled to find a pen and writing pad to transcribe the events I already struggled to remember. Clark had spoken to me in my dream. "Don't give up; the truth will surface in time. I'm sorry you got caught in my family's web of deceit. You've got to look deeper. There's evidence hidden from view." I put my pen down.

Rereading his message over and over, I broke down in frustration, thinking I must have overlooked something. He didn't say where the clues were, but I knew that somehow I had missed something and would have to closely review all the information I'd gathered so far.

One puzzling thing I'd recently discovered in the Santa Barbara Planning Commission manuals was a record where Clark's grandfather,

Otto, had obtained a direct payment from a federal grant to build two dams. This baffled me because government protocol would have a payment like this go directly to the governor's state office. The eighty-million-dollar federal grant also stipulated that fourteen acres be set aside for a nuclear waste dumping site. I couldn't find a detailed distribution of these funds anywhere or the designated parcel number for the required site.

Opening my computer, I scanned a recent copy of the *Mariposa Daily*, the local Santa Maria paper. Immediately, an article drew my attention. The headline read "EPA Fines County $25,000." Reading further, the article explained that the county Flood Control Board was fined due to high toxicity levels found in the drainage system. Chemical tests were ordered when a high incidence of multiple sclerosis and cancer cases were reported in a nearby real estate development. I recalled Clark had ordered the local Department of Water and Power to perform those same tests on another property owned by his family. I had seen the results of the final assessment in the mail after Clark died. The report confirmed that twenty-seven pesticide residuals, high formaldehyde levels and DDT were found. So much was going on then that I had just set it aside. It now occurred to me that it must somehow be connected.

"Oh, my God!" I gasped as a memory became clear.

There was a parcel circled in red in the Santa Barbara planning documents called *Federal Nuclear Waste Pit*. Could Otto have changed the parcel numbers? What if they matched the property Cynthia sold to the Santa Barbara School district after Sandy's death? It would be a death sentence for all those children. Could this be the deed Clark found that cost him his life?

Why in the hell would Otto do that? My heart was racing as the pieces came together. What about the proposed high school, which was scheduled to be built next year on that property? Could it be contaminated? Did I have the strength and drive to continue searching for the truth?

The next day I called Linda at the FBI and told her about my suspicions. "I will forward this information to a special agent from the local FBI office in California that was recently assigned to your case. Unless you can offer additional evidence, for now your file here in Oregon will be put on hold," she said.

Hanging up, I knew what I was about to undertake was a monumental task. I needed to find more evidence.

Had Clark pinpointed the evidence he spoke about in my dream? I made a cup of coffee, went upstairs and spread the pages of the Santa Barbara Planning Commission manuals across my bed. With a prayer in my heart for guidance, I began my all-night search.

Linda's words felt like a double-edged sword. Knowing too much put me in danger, yet not knowing enough kept me in the dark. I recalled once when Cynthia and Jack were out of the country, Clark had watched over their house. He showed me a large satchel of loose diamonds that he knew were kept in their vault. His mother had told him that her father left them for her, but Clark said more kept showing up. He wondered then if she might be involved with an illegal smuggling ring, but never dared to question her about it. It still seemed mind-boggling to me how our country let people travel freely throughout the world.

My head ached as I scanned the complicated manuals. When I grabbed my purse for an aspirin, the business card Donna had given me slipped out and fell to the floor. It read: *Dakota Storm, Spiritual Advisor*. I smiled, noticing the symbolic dream catcher next to her name. What have I got to lose? I thought and dialed the phone number on the card.

"Whispering Winds bookstore, may I help you?" a soft-spoken voice answered.

I requested an appointment with Dakota and was told I could see her the very next day. A light rain was falling as I headed toward the metaphysical bookstore located in downtown Portland. The constant swish of windshield wipers nearly put me in a trance while I thought about the questions needing answers. As I got closer, a sense of apprehension washed over me.

The store was located in an older part of town. Historic houses with front porches, big lawns and brick chimneys lined the side streets. I'd heard that mostly New-Age people mingled there. Bead stores, smoke shops and tie-dyed fashions were the norm. Twenty-third Street was filled with blocks of old Portland manors that were converted into local businesses. I was lucky to find a parking spot right in front of the two-story business. I pulled up the hood of my coat to protect myself from the pouring rain. As I mounted the wooden stairway leading to the entrance, I stopped to catch my breath and admired the stained glass entrance door of a large sun and moon.

The smell of incense greeted me as I opened the double brass-handled door entrance. I recognized the fragrance of lavender and breathed in the relaxing scent. Before going to the counter, I decided to walk around the large store. The shelves were filled with an expansive inventory of stones, crystals and symbolic jewelry. I picked out an Indian arrowhead, a small beaded bag and some sage to buy before heading toward the many rows of books. A young clerk wearing long dangling earrings asked, "Can I help you?"

"I have an appointment with Dakota," I answered.

She said, "Follow me," then escorted me to a back room where Dakota sat waiting at a small, round, covered table. I swallowed hard seeing her bright, tiger-green eyes that resembled Sandy's. She motioned for me to sit down and in my nervousness, I hit the table and was horrified when one of the candlesticks behind her fell to the floor. I had difficulty relaxing while I sat face-to-face with the woman whose facial features and beauty were so strikingly similar to my departed friend.

"Amber, what we will do today is open to guidance from a higher source, which can offer clarity, validation and greater understanding of your earthly journey," Dakota told me. I admired the shiny crystal hanging around her neck.

She picked up a large deck of cards lying face down on the table. "Please shuffle these tarot cards. The reading comes from your energy," she instructed.

I was nervous and dropped several of them. "Don't worry, Amber. However they fall is meant to be," Dakota smiled. "These picture cards are an age-old tool for divine communication. They represent our emotions and desires and the struggles that are a part of life. Their symbolism tells a story, like images in your dreams. Using this pathway, insights to your individual situation can be revealed."

"I need all the insight you have to offer," I assured her before handing back the shuffled deck. Her calm, sincere voice helped me focus on the task at hand.

"I know you have many questions, but before we start, I'd like to tell you something about your birth name. It represents a stone known for its clarity and ability to bridge the worlds of earth and sky."

Instantly, my whole body calmed down, and I felt as though a heavy weight was lifted from me. She had described, in a few words, the two worlds in which I had been living.

While the spiritual advisor spoke, my eyes wandered around the room. I saw a feathered dream catcher that hung down from the ceiling, a hand-painted drum and a poster that depicted a magical wizard holding a crystal ball. Overhead, the ceiling was made to look like the universe with glowing stars and planets on it. The unique room gave me the feeling that what happened there extended beyond the present moment.

"Your dreams are another tool of communication," Dakota continued. "The key is to understand and believe the messages they bring. The cards will tell us more."

Dakota turned over the first card, "*The Lovers* card." She smiled. "The issue at hand is a relationship. It is close to your heart and is being tested."

She announced the next card as the *Three of Swords*. She continued, "There is sorrow and a deep feeling of loss, but its purpose is to create strength. At this difficult time, you will be called upon to focus your mental energies and find inner faith. I see something about finding more information in a textbook that is a direct message to you."

I sat stunned. She knew nothing about Clark or my life events. As she spoke, it confirmed my decision to keep looking for more evidence. How could she possibly know anything about this? From that point on, I concentrated on her every word.

Turning more cards over, she revealed a picture of a falling tower that looked dark and frightening. "You are going through dramatic changes. Even though everything around you may be collapsing, it is actually a blessing in disguise. Working through this transformation and turmoil will teach you what is most important in your life and how to rebuild it."

Tears streamed down my face. It made perfect sense. Dakota was describing my life and showing me the purpose of those events. Whatever or whoever was guiding her, I wanted to thank them from the bottom of my heart.

A book suddenly fell to the floor from a shelf behind her. For a moment, there was dead silence, but when I looked up, Dakota was smiling, "Sometimes this happens when spirits, angels, or guides want to let us know they are present."

My arms were covered with goose bumps. As the reading progressed, the unique young woman offered me more useful information that only I could understand. One card in particular drew her attention. She called it *The Empress*. The next card was dark and scary with the picture of a devil on it. "You need to beware of a mother's actions."

My mouth went dry. I knew she was speaking of Cynthia. The validation felt like confirmation that she had an evil soul.

When Dakota unveiled the last card, which displayed a picture of a beautiful naked woman getting ready to bathe, she let out a heavy sigh, "The Star." She took my hand, "This signals a new beginning, a renewal and a greater belief in yourself that will offer a stronger hope for the future. There is a higher purpose yet to be revealed for all this work you are doing. This card is a message to have faith that all truths surface in time."

I could hardly believe that she used nearly the same words as Clark had in my dream. Nothing I'd experienced before brought me to this depth of understanding. I gave her a warm hug and thanked her for touching my life in such a profound way. Just before leaving, Dakota suggested two books that she felt I should read, *The Love Letters* and *Indian Legends and Dreams.*

Chapter Thirty-Six
Lost in Time

1989-1992
Portland, Oregon
Amber McDaniel

Dakota's words echoed in my mind as I finished the first book, *Indian Legends and Dreams.* The Native American folklore explained the existence of two worlds like heaven and earth. Ancestor spirits cross over what is called the Rainbow Bridge to guide loved ones on their journey. I wondered if that was how Clark was guiding me in my dreams.

One story in particular touched me deeply. It was about the Chumash Indians that settled in central California. The legend spoke of the time when the first settlers arrived. The Indians exchanged food and gifts with the settlers. Then one sunny afternoon, the trickster Coyote came to visit. The story said the settlers invited the entire Chumash tribe to a picnic, but the afternoon celebration turned into a massacre. Unknown to the natives, their hosts laced some of the food with poison, which only they knew not to eat. The pioneers coldly watched as all the Indian, men, women and children became ill and died. This devious plan was devised so that the settlers wouldn't have to live in fear of their savage friends.

The story made me wonder if the historic event happened on the very land that Clark's family owned. Could evil deeds leave a mark in time to be picked up by later generations? I had to look further still into Clark's family's past.

Unable to fall asleep, I decided to open *The Love Letters*. The book cover revealed it was about Albert Einstein and his love affair with his wife, Milvea Maric. The love story explained how he expressed his affections through romantic letters and poetry. In the first pages, I was struck by the fact he had an uncanny depth of emotion that was far beyond rationalization, like the connection Clark and I had shared.

Reading further, it was apparent the scientist was more than a physics genius. His mystical ideas about love—that it was timeless—mirrored mine.

His words touched me. *"Imagination is more important than knowledge. The important thing is to not stop questioning,"* he advised. *"Go with your intuition."*

I couldn't agree more. Clark had been romantic like Einstein, too. We had written each other poetry long ago. It made me want to reread some of them.

Love's Lost Memory

Life is but a flashing glimpse of Love's lost memory
Traveling through that space and time to gain eternity
Eternity is but a summary of lives good and bad
A compilation to make known the goodness we shared.

It cannot be life will not exist after Love's lost memory
For the love goes on forever and life side by side with eternity.

Clark, like Einstein, had a scientific mind. They both had pondered the complex mysteries of life and had belonged to a small minority of people who possessed an innate curiosity that drove them to seek answers to unsolved questions. I chuckled thinking this also described me.

While we lived on our farm in Santa Maria, a jet plane from Vandenburg Air Force Base had inadvertently dropped some fuel on a small portion of our land. It killed all the plants during that season, yet the next season those same plants grew double in size. This had sent Clark on a quest to find out why. Through experiments in cellular structure of how combustible material transmutes the plants' DNA structure, he developed the theory of mono-polarity and a new elucidation of the atom. I still hope to one day prove this theory in his memory.

In Einstein's equation $E=mc^2$, he documented the speed of light at a constant 186,282 miles per second, but noted it appears different depending on where you are and how fast you're traveling. This is where time plays into the picture and our perception of it. Time as we know it exists here on Earth, but not in outer space.

I grasped this reference when he described relativity this way: *"Put your hand on a hot stove for a minute and it seems like an hour. Sit with a pretty girl for an hour and it seems like a minute."*

Putting the book down, I slowly drifted off to sleep. In my dreams, I saw Einstein and Clark sitting face-to-face playing a game of chess. As they moved the carved pieces across the checkered board, I realized everything in my dream was black and white. A large clock with antique numbers appeared above them with arms moving counterclockwise. It seemed strange that the timepiece was moving backward. Both of them turned toward me and smiled.

Suddenly, the overhead clock exploded, sending small pieces flying everywhere. One piece floated down in front of me and I picked it up. With the speed of a flash camera, my mind recorded something written on it. Just then, my eyes opened and I instantly recalled the vivid letters. It was a familiar name: *Otto Preston*. It had to be a clue. I may not be as smart as Einstein, but I understood this man's past could offer answers to my questions. Einstein did say, *"The intuitive mind is a sacred gift and the rational mind a faithful servant. We have created a society that honors the servant and has forgotten the gift."*

Chapter Thirty-Seven
The Clues

1990-1992
Portland, Oregon
Amber McDaniel

Everything kept pointing me to review facts about Clark's family tree. Was it Otto Preston whose actions had brought so much pain to future generations? I knew he had been a prominent politician and lawyer and that he'd served on Santa Barbara's board of supervisors for nearly three decades. I'd read his history, but it described a perfect political record in his long, distinguished career. Though my research about his personal life was minimal, now I felt it was time to dig deeper.

I'd seen in the twelve years Clark and I were together that a legacy of money and power could breed corruption and greed. Cynthia's wealth bought political favors, and her power could persuade a one-time enemy to become an enduring ally. Maybe she had learned her manipulative ways from her father, whose shadow she walked in. I had to find out.

Living in Oregon, I'd lost touch with many of Clark's relatives. I hadn't even spoken to Barbara or Bernie since Cynthia kicked us off our ranch. I decided to call Miko, Clark's old secretary and see if she would be willing to help. She was the only one I kept in touch with that sincerely believed that Clark had been murdered and hadn't committed suicide.

I picked up the phone and dialed her number. "Hi Miko, it's Amber. I have a favor to ask. I want to find out as much personal information about Otto and Elizabeth's family that you can find. His political career seems flawless, but I'm more interested in his personal lifestyle."

"That's a big favor, Amber. The two people who know the most about him are Cynthia and Barbara. I can try, but I can't promise you anything, knowing how tight lipped they are."

"Maybe you could talk to someone at Mitchell and Blaine? I know Tony Marcello also knew him."

"I'll see what I can gather and get back to you," she promised.

Though surely this would stir things up again, I figured at this point I didn't have much more to lose. It crossed my mind to get a hold of Jack, because we always got along, but I figured he was just too close to the smoking gun.

I scanned the Internet to find Clark's ancestors. I found information to support what I already knew: they were socially accepted as a family and were well-known for their generosity and for their civic contributions to the city.

Clark once had told me that Otto also was a lawyer for the late newspaper magnate, William R. Hearst. I thought that was an interesting tie.

Several weeks later, I got a phone call from Tony Marcello. "Amber, a woman named Miko came by here asking questions about Otto Preston. What are you sending her snooping for?"

"Well, Tony, I hired the detective whose name you gave me. He advised me to stop digging if I valued my life. I want to know why he told me that."

"Amber, I really wish that I could help you, but this is way over your head. No good can come from your questioning," he paused. "Stella Barnes might offer you some insight and I can get you in touch with her, but you can never credit me as the source."

I agreed to keep quiet about Tony's help.

He gave me her phone number before hanging up. I was glad something finally came to the surface. Tony said she lived in San Francisco. It took me two days to get the courage to dial her number.

An answering machine picked up, and I left my name and phone number and said nothing else. Later that night, the phone rang.

I held my breath when the caller identified herself as Stella Barnes. "You don't know me," I started, "but I'm looking for some answers about the Prestons. I was married to Otto's grandson, Clark. People have covered up my husband's murder and I'm looking for some information."

"I'm sorry for your loss, honey, but my association with that man ended long ago," she hung up.

I wasn't sure what to think, but I knew then that I needed to make a trip to California. Donna and my step-sister's daughter, Madeline, wanted to come along. I decided that the boys would stay with my parents. We made plans to fly into LAX and rent a car. Madeline had a friend named Courtney who was a make-up artist that offered her home in the Hollywood Hills as a place to stay during our visit.

Madeline Adams, my stepfather's granddaughter was my only niece. She's a large-framed, tall girl who loves sports, works hard and has the strength and gusto to do any man's job. A few years ago, after graduating high school, she moved to Hollywood, but left suddenly to come home. I learned afterward that she only seeks out female relationships, but now openly acknowledges that she was a lesbian. We had been spending time together because she lived close by in a modular home on my step-sister's farm. We both had a strong appetite for good books and old movies.

When we arrived in Los Angeles, the temperature registered over eighty degrees. Madeline suggested we rent a convertible and we all agreed. We let her drive, since she was familiar with the area. My niece fit the California scene, wearing a black cotton sleeveless turtleneck, jeans and army boots.

There's something to be said about having your hair blow in the wind. A wild and free feeling filled the air. On our drive, Madeline told us that Courtney's house had once belonged to Frank Capra, an old-time, famous film producer.

It was a relief when we reached the San Fernando Valley where the air was slightly cooler. The fashionable car easily maneuvered the many steep curves heading up the hills along Laurel Canyon Boulevard. Gated fortresses lined both sides of the street and it made me wonder whether such security was meant to discourage trespassers or to guard devilish secrets.

The high-security stucco houses with their fenced yards greatly contrasted with the openness I felt in Portland. We arrived at Courtney's iron gate and Madeline pressed the intercom button. The edge of a red clay tile roof peeked through the thick foliage that outlined Courtney's mission-style estate.

A pretty, young, petite blond with her hair pulled back in one long braid bounced toward us. She waved us inside as the bright sun reflected her wide Dentyne-fresh smile and large, pussycat emerald eyes. She fit the typical look of a California girl with her tan skin and her off-the-shoulder white blouse, tight cut-off shorts and flip-flops. Courtney looked as sweet as the richly colored oranges that hung from a nearby tree. She flung open Madeline's door, grabbed her shirt, and ordered, "Get your damn ass out of that car, girl."

"Cut the crap, Courtney. My friends here are straight," Madeline shook her head.

"Can't you forget the past?" the young girl started to walk away.

"Only if we kiss and make up," Madeline stepped out from the driver's seat.

Donna and I didn't move as we watched Courtney plant a big, wet kiss on Madeline's lips.

"Come on in, you guys," Madeline smiled. "We just broke the ice."

It was an awkward moment for me, but it looked like a joyous homecoming for my niece. Taking Madeline by the hand, Courtney skipped back toward the house and we followed.

We were given a guided tour of her sprawling manor. White marble floors accented the deeply ginger-colored adobe walls. Large potted ferns, pillowed wicker furniture and glass tables made it feel like a comfortable vacation spot. An array of abstract wall art set a fun mood and I breathed in a unique scent that smelled like apricots and flowers.

The vibrant colors that surrounded us were as intense as the passion between the two separated lovers. They couldn't keep their hands off one another. I was relieved when Courtney offered us some iced tea, which helped cool the hot scene. Courtney's excitement bubbled over as she revealed that she had obtained day passes to United Artists studio, which was celebrating its 70th anniversary. "I think you'll enjoy the special events that are planned," she beamed.

Sitting in her enclosed courtyard, she revealed, "Make-up artists are independent and can work for more than one studio. An actress or actor can request us. Lately, I've been working on the set of Alien Nation."

"What an interesting profession," Donna expressed, and I agreed.

"When we contract to do a motion picture, we usually go on-site. The traveling is the hardest part," Courtney groaned. "But the great pay and perks make it worthwhile. The one thing that drives me crazy is the unrelenting competition between studios, actors and production companies. The ego-bashing is brutal, but I love it."

"Hollywood seems to bring out the best and worst in people," Donna commented.

"Well, it brought out the best in Madeline," Courtney reached over and squeezed her hand. "I've really missed you."

Madeline's eyes welled up as she said, "I've missed you, too."

They stood and exchanged a hearty embrace.

"Time to party, girls." Courtney excused herself, saying she wanted to change clothes.

"What a charming girl. She is so full of life," I told Madeline.

When Courtney returned, her long blond hair was flowing over her bare shoulders. Her make-up brought out her stunning green eyes. She was wearing a full-length gauze skirt and sleeveless silky yellow blouse.

Her beaded jewelry, dangling earrings and high-heeled sandals finished her eye-catching outfit.

Donna and I sat in the backseat of Courtney's Mercedes as we entered the famous studio gate. "This isn't my world," Donna whispered as an overwhelming crowd waited to see the three-ring circus of performers on several stages. Flappers with feather boas, men in zoot suits and a parade of antique Rolls Royce cars reflected the 1920s heyday.

I was drawn to an exhibit that detailed the beginning of filmmaking. There was a giant poster of Thomas H. Ince, which struck a chord in my memory. That name had come up in one of my Internet searches. It was in a newspaper article about his death. I was sure Otto's name was in the same article...

Reading through the presented facts, I learned he had developed an integrated system for the production, distribution and exhibition of films all under one roof. It stated that Thomas Ince had been the young entrepreneur who had created the factory studio system, which brought long-term contracts to the stars.

"He left a memorable legacy." Madeline slipped her arm around Courtney's trim waist.

"There is a great mystery surrounding his death," Courtney revealed. "It was speculated that it occurred while he was a guest on William Randolph Hearst's yacht, the Oneida. To this day, no one really knows exactly what happened. Rumor has it that he was shot, but that isn't what the death certificate stated."

"The article I read about him implied that he was murdered because he planned to expand the Hollywood scene to Santa Barbara. The citizens of the city were against it. It was during the time my husband's grandfather was his lawyer. I wonder if he was involved in the scandal."

"Secrets, lies and sex are all part of this crazy, make-believe Hollywood world," Courtney laughed.

For the rest of the morning, Madeline, Donna and I followed Courtney around like puppies on a leash. She often stopped to chat with people she knew, which at times made me feel like a forgotten key not knowing where to turn. Courtney had the energy of a busy bee. We ate lunch at the *Roosevelt Hotel*, toured the historic *Grauman's Chinese Theatre* and then had a drink at the *Frolic Room*.

During lunch, the flirtatious pair played footsie under the table and winked at and blew imaginary kisses to one another. Their antics seemed natural in the atmosphere, but I wondered if others may have thought we were a table of couples. Though it had been some time since I had had sex, if I ever did again, it would be with a man. Still, it did my heart good to see my niece so happy.

When we returned to the house, I told Courtney, "I'm feeling very tired. Do you mind if I take a short nap?"

She showed Donna and I our separate guest rooms. Mine was decorated in soft tones of turquoise and chocolate brown. As I took off my shoes and stretched out on the pillow-soft covers, I knew I would be giving the girls time to play things out.

Before falling asleep, muted sounds of ecstasy could be heard coming from Courtney's bedroom down the hall. Deep within me, I felt a strong yearning for Clark. When I pulled the covers up over my shoulders and closed my eyes, my mind envisioned a steamy picture of Clark and I making passionate love.

Chapter Thirty-Eight
Going Home

1992
Los Angeles and Santa Barbara, California
Amber McDaniel

The next morning, Madeline told us she wanted to stay with Courtney while we headed up to Santa Barbara.

Donna and I took off around 9:00 AM and headed North on Highway 101. I put the convertible top down and welcomed the cool ocean breeze. Donna turned to me and said, "I've never told you, but my older sister Melody is gay. She was a high-powered executive in a tech company and married for five years. Then she went on a cruise with some girlfriends, met her partner and they fell in love. Later, she divorced her husband, and my sister is still very much in love with her girlfriend today."

"Love between human beings sees no distinction between race, color, or gender. In its purest form, it only recognizes the bond connecting the individual hearts," I said, expressing my sentiments.

The hour and one-half drive went by quickly and before long the Main Street exit came into view. I drove by the harbor so Donna could see all of Santa Barbara's coastal beauty. She had never been there before. Little had changed in the three years since Clark had died. Tall palm trees swayed in the ocean breeze that lined the busy thoroughfare. Tourists strolled along the boardwalk while seagulls overhead swooped down like vultures to pick up any idle food remnants. Sailboat masts clanged like church bells on Sunday morning. Breathing in the clean, fresh, salty air brought back memories of happier times.

"Gosh, it's beautiful here," Donna, exclaimed as she took in the glistening ocean view, the harbor of sporty boats and the sunny blue sky.

"Yes, it is. But I feel empty here now. Without Clark, some of its luster is gone."

"I'm so sorry, Amber. Though I never got to meet Clark, I believe he would have wanted you to find happiness without him."

"Maybe coming here will offer me some closure."

I decided to drive by the old Preston house and stopped in front for a moment. "Clark and I briefly lived here as newlyweds," I shared with Donna. "His grandparents, Otto and Elizabeth, owned it. I never understood why the sisters never sold it after their parents died. When Barbara revealed to me what they had buried there, I finally understood."

The house looked exactly the same, but now the pain of Clark's death plunged into my heart as sharp as a shovel's edge. Though my memories often took me back to days gone by, it seemed like a lifetime ago that I had Clark by my side.

Driving away, my anger at Cynthia resurfaced. "Clark's mother took everything from me when she had Clark murdered. I've struggled to raise our two boys by myself, but that woman hasn't suffered a day. I'd never felt that kind of hate before."

"My friend, I wish you peace. Life is unfair, especially when justice is not served." Donna pressed her hand to mine.

We drove down Main Street where visitors rambled through the gift shops looking for souvenirs and mementos to take home. I found a parking spot just a few doors down from *Marcello's*. "I need to talk to the owner and we can get something to eat," I explained.

A statuesque brunette appeared to take our order.

"Is Tony around?" I inquired.

"He should be back soon from a meeting," she answered.

I asked for a glass of red wine and Donna ordered a Coke to go with our lunch of pizza and salad. As we sat in our booth, the front door suddenly opened. I could hardly believe my eyes when I saw Tony enter with my mother-in-law, Cynthia, right behind him.

Something inside of me snapped. With the fury of an erupting volcano, all the pent up anger, frustration and disgust surfaced. I jumped up, faced her, and shouted, "*Murderer!*" I drew my fist back and rammed it right into her face. If Tony's strong arms hadn't apprehended me, I would never have stopped.

Cynthia fell back onto the floor, dazed, her petite nose smashed and bleeding. Right then, a feeling of satisfaction swept through me.

"That woman is crazy," Cynthia yelled, "Arrest her. I want to press charges."

Up until the police arrived, I still felt the euphoria of a doctor who just saved a patient's life. I glanced over at Donna. Her mouth was open and her eyes were wide. She had a look of disbelief on her face. When they handcuffed me and read me my rights, the impact of what I'd done finally hit me.

"Now you're in big trouble, Amber," Tony warned.

As they hauled me away, I heard Donna say, "I'm right behind you."

At the police station, I retold my story, saying that Cynthia was responsible for Clark's murder. No one listened to me. Later, I was fingerprinted, photographed and booked on assault charges. Those events made me feel like the crazy, madwoman my actions showed me to be.

When they finally let Donna see me, her first question was, "Why did you do it?"

"I couldn't help it. My emotions overwhelmed me with the strength of a tidal wave. They just took over."

As I tried to explain, some sense of remorse began to seep in. The hardest moment came when I had to call my parents to ask them to bail me out.

Once I was released, I said to Donna, "I've learned you can't always get the bad guys through the legal system. For me, this small act brought some sense of justice."

"I understand, but it was not a mature way to do things."

"I'm sorry, Donna, to bring you all this grief. Thank you for staying by my side. I appreciate it more than you'll ever know."

I had to face the consequences for what I'd done. The assault charge might land me in jail. How was I going to explain this behavior to my boys?

"You're going to need a good attorney," my supportive friend suggested as we got into the rental car.

Immediately, I thought of Miko. So I gave her a call.

"Jim Boland is a great lawyer who once helped Clark," she said. "He is not associated with Mitchell and Blaine."

I opened my cell phone and gave his office a call. He happened to be in. I explained what happened. I set an appointment with him for the next morning at 9:00 o'clock.

"I'm so sorry about my behavior, Donna. Please forgive me for getting you involved in this," I told her as we continued our drive.

"Isn't that what friends are for?" Donna squeezed my hand, "What now?"

"Well, we have to spend the night, so I better call Madeline and let her know."

"Next time, no wine for you," Donna smiled.

We got a hotel close-by downtown and later Miko stopped by for a short visit. "I heard what happened between you and your mother-in-law. I don't blame you for giving it to her for Clark. I'm sorry, but my search for background information on Otto brought little results."

"Everyone around here is so afraid of Cynthia that they keep a tight lip. Thank you for trying anyway, Miko."

"If I hear of something you might be interested in, I promise I'll call."

The next morning, Donna and I woke up early to check out and go to my appointment. Jim's municipal office waiting room was generic compared to the elaborate one at Mitchell and Blaine. We were called in promptly to meet the middle-aged, professionally suited man with a strong square jaw and wide smile. His skin was a deep tan like Clark's, and I guessed he spent his off-hours outside.

"What brought all this on?" Jim questioned as we sat in the blue fabric office chairs facing him.

"Cynthia McDaniel—the woman I assaulted—was my husband's mother. I believe she murdered him."

"Were charges filed?"

"No. My husband's death was listed as suicide."

"What made you think he was murdered?"

"I read the autopsy report and saw that the coroner had found a single bullet entered just below and behind Clark's left ear. Clark was right-handed. His left arm had been crushed in a car accident several years before. He couldn't lift that hand higher than his chest.

"Clark had discovered some damaging information that he planned to make public. His mother threatened us, but I had nothing to substantiate the information. I've also filed a report with the Portland FBI."

"It sounds like you're dealing with some high-profile individuals, Amber. I will do some checking. This morning I got a call from Cynthia's lawyer. She's demanding you get a psychiatric evaluation. This could raise some uncomfortable accusations."

"Does she really think I'm crazy?" I stood up and paced the room. "Do I have to do it?"

"Yes," Jim sternly responded. "Just answer the questions honestly. Cynthia's attorney indicated that if you cooperated, they might be willing to drop the charges."

"I don't trust her. What if they say I'm mentally unstable? My God, she could have my children taken away."

"Calm down, Amber. You panicking is just what she is counting on," he spoke up.

"I refuse her request and will be damned if she is going to ruin my life, too."

Jim got up from his desk and gently guided me back down to my chair. He stood so close that I could smell the mint on his breath.

"We came here to get his advice," Donna put her hand on my knee.

"I'm scared, Donna. Cynthia is a powerful woman and she wants to destroy me."

"Amber, as your attorney, you need to trust me. I'd never advise you wrong." Jim's eyes conveyed a sense of sincerity. "I'll make the appointment for later today so that you can return home."

I hesitantly agreed. When we left Jim's office, I was trembling. "I've messed everything up. What I thought would bring closure instead opened an old wound. What's the matter with me?" I shook my head.

"We'll work through this. I'll be right by your side," Donna promised.

Later that day, Jim's secretary called and confirmed that she'd made a 3:00 PM appointment at a psychiatric clinic across from the county hospital. It was about ten minutes from our hotel. When we arrived, the painted letters on the door spelled out *Jenny Taylor, MD, Specialist in Mental, Emotional and Behavioral Therapy and Evaluation.*

"I'm glad she's a woman," I smiled. "She will better understand my emotions."

Jenny Taylor appeared as a tall brunette having a bobbed haircut and wearing a long white jacket. Once inside her office, she lowered her wire-rimmed glasses down her nose as she delivered her lengthy questioning and personal evaluation.

I had to complete several pages of forms and a ton of background information. Some of the questions seemed odd. Many were regarding my childhood. Knowing I had not suffered physical abuse, alcohol, or drug problems helped me relax.

The only questions that hit me hard were the ones regarding Clark, his death, and how I was processing my grief. Jenny's kind spirit and caring manner helped me realize many emotions were still bottled up inside me.

She explained, "When emotions are not released when raised, they build up like air in boiling water. Later they come to the surface, much bigger and stronger than the immediate situation calls for."

Dr. Taylor never indicated anything about her conclusions during my exam, but guaranteed me, "A report will be mailed to all parties concerned."

Upon leaving her office, I told Donna, "I'm emotionally exhausted."

"What type of questions did she ask you?"

"She asked me how I felt about Clark's death. I told her, 'I felt robbed, broken and stripped of my future. I was drowning in a sea of grief, pain and anger. I kept asking myself, can I go forward without justice being served?'"

"I can't imagine what you've been through."

"One good thing came from it."

"What was that?"

"I realized I have lost my fear of death."

"How did you come to that?"

"When she asked me about it, I told her. For years, I ran from it, always scared and looking over my shoulder. Thinking someone might be following me, or, worse yet, trying to kill me or my children like they did Clark. Lately, I've asked myself what exactly I am afraid of."

"What was your answer, Amber?"

"The unknown. But as time passed, my faith has grown that Clark and Sandy would be waiting for me at my journey's end. That faith diminished my fear of dying."

"I believe, one day, we will be reunited with our loved ones," Donna squeezed my shoulder.

"After Clark died, I read something I've never forgotten that Rudolph Valentino said, '*What the average man calls Death, I believe to be merely the beginning of Life itself. We simply live beyond the shell. We emerge from out of its narrow confines like a chrysalis.*'"

"I like that concept, too," Donna said.

"Let's head home and call Madeline to update her on the news." I started the car.

Later that evening when we arrived back at Courtney's, we found the two lovers still awake. "Aunt Amber, I'm so sorry about what happened," Madeline gave me a big hug.

"It was traumatic, but it made me realize it may be time to give up my fight."

"My mother used to say that some good always comes out of something bad," Donna added.

"Courtney and I have a surprise for you. Amber, isn't one of your favorite movie stars Shirley MacLaine?"

"Yes, I've always admired her. She has such an ageless beauty, and what I've read of her reveals a boundless strength and an uplifting faith."

"Courtney has arranged for us to meet her tomorrow."

"Really? That would be quite a thrill. I've read all her books. I loved her performance in *Terms of Endearment*."

"I think she is one of the greatest actresses of all-time, but I never imagined I'd get the chance to meet her," Donna beamed.

We met in the kitchen the next morning for an early breakfast. "I'm so excited about our plans today," I smiled.

"Shirley lives in Malibu right on the beach. I've visited her before, and she enjoys being social," Courtney informed us.

We climbed into Courtney's Mercedes wearing short sundresses, except for Madeline, who had put on a dressy jogging suit.

I was surprised that when we got to our destination, Shirley answered the door herself. When my eyes met hers, I knew she was much more than all her accomplishments. Her stunning crystal-blue eyes sparkled in a genuine celebration of life. They were brighter than any star, radiating with a glow greater than the electrons that projected images on the silver screen.

She exuded a beautiful spirit that was intense yet playful, seductive yet innocent and personified the reflection of an inquisitive mind and unconditional heart. I was deeply humbled by her open-armed welcome.

While talking, I related how I had lost my beloved Clark. She intently listened to every phrase, every incident which had occurred leading to his death. I shared with her, "I've done everything in my power to prove

Clark was murdered, but all has led to a dead end. I'm tired of fighting a system bigger than myself."

"Don't give up, Amber. You're fighting for the truth and the love you shared with Clark. Nothing is greater than that," Shirley encouraged.

Her eyes never strayed from mine. I poured my heart out to Shirley, and she held it in her hands, careful not to spill one drop or lose the essence of truth. She filled my soul with compassion and faith by being my personal, spiritual sounding board. I knew she felt my words and recognized my pain.

Shirley had also lost her husband and shared the story with me.

Our exchange showed me her life was not materialistic, unrealistic, or staged with props. She was as real and down-to-earth as my next-door neighbor. Her words instilled confidence and hope in me. The kind I'd never found before. Not even the FBI had listened to my story as closely as she did.

Shirley invited all of us to walk with her as she took her dog, Terry, out on the beach. It was a beautiful, sunny California day with a slightly cool ocean breeze and a clear blue-sky overhead. The sound of the crashing waves with soaring seagulls and the sweet pitter patter of feet hitting the water made the world seem right again. I breathed in the fresh salt air and thanked Shirley for her encouraging words.

"Never give up on your dreams," she advised.

Before we left, we exchanged our mutual views on everything from past lives to UFOs. Donna, Madeline and Courtney were gracious to let me shine in the limelight.

Shirley told me, "Your story would make a great book."

"If it ever became a movie I'd be honored if you'd play a part," I told her.

Shirley smiled her impish grin. "You never know."

Upon leaving, I realized that Shirley's hopeful words had given me the motivation to continue my quest for justice. Jim Boland called and I was relieved that Cynthia had agreed to drop all the charges. He told me that she didn't want the embarrassment of any negative publicity.

On our plane ride home, I asked myself if I'd left a stone unturned or missed an important clue. One question never answered was how Sandy's and Clark's murders were linked. Was there a secret from the past I hadn't uncovered? Shirley mentioned that the diamonds my mother-in-law wore might have a suspicious international connection. This triggered thoughts of our Asia trip and the Shariff family. The one thing that linked both Sandy and Clark was Kaseem.

Chapter Thirty-Nine
Suspicions

1992-1993
Portland, Oregon
Amber McDaniel

At home I had time to review the events of my trip. My parents weren't happy about my bad behavior, but they were forgiving. Brian made a comment, "You go, Mom." Paul was just glad that I had returned safe and sound.

It occurred to me, when I saw Cynthia and Tony together, that their connection may have been the piece of Clark's and Sandy's murders that I hadn't connected before. Even when I lived in Santa Barbara, there were rumors that Tony had an affiliation with the mafia. I recalled seeing many tough guys hanging around at *Marcello's* restaurant.

Why would Cynthia have an association with Tony? Could he have set up the plans to get rid of Sandy and Clark? That would leave her hands clean of the crime. How in the world would I ever find any proof?

Or was I on the wrong track and the hits on my friend's and my husband's lives had come from Cynthia's overseas affiliation? I had notified Kaseem about Sandy's death, but I never heard back from him. Was Cynthia's involvement in Thailand tied to international organized crime?

I felt the least I should do was notify Linda Langdon at the FBI. She could document my suspicions. One week later, I called her and made an appointment.

Linda told me, "This information will be added to your file. Also I will forward it to the Santa Barbara agency. Beware of the fact you are dealing with criminals, Amber."

"I just want justice served," I told her.

After leaving her office, I felt I had to decide whether justice was worth any price. Would I ever be able to bring down the whole nest of vipers? Maybe believing that Cynthia had made her own version of hell was enough. She would reside there no matter what I did.

Chapter Forty
Victims

1994
Portland, Oregon
Amber McDaniel

At home upstairs in my bedroom, I stared at my computer screen and reviewed the cross-reference of information linked to Clark's murder. The facts were like pieces of a puzzle that I was trying to fit together.

Finding a motive and evidence to prove my case was proving my greatest challenge. I'd confronted the complexities of the legal system, of political corruption and of hidden secrets. It had taught me the determination of an archeologist, the dedication of a detective and the courage of an undercover cop. Finally, I had found the last piece of the puzzle. But would the international connection between the Prestons and the Shariffs prove my case? I couldn't help but wonder if the details of their mysterious agreement were so awful that Cynthia had killed Sandy and Clark to keep them quiet.

The following evening when my parents took the boys to a church potluck dinner, I declined to attend. As the sun set, I sprinted toward the barn and shoved open the heavy, weathered doors. A stale, musty smell filled the air as I passed my father's John Deere tractor, still as picturesque as any in the old photographs. I flipped on a small hand-held flashlight and proceeded to carefully check the marked contents of the dusty boxes I had stored there.

In one of them, I'd put Sandy's personal address book. I had used it to inform her friends about her untimely death. I even had left a message for Kaseem, but he never had returned my call.

Quickly, I found the box marked *Sandy's Personal Effects* and pulled it down from the stack. My heart beat loud as a drum as I used my father's sharp utility knife to open it. Carefully, I began to take out the contents of old paperwork. When my eyes fell upon her old address book my breath caught with the anticipation of a treasure hunter.

I opened the tattered journal. Seeing Sandy's familiar handwriting, I reeled back, caught in a wave of grief. I lowered my head, taking a moment to recall her bright essence. I still missed her dearly. Sandy and Clark had been too young to die, but at least I could find comfort in the fact that they were together forever.

My finger traced down to S for *Shariff*. Sandy had emphasized Kaseem's name with a star. I was relieved to find that his international phone number was still readable. Hearing the hum of my parent's car's engine as it entered the nearby driveway, I quickly tore out the page, tucked it inside my pant pocket and headed for the door.

"How was dinner?" I asked my family.

"Good," my father answered.

"Lots of food," Brian smiled and gave me a hug.

"Maybe you can come with us next time?" Paul looked up at me with sadness in his eyes.

There was no doubt that my children had suffered the most in the years since their father passed away. Not only had they lost him, but I was guilty of not giving them enough of my time. My parents contributed more than enough support to compensate for what they missed from me, but that was not my parents' job.

Paul had isolated himself from others his own age. I longed for Clark's advice, often sensing Paul's struggle with his sexual orientation. I'd recently come to terms with the fact that he was gay. My parents had encouraged me to let go of the past and get on with my life. I planned to...when the final link had been explored.

Later we all sat together in my parent's living room near a crackling fire and watched *Highway to Heaven*. Brian, upon its ending, looked over at me and said, "Dad would be that kind of angel, helping others."

"Yes, your dad was a good man," I smiled. "I miss him so."

"I wish he hadn't died," Paul lowered his head.

"He didn't have to," I told him.

But before I could say anything else my mother broke in, "Enough of that, let's all get a good night's sleep."

I hesitated to make the final call to Kaseem, afraid of what would happen if I came up against another dead end.

Two weeks later, something far more pressing grabbed my attention. I'd noticed that Paul had been losing weight. Even with my mother's homemade chicken soup, strong cold medicine and added vitamins, he couldn't shake his recurring cold. The previous night at supper, he had complained about constantly feeling tired, and my medical training told me something was wrong. He'd been extra quiet lately, would eat little dinner, and often said he had the chills. One night after dinner, I went upstairs to his room where he was studying and knocked on the door.

My stomach clenched, "Paul, can we talk?"

"Yes." His voice was weak.

I opened the door and studied him for a moment. His cheeks looked sunken and his eyes were heavy as though he burned with fever. "I'm worried about you. I think it's time you saw a doctor."

"There is a lot of stress at school," he lowered his head and set down his pencil.

Paul wouldn't look me in the eyes.

"Please tell me if something else is bothering you," I pleaded. "I'm your mother and a nurse. I could help." I sat down on the side of his bed.

His eyes were filled with pain. "I'm fine, Mom. You have other things to take care of," his voice quivered.

I got up and put my hand to his forehead. He was burning up with fever, "You need some aspirin, sweetheart."

I saw a tear run down his cheek. He stood up and faced me, "I'm scared to death, Mom. I'm gay, and my boyfriend told me he has AIDS."

I wrapped my arms around him. We held onto each other, both releasing gut-wrenching sobs of sadness. How I wished Clark could have been there to help me find the right words. My heart was breaking. I prayed for the strength to be strong.

"We'll get through this," I hugged him ever so tightly.

"Promise me you won't tell anyone," Paul begged as he let go.

"Honey, you'll have to get some help. They have medicine and treatments available."

"I'm so ashamed. How can I face anyone?"

"I don't think hiding the truth is the answer," I squeezed his hand.

"Mom, I'm going to die." I could not see an ounce of hope in his face.

"Don't say that. I lost your father and I'm not going to lose you," I wailed. Suddenly determined, I commanded, "Get ready, I'm going to take you to the hospital right now."

"What will you tell Brian, Grandma and Grandpa?"

"For now, I'll tell them my concern is your high fever."

With that promise, Paul agreed to go with me. We drove to the emergency room at OHSU because we had no health insurance. They put him in a private room right away. The doctor asked me to leave. He had to ask my son some private questions.

To me, it wasn't about how Paul got the pandemic disease. Acquired Immune Deficiency Syndrome was one of the dangers he faced being sexually active in that day and age. I knew little about the recent advancements in the treatment of HIV, but I felt certain some would be available by now. My fear was that he wouldn't survive the onset of his disease or that he wouldn't adjust to this life-changing event.

They admitted him into the hospital and put him in ICU. His viral load was critically high, and the CD4 was 40. No one had to tell me he was dying. I recognized the shadow of death, and it was unmistakable on Paul's face when I stood by his bedside.

I desperately wanted to call Brian and my parents and tell them the truth, but I kept my promise and said he was having extensive tests and that they shouldn't come to the hospital.

Even though I was completely exhausted, I refused to leave that night. So many thoughts crossed my mind. If a spark of life lingered in my son, I would fan it. As his IV brought hope to his body, my prayers to God begged his life be spared. I offered my soul for his and promised if he lived, I'd make every day of our lives count for something.

Watching him lay there hooked up with tubes and a ventilator, the guilt of my neglect overwhelmed me. I kept whispering in his ear, "You can fight this. I can't lose you, Paul. I love you so much."

It was no excuse that I was a young widow trying to prove that her husband was murdered. Was I so caught up in my own suffering that I hadn't seen his? I couldn't change the past, but I promised then and there that any mistakes I'd made would not be repeated in the future. How foolish that I had mindlessly been chasing after a mother who killed her son, only to turn my back on mine.

I vowed to change. I had to be a survivor and make sure my son would become one, too.

In the days that followed, Paul slowly gained more strength. The potent antibiotics, the loving care of the hospital staff and my prayers brought him through.

A saying came into mind as we left the hospital. *Life isn't about how to survive the storm, but learning to dance in the rain.*

Chapter Forty-One
Survivors

1995-1996
Portland, Oregon
Amber McDaniel

While Paul was ill, I stayed by his side constantly. Once he came home, my parents were relieved that he had finally regained some weight and that his face had color again.

I tried to get back into a normal routine. My part-time, caretaker job with Mary resumed. I found I had a week-old message from Donna, who was concerned why she hadn't heard from me for some time.

"Where have you been?" she enquired when I called her.

"I had a family emergency," I told her.

"I hope everything is okay. When would you be available to get together? There is someone I'd like you to meet."

"Soon. I'd love to meet for lunch, as long as you tell me it's not a man," I kidded.

"I'm bringing a woman my friends call Mystic Michele. She can intuitively read energy."

"She sounds interesting. I do have some questions right now about moving forward. Maybe she can advise me. I'd like to bring along the manuals Clark left me and ask her about a person I want to contact. Is that okay?"

"That would be great. I hope she can offer you some insight."

"Can you meet us this Saturday afternoon at the Wholeness Center?"

We set the date. I looked forward to meeting Donna's friend.

The day I was meeting Donna, Brian was taking Paul with him to the shooting range. Paul liked to sit and watch his brother practice in preparation for his upcoming military career. Brian was excited about joining the Army after he graduated from high school. He was fearless, just like his father was. I was proud that he wanted to defend his country's freedom.

Even though it was March, the sun shone brightly as I set out for Portland. Blooming yellow daffodils, fluffy pink blossoms and warmer weather were happy signs that spring was in the air. When the winter came to a close, the city's habitants celebrated the beauty of the Pacific Northwest by walking, biking, or just being outdoors. It was so nice that our farm was located only twenty minutes from the city.

I grabbed a grande coffee at my favorite drive-through coffee stand in Multnomah Village.

As I entered the Wholeness Center, I breathed in the apple-scented candles burning inside as I removed my shoes. Donna welcomed me with a big hug. She tucked her long ruffled shirt over her bare feet as she sat down on the soft, cotton sofa.

I quickly glanced over at the colorfully dressed woman sitting in the chair beside her. Michele's short, dark brown, bouffant hair glistened with sunlight coming from a window behind her. It made her look as though she had a halo around her head.

Michele stood up when Donna introduced me to her. "You have the heart of a warrior." She warmly smiled as her angelic eyes scanned my entire body with the precision of an X-ray machine. Michele's long bangle earrings, bracelets and beads jingled as her buxom frame sat back down. "You are walking a tightrope. That takes great courage," Michele said. "The energy you carry is hopeful, but there are many scars inside your heart."

"How do you know that?" I was so impressed.

"Everything is energy. Like the aura above a candle flame," Michele paused and pointed to a nearby taper. "Each living body emits energy created by our heartbeat. As a nurse, you know that can be electronically read."

"Yes, I understand."

"Well our brains are like computers. I just read your energy through my intuition. Something I do not totally understand, but I know it is as real as the bones in my body."

"Even in medicine there are some things that can't be explained," I admitted.

"I've learned you have to have faith in all things, even when you cannot see them." Michele's brown eyes flickered back and forth.

Donna interjected, "Michele has had her own struggles in life, like us. She had a twenty-one year old son that died in a tragic car accident."

"I'm so sorry," I told her.

"Losing my son has taught me many lessons. It showed me what matters most in life and that love is a bond that once created in life, somehow remains."

I felt humbled by her words. They made me think of the love that Clark and I had shared.

Michele patted my friend's knee and said, "Donna too has lost. Her home in Columbia was taken over by armed guerillas, and she's endured the pain of infidelity, betrayal and divorce."

"Here we are, all of us survivors," Donna smiled.

"Amber, you have suffered injustice. But with all that you endured, I still sense a strong faith in your being even though you've experienced the heartache of nearly losing your son. This, I recognize personally."

"What is she talking about, Amber?" Donna asked.

I was speechless. While trying to catch my breath, words rolled off my tongue with the speed of a moving train. "My son Paul has AIDS and nearly died." It was as though the secret within me screamed to be revealed.

Donna held me until I stopped crying.

Michele took my hand, "Your faith will carry you through this, too. It is the umbrella during life's storms."

I appreciated that we all shared our sorrows. Somehow it helped ease my pain. For a while, we sat acknowledging the fact that each of us was a survivor, each of us had a heart overflowing with faith, and each of us had loved and lost.

Before we parted, I asked Michele if she would look at the Santa Barbara Planning Commission manuals I had brought to see if she could offer some advice about Kaseem.

"I'll tell you exactly what I sense," she affirmed.

I pulled out the manuals and the torn out page from Sandy's phone book and set them down on the coffee table in front of us.

Michele closed her eyes and held the ripped paper with Kaseem's phone number in her hand, "I see this man as a Pandora's box. He holds answers, but also danger. Amber, beware. Sometimes secrets are better left unknown."

Michele then pressed her hand onto the manuals. "There is a desperate man willing to sell his soul for financial survival. He rules a city by the sea. Beneath the city's sparkling beauty lies a dungeon of criminals."

She was quiet for a while.

Then at the last she made one final revelation. "I envision a book that will reveal many secrets and truths.."

Chapter Forty-Two
Opening Pandora's Box

1996
Portland, Oregon
Amber McDaniel

The fight to avenge Sandy's and Clark's deaths had taken its toll on my family, but I had to follow the last clue. If the final call to Kaseem went nowhere, I would accept that the time had come for me to finally put my fight to rest.

Upstairs in my bedroom I used my cell phone to dial Kaseem's international number. I sat down on my bed as the first ring began. There were two more before the machine picked up. I didn't recognize the voice, but the number was confirmed, so I decided to leave a brief message. "Kaseem, this is Amber McDaniel. Please contact me regarding Sandy Preston McDaniel. It is urgent." I left my phone number and hung up.

Several weeks passed without word. I told myself to be patient, that maybe Kaseem was out of the country and hadn't gotten the message.

The next Saturday, Donna called me and suggested, "Let's take the boys to see the salmon run at the Bonneville Dam. It might help take your mind off of things." I agreed, needing the distraction.

She arrived with a Starbucks coffee for me in her hand. Donna's warm smile and upbeat attitude always brightened my day. We sat in my mother's fifties-style, lemonade-yellow, Coca-Cola-themed kitchen with the cowboy-shaped salt and pepper shakers between us.

"My friend, our emotional hardships have given us broad shoulders," she smiled as we talked about old battle scars like two army veterans.

Donna pulled out a small stone from her purse and handed it to me. Embedded inside was a beautiful gold angel. "May she carry your burdens." We hugged.

Just then Brian and Paul flashed through the back door with their overloaded backpacks. They threw them down and went directly to the fridge. Brian grabbed an apple and threw one to his brother.

"Donna had a great idea to head out to the Columbia River Gorge. We can stop and catch the salmon run," I announced.

"Can we bring our fishing gear?" Paul questioned before biting into his snack.

"Sure. Round up your things, and we'll stop by the Sandy River before heading home." I looked at Donna and said, "They used to love to fish with their dad."

We loaded up my 1985 metallic blue Jeep Cherokee and headed down the driveway. Immediately, I noticed a black car with tinted windows was following close behind us. I didn't want to alarm the boys, but I asked Donna to check and see if it turned with us onto the entrance ramp of

Highway 84. When she confirmed it had, my heart skipped a beat as I put my foot down on the accelerator and jetted into the fast lane.

Just then my cell phone rang. "Give up your fight, Amber, or we'll kill you," a threatening voice blared from the other end.

"I'm not afraid of you!" I yelled back. "I'll make sure one day the truth will come out." Then a shocking realization struck like thunder; I realized that the voice came from the Lincoln Town Car behind us. The phone went dead.

In that moment, my rearview mirror revealed that the black vehicle was lunging toward us with the speed of a bullet. We were rear-ended with the jolt of an electric shock. A roar of crushing metal mixed with screaming panic filled the air.

"Mom, what's happening?" Paul shrieked.

"Why'd that guy hit us?" Brian slammed his fist on the back of the seat.

"Stay calm," I ordered while trying like hell to keep control of our automobile. The damned attacker stayed on my tail even after I had pressed the gas pedal down to the floor. A horn sounded like an alarm when I passed a slow-moving semi, speeding at 100 mph.

"They're still behind us," Donna screamed, her face pale with fear.

"Oh God, they're trying to kill us," I swallowed hard. My heart beat hard from the adrenalin rush. I tried to calm myself in the terror-filled car. I instantly knew the threat stemmed from the phone call I'd made to Kaseem.

"Get away from him, Mom," Brian's hand reached over the seat and gripped my shoulder.

Just as he finished his sentence, the car hit us again, pushing our car out of control and into the next lane. Screeching tires, billowing smoke and cries of terror filled the air.

The scenic highway's beauty flew past us faster than the swift current of the Columbia River. My inner voiced screamed that we had to escape—but how?

Beads of sweat ran down my forehead as I envisioned the next hit would send us off the highway and into the ravine.

Not missing a beat, I grabbed my cell phone and dialed Linda's personal number at the FBI. "Stay down and brace yourself for impact," I cried out.

Hearing Linda's voice, I frantically shouted, "It's Amber McDaniel. I'm on Highway 84 ten miles west of Multnomah Falls. A black Lincoln Town Car with no license plates has already rammed us twice. We need help. Those bastards are trying to kill us."

"Amber, stay on the line. I'll get help on the way. Can you give me your exact location?"

"I'm five minutes from the Falls, and he's right on my tail."

"Can you exit?'

"I can try."

"Let's hope he won't follow. Just in case, I've just called for a chopper to track them down."

"How'd you know about this?'

"We tapped your phone. The caller's family name, Shariff, came up in our databases. Adan Shariff is involved in international crime."

"I see the Multnomah exit. There are other cars and pedestrians ahead. What should I do?'

"Brake hard and make the exit, then slow down and let me know if they follow."

"Hold on!" I yelled out and slammed on my brakes as I sharply turned off the highway. The smell of burning rubber filled the air. Donna popped up to take a quick glance behind us.

"I don't see them," her voice sounded hopeful.

Then seconds later the black marker appeared in my rearview mirror, but this time I watched in horror as the side window rolled down. I gasped, seeing the shiny end of a high-power rifle.

"Stay down!" Donna shrieked to the boys. "Move it, Amber. We have to get out of here!"

Her instructions were impossible. Several pedestrians blocked our way. I pressed hard on my horn to warn them.

A moment of sheer terror came as our back windshield shattered. Around us, the local tourists hit the ground for cover. My foot jammed down to the floor as we ripped though the parking lot at record speed. I lifted the phone back to my ear and frantically pleaded, "What do I do now?"

"Get back on the highway as fast as you can," Linda ordered. "Help is on the way."

Suddenly overhead the whirling blades of a helicopter sounded. It dipped low to try and stop our pursuers. A trail of flashing lights could be seen in the distance. I thought we were going to make it.

Then, with blunt impact, our vehicle went airborne. There was nothing I could do to stop us from leaving the road. It was like a nightmare in slow motion as the Jeep rolled over and over with metal and glass crashing around me. Then everything went black.

Chapter Forty-Three
End of the Road

1996
Portland, Oregon
Amber McDaniel

I breathed in the familiar scent of the hospital room. Panic took my breath away as I tried to raise my head. It felt like it was filled with sand. My injuries were keeping me from getting out of bed. I shivered thinking, oh God! What had happened to my boys and Donna?

I quickly pressed the button for the nurse and was glad my hand still worked even though it looked discolored and twice its normal size. There were many places on my body, especially my midsection, where a constant pain warned me not to move.

It seemed like forever until a nurse arrived. I sobbed my first words, "Please tell me what happened to my boys and Donna."

"Your children sustained no life-threatening injuries, Mrs. McDaniel. Brian does have a broken leg, and both were treated for lacerations and bruises. They were discharged into your parents' care two days after the accident. I'm sorry to tell you, but your friend Donna is still here in ICU. Her condition remains critical."

"How long have I been unconscious?"

"You suffered a severe head injury and four broken ribs. Your accident took place five days ago."

"Oh, my God." I sank down into my covers as tears streamed down my cheeks. This was my fault.

I silently cried out to Clark, why did this have to happen? I had caused so much pain to those I loved the most. My body moaned with inconsolable grief.

Later when my parents came with the boys, I watched Brian hobble in on crutches. Paul looked like a wounded soldier with a bandage that went around his head.

"It didn't hurt that bad, Mom," he told me, even though the wound had required twenty stitches.

Their bruises and surface cuts broke my heart. The next few minutes were filled with hugs, kisses and tears.

"We're just glad you're still with us." My mother's eyes glistened as she reached out to touch my arm. "We are worried about Donna. She didn't fare as well."

"Has anyone seen her? She doesn't have any family here."

"They won't let us in ICU, Amber. They say her prognosis isn't good."

"Oh God, she was just an innocent bystander in all this. Did they catch them?"

"Don't get too upset, honey... Linda told us the culprits took off and headed onto mountain roads where they lost them."

"Damn it," I cursed. "Is there any justice on this planet?"

I wanted to shake my head, but knew better. Being a nurse, it was clear what was best for my injuries. I had to stay put for now.

Several more days passed before I could get out of bed, but the first thing I requested was a wheelchair so I could get to ICU. I begged, pleaded, and demanded to see my dear friend. The image of tubes and machines surrounding her barely gave a glimpse of the person she used to be. Still I wheeled close by and had to speak to her.

"Donna, please forgive me," I reached between the bars and touched her cold hand. "If only I could turn back the clock and make things the way they were. I pray for your recovery and promise to do whatever it takes to get you through this." I burst out crying.

I visited her every day to see if there were any changes. Three days later, they had to do brain surgery to release pressure in her skull. After that, it was all in God's hands.

Linda sent flowers and came by one day before my release. "We have a special task force working on your case. The name, Shariff, came up in our files. We already knew about Adan Shariff's association with diamond, guns and drug trafficking. The problem is the federal government's authority is bound by international laws and policies, which more often protect the guilty than the innocent."

"Is there anything else I can do?" I asked.

"You have to leave this in our hands now, Amber. If something further comes up, I'll contact you," Linda assured me before saying good-bye.

I knew the boys would bounce back fast at their ages, but the emotional toll played on all of us. My parents looked tired and older. The children were scared for their lives. Donna's life had been permanently altered. The cost for justice was just too high, and it took the accident to make me realize it.

A nurse arrived with a large bag of personal effects gathered from the accident. When I went through them, I came across the stone angel Donna had given me. When they came to take me home, I asked if we could stop by the ICU floor so I could see her one more time before we left.

I carefully wheeled my chair next to her bed and bent down close enough to kiss her cheek. "May she carry your burdens now," I whispered and set the stone angel in her hand.

To my astonishment, she squeezed it lightly.

Chapter Forty-Four
The Legacy Continues: Two

1997
Portland, Oregon and Santa Barbara, California
Amber McDaniel

The boys and my healing were complete, but Donna's remained another story. After two months, she awoke from her coma, but she'd sustained brain damage and needed convalescent care for the rest of her life. I visited her at the nursing home every day, and she recognized my presence with her warm smile, but no words could pass from her lips. Many times I fed her, bathed her, and walked her down the hall. Sometimes she lost her sense of balance, and she leaned on me for support.

In time, I got to know the staff and told them I used to be an RN. One day, my mother suggested that I go back to school and update my nursing license. They offered night classes at the local college and I enrolled.

During this time, Brian graduated and enlisted in the Army. Later in the year, the word was he'd be deployed to Iraq. Paul was thinking about college, and we both became volunteers for the AIDS foundation.

The convalescent home where Donna lived offered me a job once I was certified. I hoped someday to open an adult foster care home where my friend could stay full-time with me.

I made a promise to make Donna's days the best they could be. As a nurse, it has always been my job to heal the sick and take care of the wounded.

A year quickly passed and one afternoon, my phone rang. It was Harry Mitchell's son Alan who took over for him at Mitchell and Blaine. "I'm calling to inform you that Cynthia McDaniel has passed away of a heart attack. Your sons Brian and Paul McDaniel are listed as heirs in her will. Your presence is requested on Friday, March 30th, for the reading of her will at the law office of Mitchell and Blaine in Santa Barbara."

I had to sit down. The starling news took my breath away with the speed of a sharp needle. My mind swirled with emotions of joy and sorrow that left me speechless.

Alan further explained that Cynthia had never retired and had dropped dead at age sixty-nine while visiting the Santa Barbara County Courthouse. I barely got out the words, "We'll be there," as I hung up the phone.

Now Cynthia would face her final judgment. I asked myself, "What would Clark want me to do with the rest of my life? Did he think I failed to find justice for him and Sandy?"

Twelve years had passed since Clark died. Most of my time and effort were focused on exposing the truth about his murder. Yet, with Cynthia's death my struggle comes to an end. This would bring change.

I focused on making the reservations for our trip to Santa Barbara. It worked out that Brian got leave and we all could travel together from Oregon.

We landed at LAX, rented a car and headed up the coast. The bright sun shined like diamonds off the Pacific Coast's horizon. Tall palm trees swayed with the grace of hula dancers as we passed by the county courthouse. As we pulled up to the offices of Mitchell and Blaine, I wondered how the Preston legacy would continue.

We entered the plush four-story law office and a security guard had us register our names before we took the glass elevator to the penthouse suite of David Blaine and Alan Mitchell who had taken the business over for their fathers.

I could hear my stomach making noises on our way up. Brian looked so handsome dressed in his full uniform. Paul had color in his cheeks in a fine tailored suit. I chose to wear a red dress that was a favorite of Clark.

Upon our arrival, their secretary escorted us to a nearby conference room. Mr. David Blaine greeted us, "Amber, you look wonderful. The boys have grown up nicely."

"Yes, I'm very proud of them."

"Jack, Claire, Barbara, Bernie and Joel will be here shortly."

I swallowed hard when the double doors opened and Jack appeared. His dark hair was now snow white, but he looked even more handsome than I remembered. Claire followed behind him. She was the mirror image of her stunning mother. Her sultry hazel eyes flashed our way, but she didn't utter a word. It didn't surprise me to see that she carried on the traditional diamond accessories. Alan had mentioned while we waited, that Claire had followed in her mother's political footsteps.

Not long after, Barbara appeared. She looked me in the eyes and smiled. I bowed my head as a gesture of sympathy. She had aged nicely, kept her figure and I was glad to see that she had remained by Bernie's side.

Who did surprise me, was their son, Joel. His football physique and dashing looks struck an interestingly familiar cord as he stood next to Jack. He walked over and shook Brian and Paul's hand, with the enthusiasm of an incumbent politician. I recognized the charisma reflected in the pictures of his grandfather, Otto Preston.

Even though they were family, I felt very uncomfortable. Not one of them had reached out to us after Clark died. I just wanted this to be over as soon as possible.

Mr. Blaine stood up. "We are gathered here to read the final will and testament of Cynthia Lynn McDaniel, daughter of Elizabeth and Otto Preston. The heirs to her estate are listed as: Jack McDaniel, husband; Claire McDaniel, daughter; Barbara Baumgartner, sister; Joel Baumgartner, nephew; and Brian and Paul McDaniel, grandchildren."

I was very surprised to learn that neither Claire nor Joel were married or had any children. Bernie and I were the only ones there whose names were not read. As far as the Preston family trust was concerned, spouses were not included, though it sounded like Cynthia may have written a separate will to include Jack and her sister.

Mr. Blaine continued, "Provisions for the Preston family trust remain in place. Due to the death of Cynthia Preston, land sales can be made at this time with the consent of all heirs. Monies from any sale and from leases of the agricultural land in the trust will be distributed evenly among all surviving heirs, including grandchildren."

I sighed. This meant that Brian and Paul would finally receive a part of their family legacy, which he explained would be paid in monthly payments.

The professional lawyer resumed his outline. "Cynthia added an amendment to her final will, that I believe no one here is aware of. Jack McDaniel, husband of Cynthia Preston McDaniel, is the beneficiary to all Cynthia's personal property and assets, and Barbara Baumgartner will now be the sole trustee of the Preston family trust. Each of you will receive an endowment of $10,000 a month for as long as you live, with the stipulation that if either one of you, divorce or remarry, this payment will cease."

Barbara looked over at Jack and I noticed his face was blushed red. I heard him curse under his breath.

Mr. Blaine paused and then continued. "There are packages in a safe deposit box designated for Barbara, Claire, and Joel to be opened only upon her death," Mr. Blaine added.

The three packages, each about the size of a coffee pot, were handed to the recipients, though none proceeded to open them.

At the conclusion of the meeting, Barbara walked up to me, "Amber, I'm so sorry I never kept in touch. Please forgive me. Cynthia told us that you were crazy, though I never believed it."

"It wasn't easy, but my life went on," I responded and added, "You have my sympathy at your loss."

"Here's my card and phone number. I hope, in time, we can get to know each other again," she smiled.

I took the card and tucked it away in my purse. Moments later, Jack came over and re-introduced himself to my now-grown boys.

"Nice to see a military man in the family," he shook Brian's hand. "You've done a fine job of raising our grandsons, Amber. They are clean cut and well mannered, and I know Clark would be proud. One day, I'd like to fly up to Oregon and get to know them."

Tears filled my eyes. "Clark would have wanted that," I confirmed. As we said our goodbyes, some hope filled my heart that maybe something good still might come from the legacy of the Preston's blood money.

On our plane ride home Brian encouraged, "Mother, I want you to put this money in a savings account, so that one day you can again have your own home."

"I will save it for you until you return home," I promised.

"It will help pay my medical bills and for my college. I hope to become a lawyer and help others find justice," Paul smiled.

That night alone in my bedroom I turned on my desk light and sat down. So many thoughts and feelings churned inside me. They begged to find a voice and I pulled out some stationary and a pen. I knew the empty pages before me would be the right forum to free them.

I sat down and began to write:

Dear Clark and Sandy,
If you were here, I would say, "Please forgive me for failing to find justice."

I never had a thirst or hunger for anything more. I've learned that I cannot and should not judge the ways of this world. I now believe there is a higher judge your perpetrators will face.

This journey without you has changed me. At first, I was filled with pain and rage. Your deaths were unfair. I would have done anything to prevent them. I was fighting to make things right; yet I never stopped to recognize its personal cost.

Being alone and missing you has been the hardest part. I've been guilty of neglecting the two most precious people left in my life, Brian and Paul. I vow not to waste another moment on the past and promise to be conscious of what the present has to offer.

I've come to terms that I will never understand why this had to happen. My faith has offered me the comfort of believing that one day, at my journey's end, you will greet me with open arms.

Though it doesn't take away the missing, this thought brings joy to my heart.

As I sit here, I wonder what you would have wanted me to do with the rest of my life. Sandy, I will heal all those I can, in your name. Clark, I will seek the happiness we wanted for our family. You will never be forgotten and I will treasure our time together for the rest of my days. I believe that our bond of love created in life, somehow remains. It can be seen in nature's beautiful landscapes, bright flowers and magical sunsets. It can be heard in the whistle of the wind, the laughter of a child and the melody of song. It can be felt in a butterfly kiss, touch of the hand or warm hug.

My lesson learned is that love and time can heal most wounds, no matter how deep.

Clark and Sandy, a part of you will always remain in my heart. For now I will set the past behind me and with hope I look forward to what tomorrow brings.

Forever,

Amber

God grant me the serenity
to accept the things I cannot change;
courage to change the things I can;
and wisdom to know the difference.

–Serenity Prayer

For updates to this story and the upcoming sequel, go to
MicheleMarieTate.com

About the Author

Michele was born in Cleveland, Ohio. For the past fourteen years she has lived in Portland, Oregon with her husband of forty-three years, their daughter and her family. She pursued a career as a health professional, but always made time for what she loves most—writing.

Recurrent childhood dreams, unexplained visions and questions about life and death drove her to read Edgar Casey and others who could transcend the physical plane. On her spiritual journey she took classes in Tarot, which opened her dyslexic mind to receive higher guidance. Later she also obtained a degree as a certified Hypnotherapist specializing in past life regression.

When her son died in a tragic car accident at the age of twenty-one, she longed to have an even greater understanding of the bigger picture of life. Her son, Irwin, had composed over forty songs and written a screenplay. Together they had begun writing a children's book called Pizarus. Michele finished it and hopefully one day that too, will be published.

In 1998 she joined Willamette Writers and has attended writers workshops and conferences. After meeting a new friend in Oregon, who read some of her writing, she was asked to give life to the heart-wrenching story of her husband's murder. Thus began her debut novel, Blood, Money, Power. Many hours of research followed to give this historical novel's readers a trip back in time.

Michele continues her spiritual growth by studying the Kabbalah, meditation and being a mystic guide and energy reader. Her travels to China, Chile, Europe and Machu Picchu offered ageless understanding about our world. Most recently she has begun a sequel that promises to keep her readers asking for more.

"My daily aspirations are to support our planet and live in kindness and consciousness. I always seek the truth, justice and peace for all humanity." *–Michele Marie Tate*

www.ingramcontent.com/pod-product-compliance
Lightning Source LLC
Chambersburg PA
CBHW070401260626
47161CB00001B/221